Beg For It

A Billionaire Boss Romance

Chicago Billionaires

Alexis Winter

Thank You!

A wonderful thank you to my amazing readers for continuing to support my dream of bringing sexy, naughty, delicious little morsels of fun in the form of romance novels.

A special thank you to my amazing editors Kimberly Stripling and Michele Davine without whom I would be COMPLETELY lost!

Thank you to my fantastic cover designer Sarah Kil who always brings my visions to life in the most outstanding ways.

And lastly, to my ARC team and beta readers, you are wonderful and I couldn't do this without you.

XoXo,
Alexis

You know that feeling—the one where you tell yourself it's a terrible idea but you're going to do it anyway?

Even though you know that this man isn't just your father's best friend who's twenty years your senior...he's your new boss.

I'm the girl that's always done the right thing, made the sensible and safe choices and yet here I am, fresh out of grad school feeling directionless in life and love.
So at the suggestion of my once estranged billionaire father, I agree to an interview at his best friend's company.

The moment I step into Beckham Archer's office I recognize him as the mysterious man I shamelessly flirted with and gave my number to only a few nights ago.
As much as we both try to ignore the fiery attraction between us, I can't shrug the nagging question that lingers...if he didn't recognize my name that night, would he have called me?

The power and control he possesses drives me absolutely wild, making me want to cross the boundaries he demanded we put into place.

Our resolve is hanging by a thread, stretched so thin with desire it was only a matter of time before we gave in.

I know it's a mistake.
I know I risk losing the relationship with my father I've worked so hard to repair.
I know he's going to rip my heart out and possibly destroy my life but it's too late to turn back now.

While he thinks it's just my repressed rebellion, acting out against my father for abandoning me as a child...it's so much more.
He listens to me, offering to mentor me and providing me the guidance I lacked in my childhood.

The more I get to know him, the more I realize there's more to this man than a billion dollar empire and a wall around his heart and the harder I fall.
Even his warning that all he can offer me is a fantasy gets drowned out by lust the second our lips finally meet.

But our little secret doesn't stay quiet for long and the reality that this could all come crashing down is staring me in the face...along with Beckham's pregnant ex.

I want more than the fantasy or one night, I want it all. But does he feel it's worth the risk or worth fighting for?

One thing I've learned about Beckham Archer—he's the type of man that doesn't wait for people to do something; if he wants it, he makes it happen.

The type of man that has me wanting to break all the rules.
The type of man that can make me *beg for it*.

Chapter 1

Brontë

"Congratulations to my daughter, Brontë, on her graduation from grad school. Your stepmother and I are incredibly proud of you."

My father, Jonas Ramsay, lifts his champagne flute toward the sky as he toasts to me. The room fills with cheers and echoes of congratulations as I smile shyly and nod my thanks.

I'm still not used to this kind of wealth. The kind of wealth where spending probably fifty thousand on a graduation party at one of the most exclusive restaurants in Chicago is merely a gesture.

"Come here, sweetie." My dad approaches and wraps his arm around my shoulders. "Have you thought any more about my offer to join Ramsay Consulting?"

I look down at my glass of champagne and shrug.

My dad is one of the most, if not the most, powerful billionaires in Chicago but he's only been a part of my life for the last year. He and my mother met when they were young and had me at only twenty-five, something I later learned was unplanned and a source of contention between them. As expected, they divorced when I was seven after Dad was unfaithful and Mom moved us to the suburbs where we lived a quiet, normal middle-class life away from the glitz and glam of the world's elite.

"I've thought about it a little but I'm still just—unsure."

"Well, that's why I think it's a great idea. You can come in at an entry level position, feel it out, see if finance and business are what you want. I can tell you for sure though that they're in your blood." He squeezes my shoulder and I look over at him. He's referring to my mother.

My mom, Nadia Spencer, was an accountant for as long as I can remember and she loved it. That's how she met my father. In college they were both finance majors and they hit it off. After I was born, Mom stopped working to raise me, but once she and Dad divorced, she went back to work to support us. Dad wasn't yet the billionaire tycoon he is now but I do know she received child support and alimony payments every month; however, she always said she refused to be beholden to a man and wanted to show me that a single mom could do it on her own.

She was fierce and incredibly brave. It's been almost three years now since she's been gone and not a day goes by that I don't miss her. It's actually because of her that I'm working on my relationship with my father... or that I even have a relationship with him. On her deathbed she made me promise that I'd forgive him and try to get to know him and my half-siblings. I put if off for about two years, but now here I am, having this elaborate graduation party thrown by him in my honor.

"That's part of the problem though. I know everyone will just assume I'm working there because you're my father which will probably lend to some resentment by my peers because they'll assume I can get away with anything or they'll just wonder why I'm working in the first place, like I'm trying too hard to prove myself to everyone."

I gulp down the half a glass of champagne I've been nursing and grab a fresh one off a waiter's tray as they pass by. Even talking about my future instantly stresses me out. I feel like an asshole, like I'm complaining about my gold shoes being too tight with the amount of opportunity that's sitting in my lap, but I want to be fulfilled with my career, like my mom was.

I want to know that I'm making a difference in the world.

"I think you nipped that fear in the bud when you took your mother's last name." He doesn't have to tell me that it disappoints him that I'm not proudly a Ramsay.

"Oh, trust me, with social media nowadays, everyone will know who I am the second I get hired on at your company." He nods once, giving a half-hearted smile before looking down at his shoes. I feel guilty. "I'm not ashamed of you, Dad; that's not it." I reach my hand out and touch his arm. "I'm just feeling a little lost is all. You know how it is to be twenty-four."

I give him a smile and his eyes brighten, his own lips curling into a smile. The truth is I am ashamed of the Ramsay name. For years my dad didn't have a great reputation. I know he's changed, or that's what his new wife Chantelle says, along with a few others, but it's hard to trust that when the only version I'd known of him was an angry, cheating liar who walked out on me when I was seven and barely showed back up, only to drop off a check or make a half-hearted attempt to celebrate a birthday or milestone too late.

"Okay, this is my last resort. My good friend, Beckham Archer, owns Archer Financial just across the street from my building. He's looking for an admin immediately. His last one left unexpectedly. I could send him your resume and set up a meeting, if you'd like?"

"Now you're pawning me off onto your friends who need assistants?" I crook an eyebrow at him. "Dad, I appreciate the offer, but I'm just not sure."

"Okay, just promise me you'll think about it."

"I promise."

"Come on." He motions with a quick nod of his head.

"Where?"

"To your gift." He smiles and grabs my hand, leading me toward the center of the room.

"Dad," I groan, feeling like I'm that young girl all over again who just wants to spend time with her dad, instead of being showered with elaborate gifts. "I told you I didn't need or want any gifts besides donations being made to the Chicago Boys and Girls Club."

"Oh, pish." He waves away my suggestion in classic Jonas Ramsay fashion. Sure, he gives to charity—what billionaire doesn't donate more money in a year than most of us will see in a lifetime to various causes—but do they care about them?

My dad doesn't. Which is why I haven't told him that for the last several years, I've volunteered at a few different nonprofits in the city for underprivileged children, something that has become such a passion of mine I can't help but keep going back to the idea that maybe I should start my own nonprofit.

"Ladies and gentlemen, it's gift time!" He grabs a spoon off a table and clinks it against his glass, the guests turning to listen to his announcement.

"I cannot wait to see what he got you for a gift." My best friend Sylvia stands next to me along with our mutual friend Taylor, who are both giggling.

"Stop it." I give them both a glare, but it only eggs them on.

They've been by my side for this entire journey with my father and they've been in the room with me while he's on the phone trying to talk me into letting him buy me a new house in the suburbs, a penthouse downtown, or even a flat in London or Paris.

"I wanted to do something special for my baby girl because she not only deserves it, but she's always wanted one." My dad smiles at me and motions for us to head outside.

I'm so confused as to what might be on the other side of these walls. I walk next to him as the host walks ahead of us and dramatically opens both doors of the restaurant in a sweeping gesture.

I gasp when I see it.

Parked on the street in front of the restaurant with a giant bow on top is a brand-new cherry-red Porsche 911 Carrera Cabriole.

"Dad, this is too much."

"Nonsense." He walks me over to the car and slides the key in my hand. "Remember when you were just a little girl and you'd beg me to take you driving in mine with the top down? You couldn't get enough of that car."

He smiles so proudly as he looks at it and for a second I think I almost see a tear in his eye. I'm not sure if it's a tear about my childhood or if it's because he loved that car so damn much. He conveniently doesn't mention when I accidentally crashed my bike into the rear fender and he screamed at me like I did it on purpose. I remember sobbing in my room for hours, my mom coming to rub my back and comfort me, but my dad pulling her out of my room because I needed to think about what I did.

"It's a hundred-thousand-dollar car, Dad. I don't have anywhere to put it."

"We can sell your old car."

"I like my car," I say nervously. "And it's only three years old."

I feel guilty for not being super excited about a gift I not only didn't want, but one I don't need. I like the fact that I saved up and worked hard, busting my ass doing double shifts at the restaurant I worked at to buy my Kia. I was so proud when I did buy it since it was not only new, but had cooled and heated seats, plus a moonroof.

"Chantelle enjoys having a few different cars. She says it's nice to have one as a daily driver and one when the weather isn't so great."

"Yes, well, you two have a ten-thousand-square-foot garage. I have a single parking spot."

I can see his smile fade again as he leans in to plant a kiss on my cheek.

"Tell you what," he says, taking the key from my hand, "you can keep it parked at my house. When you come over to our neighborhood, we can drop the top and take her out for a spin; how about that?"

"Sounds good, Dad."

I stand there staring at the car along with two valet guys who are admiring her from every angle.

"That's what he enjoys doing, you know?" I turn to my right

where Chantelle, my stepmother, has sidled up beside me. "Giving gifts is one of his love languages."

"Or maybe that's an excuse that rich people give instead of actually taking the time to think out something thoughtful or meaningful or just respect the person's wishes when they said no gifts?" Her lips form into a thin smile and I shake my head. "Sorry, that was rude. You're just being kind."

Chantelle is clearly a lot younger than my father, but she's also probably one of the best things that has ever happened to him. I still struggle with the notion that people can really, fully change who they are at their core, but I also feel like a hypocrite when I see the way my father has changed because of her. When I heard that he was forty, marrying a woman who was my age, I laughed. I didn't think for a second that it would last; it was merely a cliché life crisis move. But here they are, ten years and two kids later and he couldn't be happier.

"He's working on it, Brontë. I know it's practically a slap in the face to ask for your patience and understanding with him, but I promise you," she says softly, reaching her perfectly manicured hand out to rest on my arm, "he wants a genuine relationship with you. He talks about it all the time."

"I know. Sometimes it's just hard to forgive and forget."

"I have no doubt. You're justified in those feelings, Brontë. The boys were upset they couldn't come tonight by the way, Silas in particular. He and Jenson made this for you." She reaches into her clutch and pulls out a hand-drawn card that brings a huge smile to my face.

Silas and Jenson are the two little gems that came out of my family's toxic breakup. From the first day I got to meet them, it's like I've always been their big sister. And one thing that Chantelle always makes sure they know is that we are brother and sister, no half this or half that.

"Aw, those boys. I need to come see them this weekend."

"They would love that and your father would love it too, so he can take you out in your new car." She winks at me. "I better go find him, but I want to throw a fun little family cookout in the next few weeks, kick off summer right and celebrate your birthday. The boys will want to show you all their new flips and tricks they learned in swim lessons over the winter."

"That sounds lovely, Chantelle." I pull her in for a tight hug. "Tell the boys I missed them and I'll see them soon."

I head back inside to find my friends. "Hey, you guys want to go grab a drink somewhere else? I'm feeling a little celebrated out."

"Oh yes, please!" Taylor says, grabbing her clutch and hopping down from her stool.

"Just a second," I say, looking around for my dad. I spot him and head over to let him know we're leaving.

"Thanks again, Dad." I give him a hug and he squeezes me so tight, like he's trying to make up for years lost.

"I'm so proud of you, Brontë. Your mother would be too."

This time I can clearly see the tears and for some reason, maybe because I don't want to disappoint him or maybe because I'm tired of feeling guilty, I agree to the meeting with his friend.

"I'll do it. I'll meet with Beckham Archer for an interview."

A few moments later, Sylvia, Taylor, and I are making our way into a dimly lit speakeasy type bar in The Loop. This isn't our usual neighborhood and the bars here are filled with finance bros in over-priced suits and clearly veneered teeth, all trying to shout over each other about their "big win."

"You sure you want to stay here?" Sylvia asks, looking around, and I shrug, grabbing a high-top table. "Doesn't seem like our vibe."

"Yeah, but it's close by. I don't feel like Ubering anywhere. I just need something stronger than the glasses of champagne I downed."

"Did your dad manage to talk you into working at his company?" Taylor asks.

"No, but I did something stupid." I roll my eyes. "I agreed to take an interview at his fellow billionaire friend's company, Archer Finan-cial. I guess he needs an admin or something. Ugh, I'm so disappointed in myself that I didn't just tell him I want to work in nonprofit and maybe start my own someday."

"Honestly, Brontë, I think it's a smart idea." Sylvia shrugs and I look at her sideways. "Remember when you met me in undergrad? I was the teacher's assistant and I told you that I was unsure about getting my master's in education? Well, I didn't listen to that gut feeling and now I'm a teacher and honestly, I kind of hate it."

"You hate it?" Taylor's ears perk up.

"I don't *hate* it all the time, but it just doesn't feel like it was my passion, what I'm meant to do; it's something I'm good at so I convinced myself it was my dream. Sometimes I don't think I've even figured out what my dream is yet, but I know it's not in the education world."

"So you think taking this job, if I get it, would be a way for me to try out the financial world before I either fully commit or walk away?"

"Exactly!" She slaps the table dramatically. "And if you think there's an interest there, I'm sure you could move into a financial position within the company. With your forensic accounting master's, you'll be able to find work at any financial firm. Fraud is always going on. You know what they say, scammers are the new serial killers."

"True," I say, laughing at her comment. I'm feeling better already about my decision.

"But first," Taylor says, looking around the bar, "we need to get you laid because it's been over two years now and you've graduated so no more excuses."

I duck my head in embarrassment. "Okay, maybe yell it a little louder next time so the bartender can hear you?"

I slide off my stool, flipping her the bird as they both fall into a fit of giggles.

"I'm getting a round of old-fashioneds."

I walk to the bar and wait for the bartender to notice me when a shadowy figure to my right catches my eye. This guy is not your average twenty-something frat boy. His suit looks expensive, bespoke

8

like it was made for him. It hugs his arms and shoulders, accentuating a very toned physique. A lock of his dirty-blond hair has fallen over one eye as he reads something on his phone.

I take the advantage of going unnoticed by him to really look him over. His jaw is rough with stubble, but it's cut and angular. His lips full. He reaches for his cocktail, bringing it to his mouth to take a sip before placing it back on the bar top without looking away from his phone.

"What's with you finance guys?" A burst of confidence surges through me as I make small talk with the stranger. "Always working." I shake my head and place my order as the man turns to look at me.

He glances over his shoulder to make sure I'm speaking to him before sliding his phone in his pocket and turning on his stool to look at me. He doesn't hide his gaze as it slowly travels down my body, then back up again before he replies.

"Guilty." He smirks.

The dim light catches his icy-blue eyes and makes my stomach do a little flip. Maybe that champagne hit me harder than I realized because this man is so sexy I feel my mouth grow dry.

"Married to the job?" I say coyly, dragging my teeth over my bottom lip seductively like I'm in a cheesy rom-com. I brush my hair back in a flirty manner, leaning a bit forward on the bar top so it presses my breasts together.

Who the hell am I right now?

"Afraid so. She's my wife, mistress, and lover." He tosses back the rest of the amber liquid in his tumbler and places it on the bar top.

"Shame." I smile as the bartender places my drinks down in front of me and I go to hand him my credit card.

"Allow me, please?" he says, nodding toward my card.

"Thank you." I pull my card back and place it in my wallet. I gather the three tumblers between my fingers, and then I set them back down on the bar, not yet ready to break up this little flirt fest.

"So what brings a beautiful young woman like you to a place like this?" The way he looks at me has my stomach doing all sorts of little flip-flops.

"You mean to a bar in The Loop filled with young finance gurus foaming at the mouth to be the next Wolf of Wall Street?" He chuckles and I shrug. "Just something in the way they all brag about how they can really see Jordan Belfort in themselves gets me going. Like it's going to make a woman's panties drop that they can resonate with a selfish, narcissistic scam artist like they really are Leonardo DiCaprio in the movie."

"You're fiery. Funny as hell too." His eyes do that lazy perusal of my body again and it sends my stomach into somersaults. "Please tell me a woman as gorgeous as you hasn't been lured into the soul-crushing world of finance?"

"You mean because I'm pretty it would be a shame?"

He nods. "Not a shame. We need more women like you who call it like it is, but you're young. Seems like there's probably more fun and exciting things to fill your time than long hours and hanging out at bars with men like me."

"Men like you, huh?" I cock my head, bringing back my flirty demeanor. "And what kind of man are you?"

"The kind your dad wouldn't want you talking to." His voice is deep and a little ragged as he leans back in his seat, running his hand through his hair as his eyes drop down to my lips. I stare at him, debating my next move, when I notice the sexy lines at the corner of his eyes. It was obvious he wasn't a fresh graduate when I first saw him, but it's only now that I can see he definitely has a few years on me.

Damn, an older man—my kryptonite.

"Look, I don't normally do this." He laughs at my statement. "Right. Cliché, I know, especially after your little ominous warning but..." I rummage through my wallet for an old receipt and grab a pen from the bar, scribbling down my first name, last initial, and my phone number and hand it to him.

"Is that an initial?" He looks at the paper, then to me.

"Yes, I figure a man who looks like you must have at least twenty different *I don't normally do this* women's numbers in his phone. So, with a last initial, maybe I'll stand out."

"Only twenty?" He hooks an eyebrow at me, making me laugh. "Why only the initial? Scared to give me your last name?"

I grab the paper and write out the rest of my last name before handing it back to him.

"There."

He looks at it, then his smile falters a little. "Brontë Spencer?"

"Yes, that's me. I guess you probably don't have a lot of Brontës in your phone so the last name is a little redundant now that I think about it."

"Yeah," he says almost nervously as he runs his hand over his jaw. "That's for certain."

"I'll be right back. The ladies are frothing at the mouth over there for these," I say as I look over at my friends who are giving me ridiculous hand signals and eye gestures, thinking they're being subtle.

I walk the drinks over to the table and place them down.

"Holy shit, you guys. I just met the finest man I have ever seen in my life. I think I almost blacked out and peed myself talking to him," I whisper as if he could hear me over the loud ruckus the frat boys are causing in the center of the bar.

"And of course he's older." Taylor bounces her eyebrows. "Daddy issues coming in stroooong." They both laugh. They've always teased me about my affinity for older men.

Is it daddy issues? I'm ninety-nine percent sure it is. We can thank Jonas for that.

"I gave him my number!" I shriek just as both of their faces fall. "What?"

"Uh, I think he just left?"

"What?" I spin around and sure enough, he's nowhere to be found. I walk back up to the bar and look around. "Where did that guy go?" I ask the bartender who shrugs and turns to help someone else.

And then that's when I see it, the crumpled-up piece of paper left on the bar top with my name and number.

———

I GROAN AND STRETCH MY ARMS OVERHEAD, TRUDGING TO THE kitchen to make a much-needed espresso before getting ready for my interview at Archer Financial... a decision I'm now regretting giving in to.

Instead of taking time to learn about the company, I've spent far too long thinking about the rejection from a total stranger this weekend.

I make myself a latte and open my iPad to do a little research, but my mind keeps drifting to that sexy smirk from Mr. Daddy Issues at the bar.

"Ugh." I shut my iPad and march to the bathroom for a shower, hoping if I get my day going it will take my mind off Taylor's all-too-true comment that I haven't been laid in over two years and if I'm not careful, my virginity will grow back at any second.

I finish applying my makeup and pull my long hair up into a professional high ponytail. I slide my feet into a sensible pair of black pumps and do a quick spin in front of my floor-length mirror to double-check my pencil skirt isn't tucked into my panties or there isn't a hole in my white blouse.

After this weekend's rejection, I really don't need a double dose of embarrassment for my self-esteem. I look polished and professional.

"I'd hire me." I smile at my reflection before grabbing my portfolio and heading to Archer Financial.

I stop outside the reflective building and stare up at the towering skyscraper. My dad was right; it's literally across the street from his building. I feel my chest tighten as I watch several people walking into the building, their heads turned down as they stare at their phones, completely oblivious to the world around them.

Is this really the life I want?

I square my shoulders and march into the building, reminding myself that this is a good opportunity and like my dad and my friends mentioned, a way to feel out if a life in finance is really what I want.

"Hi, I have an interview with Mr. Beckham Archer at nine thirty."

I smile at the man sitting behind the front desk, but he doesn't reciprocate.

"Name." He doesn't even look up from his computer screen.

"Brontë Spencer."

"It's the fortieth floor. Take the elevator bank behind me to your left. Here's your visitor's badge. Make sure it's visible on your person."

"Thank you."

I walk timidly around the massive desk, my heels echoing against the marble floor as several others rush past me to enter the elevator. When I arrive on the floor, there's a second reception desk with two women smiling at me. I repeat the process of introducing myself.

"Mr. Archer is ready for you." One of the ladies smiles as she stands and walks around the desk. "I'll show you the way."

She brings me to two massive wooden doors that she opens and ushers me inside before turning to walk back down the hallway.

I step inside the office, nervously looking around when I spot him. His back is to me as he faces the floor-to-ceiling windows. He's clearly typing furiously on his phone but finishes and slides it into his pocket to turn around and face me, a casual smirk on his face as he speaks.

"Thanks for meeting me, Miss Spencer."

Holy fucking shit, you have to be kidding me. This cannot be real.

I almost want to pinch myself, convinced I'm having a nightmare right now. Before I can stop myself, the words fall from my lips in a somewhat whisper.

"Mr. Daddy Issues?"

Chapter 2

Beckham

Her face says it all and it's fucking priceless. "Pardon?"

I watch her delicate throat constrict as she attempts to swallow down the realization that the man she tried to pick up last night, is not only her dad's best friend, but I very well could be her new boss.

"Uh, nice to meet you," she says, clutching the folder to her chest, her cheeks flaming.

"Brontë Spencer then, I presume?" I take her hand in mine.

"Ye—yes, that's me." She smiles nervously, shifting her folder and purse to shake my hand. "Pleasure to meet you, sir. And thank you."

"Pleasure's all mine." Her hand is thin and soft, and I'm tempted to hold on to her fingers longer than professional or necessary. I gesture for her to take a seat in the chair across from my desk and she does. Crossing one slim ankle over the other, she smooths out her black pencil skirt.

"I've heard a lot about you from your father, all good things of course." I offer her a genuine smile to ease her tension but it doesn't work. In fact, it seems to have the opposite effect. Her shoulders lift as she hugs the folder in her arms a little tighter.

"So why don't you tell me about yourself, Brontë, what your background looks like, what interests you, what line of work you think you want to end up in."

I lean back in my chair and fold my hands in my lap.

"Well, honestly, I'm a little unsure what I want to do with my life which is why I'm here. My father suggested I come work for you till I figure out what I actually want to do." I chuckle and she nervously tries to backpedal. "Not that I don't think that this is a real job or anything; I'm extremely grateful for the opportunity and for you even taking the time to speak with me."

"No explanation needed." I hold up my hand. "I've been in your shoes before and I think it's a smart plan. Too often we're pushed into specific careers based on what we decided to study when we were eighteen years old. A lot can happen between now and then."

"I studied finance and accounting in undergrad and just graduated from grad school with my master's in forensic accounting. My mom was an accountant and she loved her job so I followed in her footsteps."

"But now you're unsure about that path for yourself?"

"Yeah, I guess so."

I lean forward in my chair and intertwine my fingers. "What is it that excites you? When you picture yourself twenty years from now, what career do you see yourself in?"

Her shoulders finally drop as she chews on the corner of her lip.

"Helping people. I like volunteering and I think nonprofit is something I could see myself in long term."

"Well, that's good news. We have some great relationships with a few here in Chicago. In fact, we have a foundation. The Archer Foundation focuses on single mothers or women in need of prenatal care... basically families in need. We do fundraisers and group volunteering throughout the company. We also offer five paid days off per month for volunteering."

Her eyes grow wide as I explain about our efforts here at Archer Financial to give back to our community and help those in need.

"That sounds wonderful. My mom was big into volunteering and took me even before I can remember. Anyway, I do like finance as well. I enjoy solving problems and finding errors. I just—it's a big commitment to choose a career and jump in when you're not one hundred percent certain."

Gone is the bold, flirty woman from last night who shamelessly approached me at the bar—replaced with an almost timid and nervous little creature. Her eyes dart from mine to the floor and back again as she speaks. They sparkle when the sun hits them through the blinds behind me. Her lips are full, almost too large for her delicate features, yet they fit her perfectly. Everything about her seems ethereal, like she could be a Disney princess locked away in a tower by an evil witch... a far cry from her commanding and at times tyrannical father.

"Tell you what, Brontë. If you were to accept the position here at Archer, you would be hired on as my assistant. I am in desperate need of someone who can help me manage my calendar and gatekeep my time, also someone who can attend meetings with me, book travel, manage my emails and messages. Basically, my right arm. I'm not looking for someone to work twelve-hour days or pick up my dry cleaning. I'm pretty easygoing and approachable. I do—"

"I'm really sorry about last night," she interrupts me, blurting out her apology nervously. "I had no idea who you were and I *never*"—she gestures with her arms like she's an umpire calling a runner safe—"do that. I had some champagne at my graduation party; that's why we were there, we were celebrating. I don't know what came over me, but I wanted to be bold and felt confident and I just... I'm so sorry."

She shakes her head and I can see the shame on her face but it doesn't stop me from chuckling.

"Absolutely no need to apologize about it, Brontë. We are two adults and asking someone out is part of life. I, uh, I feel like I owe you an apology actually. When you said your name, I recognized it immediately and because of who your father is... and because he's one of my closest friends, I removed myself from the situation."

"My ego appreciates the explanation." She looks down as she says it, a sly smile on her face and it feels like her nervousness is melting.

"I should have offered you an explanation, but I panicked. I think I was just in shock at the coincidence considering you were on my calendar this morning. Guess I should have just explained that right then but felt it might have been embarrassing... Then again, showing up to find me behind this desk today probably wasn't any better." She shrugs and we both laugh again. "So, water under the bridge on both our parts?"

"Deal." She smiles.

"Great. So back to the job, how does all that sound? And for the record, I am fully aware that if you took this job, you could realize in a month that you hate it and want to leave. That is completely fine and won't be an issue. I just wanted to extend the offer to you if it was in any way something you feel you would be interested in."

"I appreciate it. I think it sounds perfectly manageable on my part. When do I need to give an answer?"

"How about the end of the week? Give you enough time to think things over?"

"Yes."

"Perfect. Here..." I grab my business card and scribble down my personal cell number on it. "This has my email and work phone, but this is my personal cell. If you have any questions or need more time to make the decision, just shoot me a text or email."

My fingers graze hers as she takes it from my hand. The touch is quick and subtle, but it instantly sets my nerves ablaze. Her fire-red nail polish isn't helping the matter because all I see when I look down at them is having them wrapped around my cock.

"Looks like I got your number after all." She giggles, that blush spreading up her neck and over her cheeks again. "Sorry, that wasn't professional. I don't know why I said that."

It makes me laugh again. "Don't apologize; we're not that uptight here." She looks up at me from where she's still sitting in her chair. I'm towering over and for some stupid reason, I take it a step further. I reach out and tip her chin upward so she's looking up at me. "I promise I don't bite, Brontë. You can relax."

The tension in this second is palpable, but just as quickly it vanishes when she clears her throat and stuffs the card into her purse as she gathers her things to stand up.

"Thanks again for your time, Mr. Archer. I will be in touch with you shortly."

"Beckham," I correct her.

"Beckham." She nods and heads toward my office door. She stops just before she reaches it and slowly turns back around to face me. "Just one other thing."

"Hmm?"

"Could we keep last night between us? As in, don't tell my father."

I want to say I wouldn't dream of it because if your father knew that I even contemplated for one second taking his daughter home, he'd cut my balls off and feed them to his dogs.

"Of course, it'll be our little secret." And just to make things even more tense, I throw in a wink for good measure.

———

I'm not proud of it, but I've spent the last three days thinking of very little but Brontë.

Something about her, beyond her obvious beauty, is so compelling to me. The way she seems to hold herself back, the way she presents so innocently, yet lurking beneath that surface I sense a curious woman begging for a man to coax out her naughty side.

I grip my golf club tighter as I imagine being that man. It excites me to imagine helping her find that confidence again she displayed the other night in the bar. To see her ask for what she wants, to demand it from me.

"Something on your mind? You're awfully quiet today," her father, Jonas, asks me, snapping me back to reality.

Is it fucked up beyond measure that I'm standing fifteen feet away from Brontë's father, imagining doing all sorts of debase things to her? Yeah, I'd say that's about as fucked as you can get, but maybe that's part of the allure.

The forbidden fruit.

"Heard anything from Brontë about the job?" I ask as I take my position at the tee.

"No, haven't spoken to her since the graduation party. I can give her a call if you want?" He holds his cell phone up, but I shake my head no.

"That's okay. I don't want her feeling pressured. I told her to let me know by Friday. I'm sure she will."

"She's a very bright woman, just like her mother. I just worry she'll end up wasting her aptitude for finance and problem solving on some silly do-good endeavor in nonprofit. Now I know," he says, lifting his gloved hands, "others need help and don't have the opportunity like I had but still, she's got something and it would be a shame to toss that aside. Even her professors have said as much, that she's gifted."

I smile, not surprised at all that she's whip-smart. I could tell just from our short interaction she's the kind of woman who has it all.

I'm trying to play it cool but I'm hoping she takes the job. I don't know why because I know that no matter how much I want to, no matter how much she wants me to... I can't touch her.

I *won't* touch her.

I tee off, the ball sailing down the fairway.

"Not a bad shot but still won't be enough to beat me. Get that checkbook ready." He laughs as we climb inside the golf cart.

We've had a long-standing bet between us when we play golf. Loser has to donate winner's chosen amount to winner's chosen charity.

"We'll see about that."

"Wouldn't bet money on a shot like that."

I turn when I hear the grating voice of Mitchell Reardon, a joke of a man, pulling up beside me in his golf cart. I look to his left and see my ex, socialite Venus Davenport's father Miles sitting shotgun.

Venus Davenport's father, Miles, sitting shotgun.

"I see Miles has you being his little bi—I mean caddy today, Mitchell. I'm sure he'll tip you well." I give him a hearty grin and his freckled face flushes.

"Beckham, Jonas," Miles says dismissively as if we're bothering him.

We both tip our heads toward him and Mitchell drives off, flipping me the bird behind Miles' back.

"What an arrogant little shit," Jonas says. "What's his deal? Why does he hate you?"

"He's always had something against me. I think it has something to do with my dating Venus, but I don't know for sure."

I know for a fact it's because of my relationship with Venus. Mitchell's always had it bad for her and she's always said he wasn't her type but toward the end of our relationship, there were a few clues that she might have stepped out on me with him. Nothing I could prove or even cared to prove since I moved on.

"So any more thoughts about Pierce Investments? With almost twenty nationwide locations, it's only upside for Archer if you guys acquire them from Ramsay Consulting."

"I think you're right. I'm actually going to be meeting with them in the next few weeks. They want to come to Chicago and see how we do things here. If they end up not wanting to go through with the acquisition, will you keep them?"

Jonas shakes his head as he reaches for his beer. "They've been on the chopping block for a while with us. I think there's a lot of potential with them, could easily triple their locations nationwide, but in the last few years I've backed away from investment firms. I think it would be right up your alley to acquire them and rebrand them as Archer. Already have the overhead and infrastructure in place."

He's right. I've been looking to do a major expansion with Archer

Financial and acquiring an already established company is the best way to do it.

"Bottom line," he says, "they want to expand their portfolio and footprint but they need the capital from somewhere and they know they're not going to get it from me."

We finish our game and I head back home to try and relax and push the ever-present thoughts of my best friend's daughter from my mind.

I'm just stepping out of the shower when my phone chirps at me from the counter. I look down to see a text from a number that's not in my phone. It just reads: *I'll take the job.*

I smile and add Brontë's name to my contacts.

Brontë: *Sorry. I said I would email, didn't I? Will send an email now so it's official.*

Me: *No need for the email, Brontë. Thank you for letting me know and for taking the job.*

And because I clearly can't seem to not fan the flames, I send another text.

Me: *I was actually just talking about you.*

Brontë: *Oh?*

Me: *With your father.*

Brontë: *Oh.*

I want to read into her response. Was it disappointment that I didn't say I was telling a friend about a sexy little thing I met at the bar this weekend that has my brain doing all sorts of fucked-up backflips trying to justify wanting to fuck my best friend's daughter?

Me: *He'll be happy to hear you took the job. Have a good night, Brontë. See you Monday.*

Brontë: *Thanks again. See you Monday, Mr. Archer.*

She doesn't correct it to Beckham and I don't want her to because standing here butt-ass naked out of the shower, my cock growing harder by the second, all I want is to see her on her knees in front of me calling me Mr. Archer in that slightly breathy voice of hers.

I look back over my shoulder at the shower, my cock throbbing, begging for release at the images in my head right now.

I know I shouldn't. It's fucked up. It's so wrong on so many levels that I'm pretty sure even Freud would have a field day with me.

"Fuck it." I reach back into the shower and turn on the water as I step in and begin to slowly stroke myself.

Chapter 3

Brontë

"So you took the job?" Taylor asks, dunking her French fry into a massive pile of ketchup.

She thinks that by ordering a salad and side of fries "for the table," she's somehow gaming the system when in reality, she's the only one who eats the fries because Sylvia and I order our own.

"Yup. I told him that I'd be there bright and early Monday morning."

"Well, I'm happy for you. I really think it's the best decision," Sylvia says emphatically. "Like I said before, you don't want to end up my age, hating your job but already a decade in so you feel stuck."

"Have you considered trying something else?" I ask her.

"Yeah, but it's just not possible right now. Aaron is supportive of me finding my passion but with Lucy still in pre-K, it just isn't feasible right now. Once she's in school full-time, I plan to do some soul-searching and figure my shit out."

Sylvia's daughter, Lucy, is a ball of energy, just like any other four-year-old I suppose, but sometimes it seems like she's the Energizer Bunny.

"Speaking of Lucy, what did she think of the children's museum?" Taylor asks, referring to the outing Sylvia mentioned to us a few days ago. She was so excited to take her to the museum for the first time since we all have such fond memories of going there as children.

"She hated it." She rolls her eyes and shakes her head. "Had a complete meltdown because she got overwhelmed. I should have known when she stayed up half the night before, too excited to sleep."

"Aw, poor thing. Well, maybe next summer you guys can try again."

"Anyway," Sylvia says, "back to the job. I'm so happy for you. Maybe we should plan a little celebratory dinner; it can be for your birthday too. Then after dinner, we get a few drinks in you, some dancing, and maybe you can finally meet someone and break that dry spell."

Taylor giggles and bounces her eyebrows at me.

"Yeah, that would be fun. Actually, kind of a funny coincidence about the new job." I run my fingertip around the rim of my glass, both of my friends staring at me, eagerly waiting for me to continue. "You remember that hot guy I flirted with at the bar?"

"Yeah?" they both say in unison.

"So, the reason he didn't take my number or left it on the bar rather is because, um... well, that was Beckham Archer."

They stare at me unblinking, clearly confused.

"Wait, the man you tried to pick up is your new boss?" Taylor asks.

"Mm-hmm."

"The same guy that is your dad's best friend?" Sylvia says.

"One and the same."

"Holy shit!" Taylor clamps her hands over her mouth before bursting into laughter. "What are the odds? Oh my God. Better yet, did he recognize you?"

"Yeah." I hang my head as they both fire questions at me about how it went down and what he said to me.

"We both knew the moment I entered his office and my dumb ass

24

called him Mr. Daddy Issues to his face!" Sylvia stands up, her chair shooting out behind her as she dramatically walks in a circle near our table before sitting back down.

"Go on. Sorry, this is just too much." She laughs.

"I don't think he heard me; it was half under my breath, but he acted like nothing happened. He introduced himself and we started talking about my background and the job duties and I just blurted out that I was so sorry for coming on to him and that it was because I'd been drinking and celebrating and it was completely out of character for me."

"What'd he say back?"

"He said that when he read my name, he recognized it and realized who I was and that's why he didn't take my number."

"Wait." Taylor leans in. "He said that the reason he didn't take your number was because of who you were as in, he would have if you weren't who you are?"

I scrunch up my face at the way she worded the question. "Oh, I don't know for sure actually. I mean, it kind of seemed that way. He didn't say outright that if things were different, he would have taken it and called me. He was probably just being nice, didn't want to reject me a second time to my face."

Sylvia gets a coy look on her face. "I'd ask him."

"Same."

I look at both of them. "He's my new boss. No way I'm going to ask him if things were different if he'd go out with me. Talk about awkward."

I finish my drink and toss my napkin on my empty plate. I would actually love to know if that were the case. Trust me, that same thought has gone through my head about fifty times since our interview, but I know there's no use in wondering because a man like that doesn't break the rules for an inexperienced hookup with a woman twenty years his junior.

What's that saying? *Why go out for burgers when you have steak at home?*

I can guarantee you that Beckham Archer could have the finest grade of steak at any hour, any night of the damn week.

"What's his name again?" Taylor asks, pulling out her phone.

"Why?"

"I want to Google him, duh," she says as if I should already know. "Name."

"Beckham Archer." I say it slowly, just the syllables on my tongue making me want to blush.

"God, even his name sounds hot. Like, there's no way an ugly man would have that name." She taps around on her phone for a second before gasping. "Oh, oh, hot damn." She clutches at her imaginary pearls, then pinches her screen to zoom in on a photo.

"Lemme see!" Sylvia leans halfway into Taylor's seat to look at the photo, both women bug-eyed.

"Do I want to know?" I take a sip of my ice water, praying it stops me from breaking out in a nervous sweat. Taylor slowly flips the phone around to reveal a shirtless image of Beckham with a smile on his face from ear to ear. He's coming out of the water, droplets glistening off his broad shoulders and six-pack abs. The man is fucking chiseled.

Great, just what I didn't need to know... How the hell am I supposed to focus around him now that I know for certain what's beneath those designer suits?

"How does anyone look that good in a candid shot, in the sunlight, coming out of the ocean? Probably staged by paparazzi or something." I roll my eyes, pretending to be unfazed.

"Yummy, Mr. Daddy Issues looks fiiiine in a tux." Taylor spins the phone around again to reveal him waving to the camera in a tuxedo outside the opera house in Paris.

"Is that Kim K on his arm?" Sylvia squints.

Seriously? Come on.

"Nah, just a lookalike. Damn, this man looks like Ken. Like literally Ken in his... how old is he again?" She taps a few times. "Holy shit, he's forty-five? It should be illegal to look this good."

I reach for my drink again, guzzling down the icy liquid, but it does little to suppress the desire that's beginning to burn.

"He could literally be your daddy," Sylvia teases.

"Yeah, but that's why it's so hot, isn't it?" I didn't mean to say it out loud but it's the truth. "I just mean being with an experienced man, you know?"

"Have you ever?" Taylor asks and I shake my head no.

"No. There was a professor in undergrad that I could have if I wanted to, but it felt weird and I didn't want him to risk his job."

"I have." Sylvia shrugs.

"When?"

"When I was in undergrad actually. He was this older wealthy guy who liked having me around since I was young. I was twenty-one; he was forty-something, who knows, maybe even fifty. It was nothing serious. I think we both knew it was just a summer fling but damn, was it hot." She smiles, reminiscing, I assume.

"And you have a great relationship with your father," I point out. "So not *all* crushes on older men are daddy issues."

"But yours are," she says.

"Not necessarily. I've always been into older men. My sexual awakening was George Clooney and I was like eleven at the time."

"First"—Sylvia holds up a finger—"George Clooney has always been and will always be fine. He's everyone's sexual awakening; even straight men have had shower thoughts about George Clooney. Second, your dad has been a piece of shit since before you were eleven so that negates your argument."

"Fine," I huff, crossing my arms and sitting back in my chair.

"But it's not *your* fault; it's your dad's. He's the one who fucked up."

"I know." I sigh. "Is it so bad to indulge in daddy issues? I mean so what if I end up with an older man. Can a relationship *not* work if it grows out of past trauma?"

Taylor reaches out and grabs my hand, "No, sweetie, we didn't mean it like that. If you meet someone who's older and they truly make you happy, who gives a fuck what society thinks. We just want to make sure you don't end up with some older asshole who is just going to flake on you like your dad did when you were a kid. I know your dad is different now and you guys are working on your relationship, and that's the first step to then finding healthy relationships with the men you date."

"It really is a damn shame I didn't wait to tell him my name till after we hooked up, isn't it?" I say, referring to Beckham, causing both women to burst out laughing.

————

"OKAY, YOU'VE GOT THIS."

I slick on my favorite berry-colored lipstick that makes my blue eyes pop, then I smooth down my hair. I spray a few spritzes of my signature Chanel Chance perfume and double-check my outfit.

Did I spend two, possibly three hours last night picking out my outfit for today? Yes, but it's because I want to make a good first impression at my job, *not* because I'm so attracted to my boss that I spent an additional three hours after my lunch date with my friends, doing a little—okay a lot—of my own Google research on him.

I read up on his nonprofit he mentioned, The Archer Foundation. Shockingly, their website isn't littered with photos of him cutting ribbons, posing with children or mothers or handing over giant checks. In fact, there's very little mention of him at all. I'm not sure if that's because like most of these uber rich types he only writes a check every quarter and slaps his name on it or if it's truly because he doesn't want it to be about him.

I make a mental note to send them an email inquiring about accepting new volunteers before grabbing my bag and heading downstairs to catch my train.

I tap the toe of my black pumps nervously as I triple-check my manicure for the third time in a row. I slide my camera screen to the front-facing camera and double-check that my lipstick hasn't smeared. I smile a toothy grin, looking for any sneaky chia seeds that might have lodged in my teeth when I pull back and see Beckham behind me in the camera frame.

"Good morning!" I fumble with my phone, almost dropping it as I rush to stand up and face him.

"Good morning, Miss Spencer. You beat me into work. Not gunning for my job, I hope." He flashes a flirty smirk as his eyes casually travel down my body. It's not in a predatory manner, more an appreciative perusing of my outfit selection—a fitted black dress that falls just above my knee, black pumps, and some sensible gold jewelry.

I've never been great at business attire. Pantsuits always made me feel like I was playing dress-up in my mom's closet or perhaps like I was going to guest star as a detective on a cop show, but the flowery dresses and cute skirts I'd prefer to wear make me feel unprofessional or even childlike compared to the amount of grays, blues, and blacks that everyone else wears.

"I was anxious about making it on time so I opted to take the earlier train which I now realize is probably a little too early." I smile and start to follow him into his office.

"Well, as I mentioned in the interview, there's no need to keep unrealistic hours. I get in pretty early—before eight—but I wouldn't expect you to. That being said, since you're here, let's grab coffee and have a little talk. I'd like to run something by you."

"Absolutely. How do you take yours?" I look at him, but he shakes his head and steps around his desk toward me after placing his suit jacket on the back of his chair.

"I'll go with you." He gestures forward with one hand, his other ever so lightly touching the middle of my back to guide us down the hallway toward a break room that has more snacks and coffee machines than a Hudson News at the airport.

It's just the two of us in the room and I'm now very aware at how close I'm standing to him as he shows me how to work the fancy machine that sputters and hisses before producing a cup of coffee.

His hands are in his pockets, pulling his dress pants taut against his perky backside as he waits for the machine to finish. I bite my tongue to keep myself from outright staring. The images of him wearing small swim trunks, emerging from the ocean with water cascading over his tan body, come rushing back and I bite down harder.

James Bond... or Daniel Craig rather in those tiny blue swim shorts from one of those Bond movies from years ago... that's what it reminded me of. I smile, almost giggling to myself that Beckham Archer really is like a real-life James Bond. Hot, rich, and if I had to guess, knows *exactly* how to make a woman co—

"Brontë? You okay?"

"Hmm?" I whip my head around to face him, realizing I've been standing there staring at the coffee machine with my empty cup for several minutes as he finished making his.

Now is not the time, Brontë.

"Oh, yes, sorry." I stumble forward, placing my cup under the spout and jabbing erratically at the buttons because I was clearly not paying attention when he explained it a few moments ago.

"Here, allow me." He reaches around me and presses the correct button, his expensive cologne wafting upward.

He even smells like what I picture James Bond smelling like.

I let my eyes flutter closed for a brief second before he steps back and the space between us widens.

"Your dad and I were talking about you last week at golf. I think he was curious about if you were taking the job. Have you told him yet?"

His question about my father instantly tamps down the arousal I could feel building. Nothing like being reminded that the man you're crushing on hangs out with your dad for fun.

"Uh, no, I haven't yet. I will. I need to call my stepmom back about something so I'm sure I'll tell them then."

"Chantelle? She's a very nice lady."

"Yeah, she is. Makes my dad happy." The small talk is odd but I smile and grab my coffee, then I follow him back toward his office.

He takes a seat behind his desk and I do likewise in a chair in front of his desk.

"What I wanted to talk to you about is a slight change in your role here at Archer."

"A change?" I furrow my brows as I nervously clutch my coffee.

"Yes, but it's not required. I thought I'd offer you my idea and if you say no, that's perfectly okay. We'll just have you be an assistant like we spoke about in the interview."

He pauses, looking at me like he's trying to ease my nerves.

"Okay."

"After speaking with your father and going with my gut on our first meeting, I feel like you'd benefit from more than just setting appointments and booking travel. I'd like to see you in a more mentor-type position—with me."

I swallow down the mouthful of coffee. "What do you mean?"

"Well, we are currently looking to possibly acquire an investment firm; they're like one of those chain investment firms. They want to expand but don't have the backing. If I purchased them, we would turn them into an Archer subsidiary and help them expand."

I nod. "Understood. So what would I be doing then?"

"I'd love to use your expertise to help me analyze them. Look at their financials, their performance, do some due diligence. We would meet with them, go through all of the preliminary talks, and if things proceed, you could be hand in hand with me on the acquisition process."

I'm shocked. This isn't just a mentorship; this is a huge opportunity to really get my feet wet and be hands-on in the financial world. I actually feel a tinge of excitement.

"Wow, that sounds like a great opportunity. I'd be crazy to pass it up, huh?"

"Well, I don't want to say that, but I think you'd benefit greatly from it. It would allow you to then make a fair assessment on your future."

I smile and jut out my hand. "I'll do it."

He laughs and stands slowly, sliding his hand over mine to shake it. It's not your typical handshake that's firm and deliberate; it lingers, feels sensual. His fingers glide ever so softly over my skin as he slowly pulls his hand away from mine.

"You're okay to travel, right?"

"Travel?"

He sits back down in his chair as he lazily unbuttons his cuffs and begins to roll up the sleeves of his Oxford shirt. My eyes fall down to his thick forearm, peppered by dirty-blond hair that matches his head.

"Yes, I'm sure we'll go visit the client in Las Vegas when the time comes."

Panic suddenly grips my chest when I think about nothing but a single wall separating us in a hotel.

"Brontë?" He says my name again, his voice deep and gravelly.

"Yes, that won't be a problem. I'll let you get to work." I give him a broad smile before standing and exiting his office calmly.

"I've got to get laid," I mutter to myself, trying to shake off the effect that Beckham Archer has on my ovaries.

Chapter 4

Beckham

Did I enjoy seeing the brief panic that took over Brontë's face when I offered her a more hands-on position?

Yes, yes, I did because I'm clearly a sick bastard who wallows in torturing myself.

But did I anticipate the complete agony I'd face day in and day out when she's next to me, in my space, her perfume permeating every inch of my office as she leans across a table to hand me a report, giving me a perfect shot right down her blouse to her perfect tits?

Fuck no.

"I believe that is everything for their last fiscal year. I've broken out all of the reports into quarterly and monthly as well."

She places the stack next to me. A lock of her hair has fallen from her updo down her exposed slender neck. She shrugged off her cardigan hours ago, leaving her in a silky tank top tucked neatly into her sensible skirt that hugs her hips.

"It's late, Brontë. Go home. Your first week and you're already staying late like I promised you we wouldn't. We can tackle this tomorrow."

"We actually can't tackle this tomorrow because tomorrow is

Saturday and the meeting with Pierce Investments is Monday night." She smiles and leans one hip against the boardroom table that we've taken over.

She's only been working here a week, and I've already started to see her shy walls come down, brick by brick. Bits of her personality are shining through, just enough to make me more curious with every interaction. I suddenly want to knock down all her walls, but I know that's not how it works. Slowly they'll come down as I earn her trust.

"That's right. Well, we've done all the heavy lifting so we'll have time to go over the rest Monday afternoon before the meeting."

I drag my hand over my face before pulling my loosened tie completely free from my neck. I watch as her eyes move from the table to where my hands wrap the tie around my fist. Her fingers slowly creep up her neck to that tendril of hair that she wraps nervously around the end of her finger.

"It's our annual company outing tomorrow?" she says in a half question.

"It is. You should go, you'll have fun." Every year I rent out Navy Pier in downtown Chicago for the company. They get unlimited access to the rides, open bar, and even the speed boats that take people out on the lake. "Unless you have other plans?"

"I don't." She smiles and a silence settles between us before she turns to the table to begin gathering up our paperwork.

"What does a twenty-four-year-old do for fun on the weekend these days?" I cringe at the way I worded that as I step closer to her to help. I could have certainly worded that several different ways that didn't make me sound like an old man.

"Um, go out, I guess?"

"You do that often? Clubs, you mean?"

She shakes her head. "Not too much at all really. It never really was my thing. My two close friends are several years older than me and they're out of that stage anyway so it works out well. We go to brunch, sometimes yoga, sometimes shopping."

"So you've always been into older people?" Her head snaps up, her cheeks already pink with embarrassment, and I'm not sure mine aren't the same. "That's not what I meant." I chuckle and it makes her laugh too.

"Yeah, I guess you could say that. I met my best friend Sylvia when she was my TA in undergrad and Taylor I met at the children's nonprofit I volunteer at. Just so happens they are both older. Guess you could say I have a type."

I tell myself not to, but I look over at her. She looks up at me, her lip caught between her lower teeth. I swear I can hear the rapid beat of her heart or maybe it's my own as we're caught in these tension-filled seconds together. I imagine tossing the papers dramatically to the side, reaching across the table, and dragging her toward me as I have my way with her, but the thought of Jonas Ramsay as my enemy instantly kills that thought.

"What about you? What does a forty-five-year-old man do for fun on the weekend these days?"

"You know how old I am?" I don't bother looking up at her this time, but I can feel her panicking.

"I, uh, before, er, after the interview, I did some research on the company and I think it was listed on Google somewhere."

I chuckle. I know it's fucked up, but I like making her flustered. Maybe it feels like I have a leg up since the rest of the time she's so poised and calm that it makes me feel like I'm seconds away from losing my composure when I feel the warmth of her body so close to me.

"I'm afraid my weekends are pretty boring. A round or two of golf if I have the free time but mostly I work from my home office."

"Well, that doesn't sound very fun. I thought one of the perks of being the boss was you got to have more time and money to do what-ever you wanted."

"Yeah, I thought that too." I laugh. "Sometimes I'll take my boat out on the lake if the weather cooperates... and then I'll work from there."

She shakes her head as we head back toward my office.

"Sounds like you need to find a work-life balance. Maybe pick up a new hobby or go on a date."

"A date? What's that?" I joke.

"Well, I'm going to take off for the night. I hope you have a nice weekend." She smiles. "Will I see you at the company event tomorrow at Navy Pier?"

I'm not sure why I say it because I've told myself a thousand times not to let the flirty moments turn into more, but before I can stop myself, the words are out of my mouth.

"Do you *want* to see me at the company event tomorrow?"

"Yes," she answers quickly.

"Then I'll see you tomorrow."

"Good night, Mr. Archer."

She spins on her heel and walks out of my office, a bouncy little pep in her step that has me second-guessing my decision to go. Part of me wants to keep the flirty innuendos going, convincing myself they're harmless. But a bigger part of me wants to warn her that I'm not the older, experienced boy-next-door fantasy.

I'm the wicked man who will destroy her innocence, and most likely break her heart in the process.

———

I scan the crowd, attempting to act casual and not like I'm searching through a sea of people for Brontë when I spot her, surrounded by a group of young guys from our investment division. Each one of them dressed more douchey than the one next to him.

"I've never seen so many pastel polos," I mutter to myself, remembering how I looked just like them at their age. Young, eager, and ready to fuck anything that gave me the time of day.

She's smiling widely, her eyes sparkling as her blond ponytail bounces with the movement of her laughter. She doesn't notice me so I take the opportunity to watch her. She's fully engaged with whatever they're talking about.

"Fuck me." I glance, around making sure nobody notices me creeping as the men part and I see what she's wearing.

Her bare legs look smooth as glass, exposed by her cute pink shorts that hit at her mid-thigh. Her white top has several straps going every which way and stops an inch above the waistband of her shorts, leaving just a hint of skin showing that makes my mouth water.

Everything about her teases me. The slight curl of her plump lips, the way her big doe eyes stare at me when I say anything that shocks or embarrasses her. The contrast of how she can go from a sexy siren who seems to know exactly what she's doing in one second to an innocent woman who is flustered and naive is so alluring to me. She's a puzzle—intriguing and challenging.

Her eyes shift from the man in front of her to directly over his shoulder, at me. I smile, shoving my hands in my pockets to avoid waving like a desperate idiot who's been standing around hoping she notices me.

I watch as she excuses herself, walking between the group of guys and heading straight toward me. Their eyes never even notice that it's me she's approaching; they're all too focused on watching her walk away... and I don't blame them.

"Hey," she says coyly, the straw of her drink perched on the edge of her lips.

"I hope I didn't interrupt." I nod toward the men but she just shrugs.

"Nah, I was merely entertaining them."

"With tales of great financial exploits?"

"Not exactly." She giggles as we begin to walk down the pier. "I was kind of trolling them, but they had no idea."

I hook an eyebrow at her in question.

"So guys my age, or finance guys my age I should say, loooove to impress us women with all of their advice about how we can dominate the markets and build independent wealth overnight."

"Ah, yes, I remember those days."

"They all just assume I'm an admin with no financial background so I just play dumb."

"*You* playing dumb?" I struggle to imagine that.

"It's pretty funny. This one particular time I pretended like I had never heard of crypto currency. You should have seen them when I said, *what's a bitcoin?*" She cocks her head and puts on a valley girl accent that has me rolling. "Needless to say, their heads practically exploded as they tripped over each other trying to be the first to explain it to me."

She smiles again, that wide, bright smile that reaches up to her eyes, then she takes a sip of her drink.

"You're something else, you know that?"

"Just wait till I tell them I'm rooting for a bear market because they're cute and cuddly and bulls aren't." She does the accent again before bursting into laughter herself.

These are the moments when I think she knows exactly what she's doing.

"So, besides breaking hearts and playing dumb, are you having fun out here?"

"I am. I ate a pretzel and walked through the shops. I actually haven't been here since I was a kid, at least ten years or more."

I can't help it, I shake my head. "Ten years ago you were a kid."

"I was fourteen and you were"—she hesitates—"thirty-five." We both know what we're thinking as she says it.

"That's uncomfortable," I half mutter under my breath but she hears it loud and clear.

"Why uncomfortable, Mr. Archer?" She gives me that same look she was giving those young men just a few moments ago, her tongue darting out to pull her straw into her mouth as she levels her eyes on mine.

I'm tempted. Very tempted, in fact, to say something that would make her blush but I ignore her question.

"Anyway, what's your favorite ride?"

"When I *was* a kid, it would be the swings but now probably the Ferris wheel. I haven't been on it since they redid it."

"Neither have I."

She looks at me sideways. "Do you normally not come to this? The work party I mean?"

"I have in years past, but it's been a few years now."

"Any particular reason why?"

I shrug. "Besides you asking me to, no. I guess I assumed people don't want to hang out with their boss on the weekend."

"I guess that says something about me?" She nudges me with her elbow just as we approach a few of the guys she was speaking with earlier. They're loudly shouting about something when they back up and one bumps right into my chest.

"Sorry, si—oh, Mr. Archer, sorry, sir."

"Hey, Steven, no worries." I grab his shoulder and turn to the others. "Hope you guys are having a good time."

"Yes, sir," Steven says, the others echoing his sentiment as we walk on.

"Do you intimidate everyone?" She laughs and I look over at her.

"Do I? I don't think so. Were they intimidated?"

"Yeah." She says it like it was right in front of my face. "Steven was beet red and practically choked on his words when he saw it was you he ran into."

I shrug it off. I'm not a tyrant by any means. I go above and beyond to give my employees higher salaries, better work-life balance, and reasonable deadlines more than any other competitor.

"Do I intimidate you?"

"Isn't that obvious?"

"Really? That's surprising I guess since you approached me so confidently in the bar that night."

The sun has begun to set as we walk closer to the Ferris wheel.

"Yes, well, like I mentioned, I was several glasses of champagne and that was very much not like me. I was feeling empowered and bold and decided it was my moment to go for it... which clearly backfired."

"It didn't backfire." I chuckle.

"Really? Because I recall looking back to see you gone and the piece of paper with my number on it still on the bar top."

"We both know why I did that."

I usher her toward the ramp for the Ferris wheel and we wait as an empty car approaches and the attendant opens the door for us. We step inside and each take a seat on opposite benches. The lights of the city twinkle against the multicolored sky. Ribbons of orange and pink make it look like the sky is on fire as the sun slowly sinks lower in the sky.

We both stare out over the skyline for several moments as the car travels slowly upward. We comment on the skyline, making small talk about our favorite views. After a few moments of silence, she grips the edge of her seat and leans slightly forward, the tip of her pink tongue darting out to wet her plump lips.

I try to ignore it but my eyes are drawn to her. A small smile tugs at her lips and I know something is brewing in that head of hers. So, against my better judgment... I ask, "What's on your mind?"

"If I hadn't written my name on the paper, would you have called me?"

Yup, instant regret on asking.

I lean back, crossing one ankle over my knee as I stretch my arms out over the back of the seat. I settle my gaze on her, thinking before I reply.

"Brontë." I level my eyes at her, attempting to give her time to take it back, but she doesn't. She squares her shoulders and stares back at me.

Defiant little thing.

"I don't think that's a thread we should pull at."

She doesn't break eye contact; instead, she doubles down so I lean in.

"What did you come here looking for tonight, young lady?"

40

She mimics my behavior. "Why did you agree to come tonight?"

I shake my head and chuckle, leaning back in the seat. "I think you're looking for trouble."

"Didn't realize you were such a Boy Scout, Mr. Archer." She has that look in her eyes, the same one she had the night we first met and I know she's goading me.

I let her comment simmer for a moment, running my hand over my jaw as I allow my eyes to slowly peruse her body. I can see her fidget under my stare, her facade slowly breaking. I level my eyes directly at hers.

"I can assure you, Miss Spencer," I say her name deliberately with a touch of sternness. "I am anything but a Boy Scout but there are several pretty solid reasons why we know that's a bad idea. One being I'm your boss; I'd say that's a pretty big reason. The others being the very obvious fact that your father and I are good friends and lastly," I say slowly as the car comes back down to the platform where we started, "I'm old enough to be your father."

There's a flash of something in her eyes, something that tells me this won't be the end of this conversation and as much as I know it should be, I don't want it to be either.

We exit the ride and make our way back down to the entrance of the park. The sun has fully set and the city is alive with lights and the usual Saturday night crowd looking for fun and trouble.

"Come on." I cup her elbow and point toward my driver whom I texted on the ride. "My driver's waiting over here. He's going to give us rides home."

I don't give her time to argue. I help her into the back seat of the SUV and slide in beside her.

"Evening, Carson. This is Brontë Spencer. We'll be making a stop to drop her off tonight."

"Evening, sir, Miss Spencer," Carson says before asking for her address.

"You're not getting out of answering," she whispers. I give Carson a look in the rearview mirror and he hits the button to slide the partition up. She watches as it closes, then looks over at me. "Just answer as if none of those things existed."

"Why are you doing this?"

"It's vindication. The one time I go out on a limb and ask a guy out while trying to get back out there, I get rejected. And it was in front of my friends, on my graduation night." She plays up the puppy dog eyes and I hate that I can feel myself giving in.

"Get back out there?" I give her a questioning look and she shakes her head.

"You answer first."

I stall for as long as possible till I feel the car slowing and Carson taps on the partition.

"Looks like your stop. I'll walk you to your door."

I exit the vehicle and hold out my hand. Brontë slides hers into mine as she steps onto the curb. We walk to the front of her building and she turns to face me.

"I'll drop it." She smiles. "Thanks for the ride and the company. I had a lot of fun." She turns to reach for the handle of her door when I dart out my hand to grab her arm. She stops, looking down to where my fingers are wrapped around her arm, then back up at me.

Now is the time I should release her hand. I should tell her good night and march my ass back to my vehicle, but I don't.

"No," I say, looking into her eyes as her smile fades. "I wouldn't have taken your number... Because I wouldn't have let you walk out of the bar without me that night."

Her lips turn from a straight line into a coy smile. "Bold of you to assume I would have gone home with you."

Damn this woman, she knows exactly how to push my buttons... and it's working.

I step closer to her, her back hitting the brick wall of the building and that cocky grin of hers fades.

"Bold of you to assume you would have been able to resist." I run my hand slowly up her exposed arm till I reach her chin. I hook my finger beneath it, tilting it upward so that she's looking at me. I take the opportunity to give her a taste of the kind of man I am—maybe if I call her on her bluff, it will put a healthy dose of fear in her.

"Do you think you would have said no, Brontë, if I had touched you?" I step even closer, the heat from our bodies colliding. I lean in, my lips right at her ear. "If I had kissed you?"

I hear her swallow as she tries to maintain her composure. This is what she needs, a reminder that her flirty little questions might have answers that she's not prepared to hear.

"I know you enjoy tempting me, but I've got a lot more experience in this game than you do, sweetheart, so unless you're planning on following through." I lift my head so that our noses are practically touching. "Don't fucking tease me."

I reach my thumb up and drag it slowly over her bottom lip, contemplating if I should bite it but I decide I won't be able to stop myself if I do.

"Now go upstairs and sleep well, Brontë."

Her eyes are big and unblinking as she stares at me for several more seconds before fumbling with her keys which I take from her hand to open the door. I hand them back to her, then reach past her to close the door and turn to head back to the SUV.

Chapter 5

Brontë

"Are—are you coming to your birthday party?"

Jenson, my five-year-old brother, asks me for the third time today.

"Of course I'll be there, buddy." I crouch down and grab his little shoulders.

"It's her birthday, dummy," Silas says, "she has to be there."

"Hey, let's not name-call. He's just making sure I don't forget, right, Jenson?"

Jenson nods, wiping his nose with the back of his arm.

"Do you like dinosaurs? Mom said I get to have a dinosaur party this year."

"I do love dinosaurs. Do you boys have a favorite?"

I hold each of the boys' hands as we leave the children's center where we've spent the last few hours volunteering. Chantelle has made it a point to let me involve the boys in volunteering and giving back to their community. I think she also welcomes the break twice a month on Sunday mornings.

"Silas likes the spin—Spinosaurus." He says the word slow and deliberate like he's sounding it out. "But my favorite is the T-Rex."

"Spinosaurus aegyptiacus is by far superior," Silas says, emphasizing his statement with dramatic hand gestures that make me giggle. "Everybody likes the T-Rex, Jenson."

He's always been more serious than his brother. His mom says even as a baby he was fiercely independent and insisted on doing everything himself.

"It's okay. I like the T-Rex a lot too. I think my favorite would be the Velociraptors; they're so cute."

"Actually," Silas says, pointing a finger into the air like a little scholar, "scientists believe they were covered in feathers and more birdlike than reptilian."

I burst into laughter this time. "Did you just say reptilian?"

He looks at me seriously. "Yes, meaning like a reptile, often with scales like a lizard or alligator. Speaking of alligators, they are actually decedents of dinosaurs."

"You are so smart, Silas. I need to hang out with you boys more often; you teach me so much!"

We round the corner to Burton Place where my father and his family live and make our way to the front door of the massive historic home that sits in the heart of the Gold Coast, one of Chicago's most sought-after neighborhoods.

"Hi, Mrs. Ludlow." I smile at the housekeeper whom the boys practically run over on their way inside the moment she tells them fresh cookies just came out of the oven.

"Hello, dear. Did the boys behave today?"

"Always." I smile just as Chantelle appears.

"Hey, Brontë." She steps out and gives me a hug. "Come inside. Don't stand out here like a stranger."

"Thank you, I would, but I promised Sylvia and Taylor I'd do brunch with them. Thanks for letting me take the boys. We had so much fun and they taught me a lot about dinosaurs." I laugh.

"They can't get enough of dinosaurs and don't even get me started on Silas correcting all the inaccuracies in *Jurassic Park* when Jenson watches it." She rolls her eyes.

"Silas used *reptilian* today; I was very impressed."

"They're something else. You kids get it from your father, that's for sure. I know you have to run, but I'll text you details about your birthday party. I know you said you didn't want anything big so I'm keeping it low-key. I promise."

I say my goodbyes and head over to Ann Sather to meet the girls for brunch.

"So, have you thought any more about dating? There's a woman at work who just got engaged to a guy she met through one of the apps," Taylor asks before shoveling a massive bite of the restaurant's famous cinnamon rolls into her mouth. She moans loudly, and a few patrons at the table next to us look over at her.

"Doesn't really help if you don't know which app, Taylor," Sylvia says, nudging her.

"Just saying, there's hope if you choose to do online dating; it's still successful."

"There are also murderers on those apps too, so it's kind of a gamble," Sylvia adds with her trademark sarcasm that has Taylor rolling her eyes.

"Ugh," I moan, dropping my fork to my plate. "I don't want to do online dating. I want an organic relationship."

"Nobody *wants* to do online dating, sweetie, but in today's world it's kind of unavoidable. Nobody is having those Meg Ryan and Tom Hanks meet cutes anymore where he saves you from a taxi or stops a stack of papers you dropped from flying all over the city." Taylor is always the one to paint a beautiful picture and then squash it. "It's just old balding dudes cat-calling you from construction sites or trying to grope you on the subway."

"And they say romance is dead," Sylvia pipes up, making me laugh.

"Or what about a meet cute where you hit on him at a bar and he turns out to be your boss? Just saying."

They both give me *the look.*

"I'm kidding. I'm just out of practice with dating is all. I'll do it."

"Why do I feel like you're full of shit?" Taylor eyes me suspiciously.

"We had a moment." I promised myself I was going to keep it to myself, but who am I kidding; I tell them everything. They both drop their forks and stare at me wide-eyed.

"Well, not a *moment*, but there was some tension." They wait for me to go on so I explain to them what happened between us last night.

"You know nothing more than regret and a hookup will come of this, right?" Sylvia asks cautiously.

"I know that and it doesn't matter. I'm not pursuing it and he wouldn't either. He's far too professional for that."

"Was he being professional last night?" She raises her eyebrow.

"No, but look. It's fun to flirt and fantasize about him. I realize it's because it's all so taboo for several reasons. I'm not an idiot. I don't think he's my knight in shining armor or anything like that. I just haven't been in a relationship in forever and I haven't been laid in almost two years now. I know dating apps are the way to go but it's like there's so much damn effort just to go on a single date that most likely won't amount to shit. You have to find all the right photos and fill out these quippy little questionnaires and it's all just so exhausting. What happened to getting done up and going to a bar and meeting someone?"

"Have you seen *Sex and the City* because there's like ten seasons of them doing exactly that with almost no luck." Sylvia shrugs.

I lean back in my chair and fight back the tears of frustration that threaten to fall. I feel like a child throwing a tantrum, but I do feel overwhelmed by it all. It's not only been years since I've been in a relationship, but it's been years since I've felt the spark and excitement that I feel with Beckham and I hate that it's all so wrong and complicated.

There truly is nothing worse than wanting something you can't have.

"I know, sweetie. I'm sorry I'm being insensitive and I hate seeing you so frustrated," Sylvia says sympathetically. "Maybe just go out and do what you said, meet someone at a bar casually. We'll be your wing women. You're only twenty-four. No need to pressure yourself to find your soulmate right now."

"Twenty-five in two weeks," I mutter.

"Look at me, I'm thirty-three and just now getting married. I don't regret having fun in my twenties at all, but I can tell you that if I had gotten married at twenty-five, I might regret it right now. You've got the world at your fingertips, B. Enjoy finding your passion and career and just having fun. Just maybe not too much fun with your boss."

We laugh, and talking to them about it all does make me feel better. For as much as I feel like I know what I don't want in life, sometimes the pressures of marriage and kids get the best of me too, even if I never thought they were things I wanted or needed.

―――――

I DOUBLE-CHECK MY LIPSTICK IN THE MIRROR, SMOOTHING down a flyaway hair before exiting the restroom to head to the restaurant to meet with Pierce Investments.

"Ready?"

My mouth goes dry when I see Beckham standing by my desk, one hand casually in his pocket, the other running through his silky dirty-blond locks.

"Did you change?" I take in his fitted three-piece gray suit.

"I did. The other suit didn't feel business meeting appropriate."

"How is a suit not—should I change?" I don't finish my first question, now too nervous that I'm not dressed appropriately. I look down at my red dress, then back up at Beckham's darkening eyes.

"No, you look fucking fantastic." I can see he didn't intend on saying that out loud, but he just smiles sheepishly as we walk toward the elevators.

The doors shut behind us and for some reason my eyes drop

down right to his crotch. The fitted gray pants do nothing to help the situation as I realize I think I can see the outline of his dick. No, I absolutely can and sweet baseball bats, Batman, that thing is huge!

What the fuck?

I feel myself physically jerk as I avert my eyes but it's too late.

"Did you just—check me out?" A smile pulls at one side of his lips and I shake my head violently.

"No, just thought I saw a spider in the corner. Just a thread." I smile as I stare at the floor.

"Don't be nervous about this dinner, Brontë." His hand reaches out to settle against the small of my back and instantly sweat starts to form at my temples and upper lip.

Does this man not understand the effect he has on women? Or maybe he does and this is his twisted little game to tease me.

"Your financial analysis is spot-on and you know what you're talking about. Just remember that they need *us*. We've seen their numbers. If you feel like you want me to step in at all, just tap my knee under the table."

"Wait, I thought I was just there to learn. You want me to do the talking?" My stomach does a flip.

"Not all of it, no, but I also think you can easily talk through what we've gone over. Just read the room and you'll be fine."

We exit the elevator and head to the restaurant, my nerves feeling like they're going to rip through my skin at any second.

———

"You're a bright young thing, aren't you?" I smile nervously at the gross attempt of a compliment from Chad, the younger guy at the table. I choke down a mouthful of water to prevent myself from throwing up in my own mouth.

The meeting is going well... I think. We've had cocktails and appetizers and our entrees have just been brought out. The three men that came are CEO Jack Niles, CFO Bryan Winthrop, and

Chad Bellview, their cocky president of sales who has mentioned at least three times tonight that he's the youngest executive at the company. He's also mentioned his brand-new Range Rover and the lake house he recently purchased.

"I'm still just learning, all thanks to Mr. Archer giving me the opportunity." I pick up my wine and take a healthy gulp, praying it makes the schmoozing from this asshole more palatable, but so far, it's not helping.

"I bet he was more than eager to give you an *opportunity.*" He actually winks at me when he says it and it makes my skin crawl. I glance up at Beckham and see his lips are set in a hard, thin line. His jaw is clenched tightly as he finishes off his second glass of scotch.

"Like I mentioned, we do think this would be a great opportunity for us at Archer as well as Pierce. I think we both offer some mutually beneficial assets to each other and if given the chance, we could really turn this relationship into something spectacular if an acquisition were to go through."

The CEO and CFO both agree and offer a few words before Chad interrupts again. His sleazy chuckle puts me on edge.

"I don't doubt that, darlin'. I think this relationship could really blossom if we were to consider moving forward with Archer. I know that we would really be an asset on your books and I can't help but think there's some unsaid *mutual* benefits as well. Who knows, when it's all said and done, maybe you can help me figure out which boat I should buy."

This asshole couldn't be laying it on any thicker and I've had just about enough. I'm about to say as much when Beckham lets out a loud laugh.

"Do you actually think we at Archer *need* you? That we in any way would be the ones to benefit most from this relationship?" Chad's smile fades, quickly replaced with anger as Beckham leans forward, steepling his hands on the table.

Shit.

"In case you missed it, Chad, Brontë detailed very clearly your

50

current financial situation and how you don't have the capital to grow like you would if we bought you out. So before you think you can speak to her that way, you better check yourself or you're going to have a much bigger issue than trying to figure out which boat you think will make your dick look bigger."

My mouth falls open as Beckham stands up, the chair he was sitting in shooting out behind him as he turns and walks away from the table.

Chad's face is bright red, but the two older gentlemen at the table are both grabbing for their tumblers, trying to hide their snickers at what just happened.

"I—uh, I'll be right back," I say before chasing after Beckham.

I search through the sea of people standing at the bar till I find him at the very end.

"What the hell was that?" I say angrily.

"Seriously? That piece of shit was laying it on so thick the table next to us was embarrassed. I wasn't going to sit there for another second while he spoke to you like that and fuck those fools with him who didn't try to rein him in."

I take in a few breaths, letting him get it out of his system before responding.

"I agree, he was being a complete sleaze, but you can't ruin the deal just because he was talking to me like that. I was handling it."

"You were? Didn't seem like it to me. Seemed like you were laughing and letting him get away with it."

I narrow my eyes at him and step a little closer. "If I had it my way, I would have thrown a glass of water in his face within twenty seconds of meeting him because he couldn't find my eyes to save his life, but I'm being professional and I expect the same from you. If you want me to work on a deal and say you're giving me a chance, then you have to give me a chance to stand my ground too."

He searches my face, listening to me and I can see that he gets it now.

"I'm sorry." He shakes his head. "I know how toxic the corporate world is and I guess I felt this need to protect you from that. I don't want you not wanting to work on things because you feel like it's a boys' club or like I don't have your back."

"You can't protect me from that. I know you do and will have my back, but the toxic masculinity bullshit isn't going away in the corporate world; we both know that."

He looks over his shoulder at me as he leans on the bar. "You really are—" He doesn't finish the sentence. "I'll apologize in there. We won't lose the deal. I can promise you that."

We step away from the bar and he places his hand ever so softly against my lower back, all the same exciting feelings rushing back.

"But I also want you to know that I'm not a pushover, Brontë. I'll never let someone strong-arm me into something. I'm not a pleasant man if I feel like I'm being manipulated."

A shiver runs down my back at how commanding he can be. It's alpha and masculine without the toxic trappings of a man that's all talk.

No, Beckham Archer is the type of man who delivers on his promises.

We finish dinner and Beckham pays for the bill after apologizing to the table. Chad excuses himself to use the restroom before they leave, and Beckham turns to the two older gentlemen.

"I meant what I said earlier about Brontë's financial assessment of your firm. We're all well aware that you need us; we don't need you. Don't forget that if this goes through, Archer is doing you a favor, but if you can't rein him in," he says, pointing toward Chad who's walking back toward us, "the deal is off the table."

"So much for an apology," I mutter as Beckham ushers me into the back seat of his waiting Rolls-Royce.

"I did apologize, but I won't let that bitch use you as a pawn in a business deal. That's fucked up." He shuts the door and Carson pulls the car into traffic.

"If he thinks for one second that he can flirt with you like that, say disgusting shit that makes you uncomfortable because he thinks I won't say something, then he can shove that deal so far up his ass it—"

You know that moment, the one where you know you're about to do that thing you told yourself and everyone else you wouldn't... that's this moment.

There's no partition in this car, but I don't care. Before he finishes what he is saying, I'm crawling into his lap, my lips on his as I grip the lapels of his suit coat. I know everything I've told myself and my friends just went out the window but I don't care.

I've never had a man stand up for me like that. The power and control this man possesses drives me absolutely feral and I can't keep myself from indulging any longer.

I know he's off-limits.

I know it's a bad idea.

I know he's going to rip my heart out and possibly destroy my life, but in this moment, I just don't care.

I fully expect him to push me away, to reprimand me and remind me who my father is, but he doesn't.

Instead, his hands are on my waist, then traveling up my body and into my hair where he tilts my head to take the kiss deeper. His lips are full and soft, caressing mine, kissing me like his life depends on it. His tongue laps at mine, long languid strokes as I feel his erection firming beneath me.

I want to grind down on him but the moment I start to move, his hands fall from my hair to my waist where he stills my movements before breaking the kiss.

We're both panting, our foreheads pressed together.

"I shouldn't have done that," he says.

"Technically, I did that." I lean forward and kiss him again quickly, then again, but he pushes me back.

"I have to look your father in the eyes tomorrow, Brontë."

"Yeah, but isn't that part of the fun?" I say, attempting to keep the moment going.

A *V* settles between his brows. "Is that what this is about?"

I shrug, not wanting to remove myself from him.

"It's a dangerous game."

"Maybe that's what I've been missing." His eyes finally come up to meet mine before he reaches out, brushing my hair away from my face.

"I'm not your happily ever after, Brontë."

"I'm not asking you to be."

I stay in his lap till the car slows in front of my building.

"What are you asking me to be?"

I don't answer because I'm not sure of the answer. Do I want just a one-night stand? Would that ever be enough with a man like Beckham Archer or would it just be setting myself up for heartbreak?

"I can tell you that right now, I'm not going to get out of this car because if I do, I won't be a gentleman. If I walk you to that door," he says, pointing out the window, "I'm going to fuck you so hard you can't walk tomorrow, and then I'll go home. I won't cuddle you or hold you or kiss you good night. All I can offer you is a fantasy, Brontë."

I look into his eyes, searching for any hint that what he's saying is what he thinks I need to hear. That he's just trying to scare me away, but I don't think he is. I think he's telling the truth.

He grabs the tip of my chin. "I'm not what you want, sweetheart. Go inside and put yourself to bed and dream about finding a nice young man who will give you the white picket fence, the two kids, and the happily ever after."

I don't make him tell me twice. I climb out of the car and head inside without looking back. I have no illusions about the kind of man Beckham Archer is, but he clearly is confused on what he thinks I want from him.

Chapter 6

Beckham

Walking out of the bar that night without Brontë was one of the hardest decisions I've made but the moment I realized who she was, I told myself there wasn't a chance in hell I could give in to that fantasy.

But tonight, feeling her warmth against me, feeling the curve of her hips beneath my hands as my tongue danced with hers, made me second-guess everything. How can something that feels so right, so fucking delicious, be so wrong?

I guess that saying about forbidden fruit tasting sweeter really is true because telling her no just now was a true test of my willpower.

I wasn't lying to her when I said I can only offer a fantasy. I've never wanted marriage and kids. After my father walked out on my mom and she was left to raise me alone, I saw a side of life I knew I never wanted to replicate, and not having a father has made me feel like I would be inadequate if I ever was one myself. Hell, even Jonas couldn't keep his first family together.

After hearing just a little about Brontë's past and finding out that she's just now working on mending her relationship with her dad, I won't be another man to let her down or break her heart.

I close my eyes and lean back further in my seat as Carson navigates through traffic. I try to focus on what happened at the meeting tonight, about the next steps and what I'll divulge to Jonas tomorrow, but all I can focus on is that now I know how soft Brontë's lips are and my mind spins out on how the rest of her would taste.

I imagine what would have happened had I not stopped us. Would I have had my way with her right here in the back seat? Would I have attempted to be a gentleman and waited till we were inside her apartment?

Suddenly I feel like I'm suffocating. I reach up and loosen my tie but it does little to help. Instead, I roll down the window and let the warm night air breeze across my face.

"Carson, drive around the city a little before heading back to my place, would ya?"

"Absolutely, sir."

———

"WELL, HOW'D THE MEETING WITH PIERCE GO?" JONAS ASKS as he plants his feet and takes a few practice swings before teeing off.

"Good." I hesitate to reveal too much about what went down at the meeting. Only because I've gathered that Brontë is a private person and I'm sure the last thing she'd want is me stirring up drama by getting her father involved, especially after how she reacted to me stepping in. "That daughter of yours has a good head on her shoulders. Even after just a week at Archer, I could see her financial prowess."

"Told you," he says before smacking the ball hard, sending it soaring down the fairway. "She's not only smart, but she's a critical thinker. I think we both know those bright young minds that come out of some of the best institutions, but the kids can't tell their head from their ass because they're only book smart." He shakes his head in frustration and I know where he's coming from. I've hired a few top-of-their-class graduates, only to realize they need someone to babysit them because they're too scared to take risks and make judgment calls.

"Well, I can tell you with absolute certainty that isn't the case with Brontë. Half the stuff I had hoped she would do, I didn't even have to tell her to do. Once I gave her the first stack of financials from Pierce, she ran with them. She came back with not only an in-depth analysis but projections."

He chuckles. "Her mother was the same, you know? That's why I told you last time I don't like the idea of her wasting her talents by working for some charity. Sure, it's a good cause but she could make more of an impact if she worked somewhere she could make a lot of money and help people out that way, then donate and volunteer on the weekends like you do."

I don't want to stick my nose where it doesn't belong, but I also don't love the idea of someone as young as Brontë not doing what they love because of an outside influence from a parent, no matter how well-intentioned it might be.

"As long as she's happy in her career choice, that's the most important thing, right?" I look over at Jonas in the golf cart. He nods his head like he's thinking.

"Maybe you're right. I guess I'm thinking more as a businessman than a father. Her mother, Nadine, did an amazing job raising her. I don't regret that even though I regret how things ended between me and her."

"Do you ever regret that you and Nadine didn't end up together?"

He shakes his head. "Nah. It was for the best, trust me. Nadine didn't want a life with me and I don't blame her. I was a shit husband and father at the time. I do regret cheating on her, hurting her the way I did, and not being involved in Brontë's life for so long."

Jonas and I have been good friends for many years now, but we've never delved too deep into what happened in his past with Brontë. I find myself wanting to know more now that I know her. Maybe it's out of pure curiosity or maybe it's because I want to know what makes her, her.

"So after you and Nadine split, did you just disappear out of her life?"

"Unfortunately, yes." He looks over at me and I can see the heavy pang of regret in his eyes. "I was so consumed with building Ramsay Consulting that I would forget visits and birthdays. I disappointed her one too many times and Nadine said that was enough. I'm either in or out, and I chose out because I had convinced myself it was for the best, that it would be better for Brontë to not know who her deadbeat father was... but I was wrong. I'd reach out a few times a year, show up to a school function or holiday, but it was never regular and it clearly wasn't welcome. By the time she was about thirteen, I tried to come back into her life, really make an effort to mend our relationship, but she told me it was too late. Less than a year later, her mother let her file paperwork to legally change her last name to Spencer, Nadine's last name, and remove me."

"Shit." I place my hand on his shoulder and hang my head. "I didn't realize all that, man. I'm sorry, I didn't mean to bring all that up."

"No, I deserved it. That's why I'm just beyond grateful that she wants anything to do with me now. I'm grateful that Nadine wanted her to reach out to me in her final months."

"Is that why she reconnected?"

He nods. "Nadine made her promise she would try to mend her relationship with me. I think it took a while, about two years after her mother passed for Brontë to reach out. I think it also helped that she had two younger brothers she didn't know. Thank God for Chantelle; she's been the bridge between us and she's done so much to help Brontë and be somewhat of a motherly figure to her even though they're only ten years apart."

I perk up. I had completely forgotten that Chantelle was twenty years younger than Jonas. In fact, they were about the same age as Brontë and I right now when they started dating.

So technically, if anything did happen, he couldn't be pissed about that... right?

"Her mother and I actually made up a few years before she passed, became good friends again."

"Really? Does Brontë know that?"

"Not yet. I plan on telling her at her twenty-fifth birthday party at the house. I have something else I need to discuss with her anyway. You're coming to that, right?"

"To what?"

"Brontë's birthday party. Chantelle is throwing it at the house. It'll be laid back. The kids will be in the pool, I'm sure."

"You want me to come?" I chuckle. "I'm not sure Brontë will love seeing her boss over a weekend."

"Nonsense." He waves away my comment. "It's just us and her. You're family, Beckham; you know that. You better be there or Chantelle will be upset."

I swallow down the anxiety in my throat and tell myself to relax. It won't be a big deal if she sees me on a weekend and it's not like anyone will know what transpired between us last night.

"Thanks for letting me blow off some steam about all this. Sometimes I feel like I'm drowning in immense guilt because of my past." He looks over at me. "But I got a second chance with my girl, and I can tell you without a doubt"—he lifts his golf club and points it toward me—"I'll do anything in my power to keep her in my life and damn anything or anyone who tries to ruin it because I'll destroy them."

Fuck. Yup, definitely need to make sure she and I are on the same page about our relationship because there's no way in hell I'm ending up on Jonas Ramsey's shit list.

After our golf outing, I make a mental note to call Brontë into my office tomorrow to make sure she knows how much of a mistake I feel last night was.

"You wanted to see me before I left, sir?"

I look up to see Brontë standing in front of my desk, her hands folded neatly, hanging down in front of her. She's since pulled up her hair from this morning. It's now in a high ponytail, accentuating her long, slender neck that's begging to be tasted. Her dress, a wide neckline, only drawing even more attention to it and her delicate collarbones.

"I did," I say as she sinks slowly down into a chair across from me. Her big blue eyes are staring at me, long dark eyelashes fanning out, making her almost look like a cartoon, a Disney princess.

The thing that gets me about her, that makes me so desperate to throw caution to the wind and call bullshit on my own speech I'm about to give her, is her naiveté. She's flirty, and she did come on to me after all, twice now, but it's almost an innocent type of flirting. It's coy and sweet. She has a tell, an impish little smile when she knows she's being seductive, but it's not like a woman who knows what she's getting herself into.

No, it's like she thinks a few stolen kisses or maybe an inappropriate comment will be the outcome and maybe in her past, that's all it was. And that innocence calls to me, makes me want to defile her, to show her what it's like to flirt with the big bad wolf.

"I'll make this quick. I know it's after hours, but I, uh, golfed with your father yesterday as you know. He and I had a good talk and he expressed how appreciative he was that you're back in his life and how important you are to him. It just made me want to apologize again for my behavior in the car the other night. I shouldn't have kissed you. I shouldn't have said the things I did."

She smiles. "I know. You already told me and like I mentioned before, I kissed you so technically, you don't have anything to apologize for."

There's that cute little flirty smile. I imagine it's like the one she gave the young men at the work party at Navy Pier.

"Well, either way, I just want you to know that as enticing"—I look up when I say the word—"as it might be to do something so forbidden, I think that's where the excitement lies so we're both better off not indulging in that. I won't be the man who comes between you and your father."

I stare at her, but she doesn't seem to have much of a response to what I'm saying. I don't know what I expected. Maybe she sees through my bullshit. I shake my head at the thought. No, this is serious and I mean it. Even though all the desires are still there, more than ever, I can't act on them.

"I completely understand and I will respect the boundaries. I think I've just been celibate for too long." She shrugs with a slight giggle and it hits me right in the gut.

This shit right here, this is what gets me. She says it so nonchalant like I won't instantly start thinking about fucking her when she brings up the fact that she hasn't been laid. I feel my cock stiffen in my pants.

"I think it's the kick in the ass I need to actually get out there and start dating again. Trust me, my girlfriends have been on me about it so they'll be happy to know I'm going to do it." She stands up and smiles again. "If that's all, I'm going to head out to my yoga class, and then I'm setting up my dating profile tonight. No more excuses."

"That's all, Miss Spencer."

She stands and steps closer to my desk. "Okay, I can respect the boundaries, but *Miss Spencer?* Should I start calling you Mr. Archer again?"

I know she doesn't mean to but the way her breathy voice drops an octave when she asks the question has me already wanting to throw my resolve out the window and tell her only if she says it on her knees.

"Good night, Brontë."

"Good night, Mr. Archer." I watch as she walks out of my office, her hips swaying with each step as she closes the door behind her, and I let out a frustrated groan.

The idea that she's going to go home tonight and set up her dating profile has my blood about to boil. I already know it will just be a slew of fuckboys waiting their turn to fuck her over and leave her unsatisfied.

Chapter 7

Brontë

"Are you from Chicago originally?"

I take a sip of my Aperol spritz and try my hardest to keep some sort of conversation going with Brayden.

"Nah, bro. I'm from the suburbs, Naperville. You heard of it?"

Did he just call me bro?

"Yes, I think it's actually the biggest suburb," I reply as he continues to mess around on his phone.

"Can I grab you another drink, miss?" The bartender approaches us and Brayden replies before I can.

"Nah, we're gonna head out of here in a few, right?" He looks at me.

"Did you have another place in mind?"

"Uhh, my place." He gives me his, what I assume anyway, best sexy eyes look. You know the one, where they're excessively licking their lips and look like they're about to sneeze.

I laugh into my glass, finishing it in one large gulp before placing it back on the bar with a twenty.

"Well, Brayden, it's been great, but no, I don't think I'll be joining you at your apartment tonight."

"Seriously? Maaan, I thought we were vibing though. Do you not think I'm hot?" He asks the question so sincerely and clearly confused that I can't help but laugh this time.

"You're very attractive, but I'm not really a *go home on the first date* kind of girl. I'm looking for something more long term and I guess I assumed you were too since that's what your profile said and you also told me that when we were texting before meeting up."

"Oh that, yeah, I mean I am and I'm not, if that makes sense?"

I shake my head no. "It doesn't actually but that's okay. You don't have to explain." I smile and slide off my barstool.

"It's just that, if you put that you're *only* looking for a hookup or casual, you only match with sluts, I swear."

"Brayden." I reach out and touch his hand. "I'm going to leave, okay?"

I don't wait for a response; I simply walk out the door of the bar and scurry around the corner to call an Uber to head home. I really don't have it in me to explain to a twenty-eight-year-old man why calling women sluts when they sleep with you on the first date is a double standard and also misleading and gross and a lot of other offensive words.

I bolt for the car when it arrives and sit silently in the back seat, mourning yet another wasted evening spent with yet another failed date. That's three this week and I already feel over the online dating scene... and these are the good ones I matched with.

Sylvia and Taylor both told me not to be too picky at first, to be open to going out with men I wouldn't normally be attracted to because attraction doesn't always lead somewhere. While I do agree with that sentiment, it's also proving to be a lot harder than I realized.

What's really disappointing is, on paper, the three guys I've gone on dates with sound like a dream. They're around my age, driven, love to explore the city and learn new things, want a lasting relationship built on communication, but in person, total epic failures. Even through the texting phase they can sell it, but damn, two tried taking me home after one drink and one was actively scrolling through Tinder while on our date.

I pinch the bridge of my nose and let out an audible sigh.

"Tough day?" my driver asks and I look up to see her looking at me in the rearview mirror.

"The worst. Another day, another failed date." I laugh and she joins me.

"I feel you. The last date I went on, the guy tried to recruit me to join a cult."

"What?"

"Yeah, apparently that's a tactic he uses to get new members."

"And it works?"

"I guess so." We both laugh and commiserate the last few miles to my apartment. At least I feel a little better knowing that I'm not the only one completely striking out in the dating scene.

Once home, I grab my iPad and flop down on my couch. Checking my email, I see a note from the Archer Foundation letting me know that I can come in tomorrow to volunteer and go through the orientation process.

That puts a smile on my face. Helping others always puts me in a better mood, plus I'm excited to talk with Beckham more about it next week at work.

I lie back on my couch, a random show playing in the background as I pull up the Google image results for my search of Beckham. The first picture actually makes my heart skip a beat. It's a black-and-white photo done for an interview in a well-circulated magazine. He's not smiling; he's staring into the camera, a lock of his hair over his brow as his eyes feel like they're burning through me.

I scroll down further and my eyes catch another image of him and that woman from the image I saw when Taylor and Sylvia were with me. She's stunning, the kind of woman you'd expect to see on his arm. The type of woman who looks like she takes her appearance and the way she carries herself very seriously. The type of woman who probably has a professional team to help style her. The exact opposite type of woman than me.

I swallow down the jealousy I feel forming, hating that I'm comparing myself to someone I don't even know. I'm not ugly by any stretch. I've never had a problem attracting attention from men and don't have to work at keeping my figure, but I'm more of the girl-next-door type, not the siren who leaves necks broken when she walks down the street.

I push the feelings aside and scroll back up to the first image and click on it to take me to the interview where there are several more photos. In one, he's sitting on the edge of a chair, reclining back so that his long legs are outstretched, one arm behind his head, the other resting on his thigh. His shirt is almost completely unbuttoned. I can feel wetness building between my thighs as a thin layer of sweat beads on my brow.

I've never had such a visceral reaction to someone before. It feels like more than just attraction, more than just a little crush... It's need. A deep hunger that as much as I try, I can't suppress. It's like being on a diet and craving that one thing you're not allowed to have so you've convinced yourself that if you have just one bite, one little taste, it will satisfy you and you can move on, but you know damn well, it will never be enough until you've consumed the entire thing and you're sick with regret.

I close the cover on the iPad and walk to my bathroom, flipping on the shower and not even waiting till it's warm before I jump in. Maybe the icy water will tamp down the hormones raging inside me.

––––––

"Beckham?" I grab my purse and race down the hallway to catch up to him. "What are you doing here?"

He smiles. His hair is disheveled and he's wearing a plain white t-shirt and jeans. I've never seen him look so casual.

"You mean what am I doing at the Archer Foundation? Beckham Archer?" He laughs and runs his hand through his mussed-up hair. It's so effortlessly sexy and cute.

I playfully smack his arm. "I mean—well, yeah, I guess that's exactly what I mean. I've volunteered at a lot of places and I've never seen one of the people whose names are on the foundation actually volunteering."

"Ah, well, you caught me. I am, in fact, a billionaire who actually volunteers. But let's keep it between us. Can't have people thinking I care." He winks at me and I fall in step beside him.

"Today was my first time volunteering here, and wow, I am crazy impressed with how much you've been able to accomplish with this institution. It's incredible and so inspiring."

"Well, thank you. I appreciate that and I sincerely appreciate your time. We always need more volunteers. I try to come every week, more if I can. I'm usually here on Sundays if I'm not traveling for work and even if I can pop in for an hour midweek, I do. I think it helps for people to see the face with the name. Not because it makes me feel better, but because I want them to know I actually give a shit rather than just writing a check."

I smile at him as we descend the stairs. If I thought this man couldn't get any sexier, I was wrong. A hot, successful man who not only donates millions but also his time for mothers and children in need? I almost say it out loud, but I remember our talk and keep it to myself.

"Wow, it's such an incredible day out." I shield my eyes from the sun and look up at the cloudless sky. The breeze from the lake and severe drop in humidity results in the perfect temperature. "Nice to finally have a break from the oppressive heat."

"Want to walk by the lake?" he asks, surprising me.

"Yeah. Tell me more about why you started the Archer Foundation. I read up on it, but I'd love to hear it from you, if that's okay?"

"Yeah, of course. I was raised by a single mom, something I know you can understand," he says cautiously and I nod. "My dad left when I was maybe four; I don't really remember him. I think I have these memories that resurface, but I'm not sure if they're mine or based on a photo my mom showed me of him and I doing something when I was a kid. Anyway, she struggled every damn day to not only put food on the table but just to provide basic needs for me. School supplies aren't cheap, and neither are clothes when you go from being just over three foot tall to five foot in a summer." He laughs.

"Damn, guess that explains the six-five stature."

"You know my height?" He looks over his shoulder at me and I blush. A biker whizzes by us and he reaches his hand out to grab my waist, pulling me on the other side of him to protect me. He keeps talking, completely unaware of how sexy that little gesture was or the effect it's having on me.

"I wanted to play Little League when I was a kid. I had a good arm and I was athletic, but she couldn't afford the uniform and fees so I never got the chance. Things like that really ate at her, made her feel like a failure as a mom. She'd compare herself to some of the other moms and she just never felt like she was doing enough. If she worked longer hours to make more money so I could do sports, she lost time with me and someone else was raising me. She felt like it was a lose-lose situation so I vowed that when I made enough money to start this foundation, I'd make sure we provided help to moms, and now dads as well, who needed it. We started out focusing on single moms, but there's a need for single dads, families, all of it. Our mission and goal is to make sure no kid goes without."

I wipe away a stray tear. "That is beyond wonderful. I was raised by a single mom but I didn't struggle like that. My dad paid alimony and child support and my mom had a career that paid enough. We weren't rich by any stretch and I know my mom went without some nicer things that she could have afforded but chose not to so that I could take piano lessons or go on field trips. I have such a soft spot for children and parents in need so what you're doing is beyond amazing."

"Your dad told me your mom liked to volunteer and was very charitable. He said she passed that on to you."

"Yeah, she did. Now Jonas on the other hand?" I laugh. "My dad doesn't exactly get it. He's gotten a lot better, I think. I know he donates, but what billionaire doesn't to get those tax write-offs?"

"I think you're right; he has come a long way. He's not that same man he was."

I look over at Beckham and I can see that he wants to talk more about my dad, about the man he's become, but it's not a conversation I'm ready to have.

"I went on some dates." I smile, changing the subject.

"Dates—plural? With the same guy?" His tone changes, his brow furrowing with the question as he nervously runs his hands through his hair again.

"No, three different guys actually. There will be no second dates with any of them."

"That bad, huh?"

I groan, my head falling back. "You have no idea."

"Then tell me." He playfully bumps his elbow against me.

"One guy called me *bro* the entire date."

"A grown man called you bro? On a date?"

"Yeah. He's twenty-eight. And no, before you ask, he doesn't live at home. He has advanced degrees, a good job, all of those *things* we're told to look for in a partner, but he was buried in his phone the entire date. If you can even call it a date because halfway through my drink when the bartender asked if we wanted another round, he told her no because we were going back to his place."

He looks over at me and I'm not sure what he's trying to convey. He looks curious but also pissed.

"No," I say as I narrow my eyes at him, "I did not go home with him."

"That's not what I was questioning."

"Then what?"

69

He chuckles, that low rumble that reverberates through his chest. "I shouldn't say what I'm thinking."

I roll my eyes. "You're a tease, you know that?"

"I'm the tease?" His eyebrows shoot upward.

"Yes. You tease me with little things like that, then say it's unprofessional or inappropriate. You know what you're doing."

"And you don't?" I question him and he turns his eyes from mine down to his feet.

"I was going to say that I'm no different."

"Meaning you're a one-night-stand type of guy?"

"No, meaning that I confessed to you that if you hadn't written your name with your number that night, I'd have taken you back to my place and we weren't even on a date. So being that he took you on a date and knew your name before offering to take you home, he's a better man than me."

My stomach drops. "Guess it's good that I gave you my name then, so we avoided a regretful situation."

"So are you going to continue the online dating exploits?"

I shrug. "Honestly, I don't know. I was telling my friends that I just wish I could meet someone organically. I like building a friendship first. I'm not typically a *go in search of someone to date* type of person. I prefer when things just happen naturally."

"I understand that. I'd say most of us feel that way, but then again, online dating has been so popular."

"Have you ever done it?" He looks over at me and smiles. "Sorry, stupid question. I'm sure you don't have to ever go searching for a date."

"That's not why I smiled." He shakes his head. "I'm just not really the *looking for marriage* type and I guess I assumed that's what dating apps were for."

"Seems like it's the exact opposite actually, so you might like it," I tease him.

We walk for a bit longer and we're nearing my street when he offers to walk me home.

"You know, this is starting to become a pattern," I say as we walk up to my building.

"I guess it is." He smiles again. I've noticed when we're in these types of situations, he tends not to elaborate too much on little innuendos I say.

"You're the only man who has consistently walked me home, yet never made it inside the lobby."

I place my key fob near the sensor, and it clicks. Beckham reaches around me, his hand on the door as he opens it. He places his hand in the middle of my back, pressing me forward and stepping inside with me. I turn around to face him.

"There, now I have."

We're standing so close, only a few inches between our bodies as I look up at him. The lobby is empty.

"Better be careful, Mr. Archer," I tease. "Wouldn't want you breaking your rule."

He arches a brow at me. "My rule?"

"Mm-hmm. About boundaries."

He chuckles again, stepping a bit closer. "Didn't realize I was crossing any boundaries or breaking any rules being inside your building." He reaches his hand up and brushes a few strands of hair away from my face. "Does it make you want to break the rules, Brontë?"

I hear myself inhale a sharp breath as his fingertips brush against my cheeks so lightly. I want to play it off, tell him that he wishes and casually walk away like he has no effect on me, but I can't move. His eyes search mine and I want to reach up on my tiptoes to kiss him, but I tell myself no. He made it clear he doesn't want me to instigate things so if he is going to break his rules and cross boundaries he's put in place, I won't be the one to make the first move... Yet I can't help but tease him back a little bit.

"Seems like it makes you want to more than me, but then again, I'd hate to cause you regret."

He leans down, his lips hovering near mine for a brief second before he moves further back to my ear.

"Well, that's a shame. And for the record, no, I wouldn't have regretted it had I taken you home that night. My only regret is that I didn't get the chance to before I had a reason to resist."

Chapter 8

Beckham

I spend the rest of my Sunday evening trying to convince myself that acknowledging the attraction and desires between us is okay —smart even—but also fighting off the pangs of jealousy at the thought of her now dating.

If we allow a little harmless flirtation, it will keep our desires at bay, make us less likely to act on them. Considering how we first met, it's ridiculous to pretend that given the chance, we wouldn't have fucked each other's brains out by now if we could.

Still, knowing who her father is and how young she is, even I can't manage to talk myself into not giving a fuck and taking what I want from her.

I scroll through my email at my desk, attempting to bury myself in work in my home office to distract me when I see an invite from Pierce to visit their headquarters in Vegas as soon as possible for further discussions.

I lean back in my chair and anxiously tap my foot. I hate this feeling. I'm a very in control man and the fact that even with half a dozen red flags and the risks involved, I still can't seem to shake the pull this woman has over me.

I consider not inviting her, but I know that would be a dick move, especially after I got her involved with this acquisition specifically and the work and effort she's put into it. I push back from my desk, standing up and heading upstairs to take a shower and go to bed. I'll deal with it all in the morning when I see her bright and early.

———

I PARK MY CAR IN THE GARAGE AND TAKE THE ELEVATOR UP TO my floor. Every morning I get little butterflies in my stomach the closer I get to my office, knowing that I have to walk past Brontë.

"Good morning, sir." She smiles from her desk and holds out a fresh cup of coffee for me.

"Good morning, Brontë. I told you, you don't need to get me coffee."

She stands, gathering a few items in her arms, then follows me into my office.

"What a weird way to say thank you." She smiles at me as I place the cup on my desk.

"Thank you."

"I need you to sign the retainer renewal for outside counsel," she says, handing me the contract, "so I can send that back to them today, and then I also need you to look over and approve the raises and performance reviews from HR for your executive team."

I take the items from her, our hands grazing each other in the process, and I think I see her flinch at my touch as she jerks her hand back and folds it neatly into her other hand.

"Thank you. I'll handle these today. I need to talk to you about Pierce." Her eyes grow wide as she stares at me. "They want a meeting at their headquarters in Vegas, I'm thinking next week."

"Oh, that's great." She smiles like she's relieved. "I'll get you all booked. I assume you'll be taking the private jet? I'll make sure they have a car for you too." She pulls her phone out of her pocket and begins to take notes, I assume. "Is there a specific hotel you normally stay at in Vegas? I'll reach out to them and have your suite arranged, also."

"Yes to the jet. Double-check with Pierce that a Monday through Tuesday meeting will work. Also, no, I don't have a usual place in Vegas actually so it's your choice."

"Okay, will do. I'll just see who has the best suite available for you for those dates."

"Well, if there's any place you've always wanted to stay but haven't, book there." I look at her and she blinks in confusion. "You're coming with me, Brontë."

"Oh."

"That is your job, isn't it?" I smile at her and she laughs.

"I guess it is. I was thinking more in the assistant mindset." She nods as she goes back to tapping at her phone. "So, okay, I'll book two rooms and get this all sorted. I'll shoot you over the itinerary and have it on your calendar by end of day."

––––––––

ONE WEEK LATER...

"So these are the only numbers I'm still sorting through. I can't quite make sense of the entire cash flow yet, but there are several different accounts I need to sort through before I bring it up to Jack or Bryan."

I'm trying to focus on the excel sheet she's showing me on the iPad in my hands, but her hair has fallen over her shoulder and mine as well as she leans down next to me on the flight.

"I figure I'll have everything sorted in the next few weeks once I talk with their accounts payable department which I already have on the calendar."

Her perfume smells spicy and erotic, and it's doing things to me. She goes to stand up but stumbles with a bump of turbulence, falling forward so that her top half is across me, her hands shooting forward to land on the armrest.

I reach out my hand to steady her; it falls half on her waist, half on the top of her ass and I freeze. She looks over her shoulder at me while bent across my lap with my hand so close to being able to reach down and grab a handful of her perky little ass or better yet, pull my hand back and spank her.

"Don't even think about it." Her voice is husky; instantly, my cock is begging for attention at the recognition of lust in her eyes.

I don't remove my hand; instead, I curl the tips of my fingers against her.

"Wouldn't dream of it, Miss Spencer."

Tension hangs between us for several more seconds before I move to help her right herself. She settles back into the seat opposite me, neither of us mentioning the moment again as we descend into Las Vegas and make our way to the hotel to check in.

I don't give myself time to think about the fact that our rooms are right next to each other. We both quickly freshen up, then make our way downstairs to head over to Pierce Investments.

"Mr. Archer, Miss Spencer, pleasure to see you again." Jack extends his hand to us both as we take our seats in the conference room.

We spend the next half hour talking about business before he walks us around the office, introducing us to a few key people, pencil dick Chad noticeably absent.

"Oh, Chad apologizes he couldn't make it; something came up and he had to take his wife somewhere," Bryan says.

"His wife?" I mutter, remembering the way he so vulgarly spoke to Brontë at our first meeting.

The tour and dinner go far better than our last meeting. I enjoy sitting back and watching Brontë demand respect with the way she carries herself and presents her questions and concerns to the other executives at the table.

By the time we've finished and head outside, it's just after ten p.m.

"Want to grab a drink?" I ask as we duck into our ride.

"Yes, please," she says, half-exasperated. "Our hotel has some pretty nice-looking bars."

"Perfect."

A few moments later we're lifting our glasses to toast to the successful trip.

"To you," I say and she smiles. "Your intellect and intuition are remarkable; don't ever doubt yourself if you do decide to pursue a career in finance." I wink at her and a slight blush creeps across her cheeks as we clink glasses.

"So, enough work talk," she says, turning on her barstool toward me, her bare legs crossed one over the other. "I have a question for you."

"Oh boy." I laugh as she gets a wicked little grin on her face.

"You always ask me about my dating life; what about yours?"

"What about it?"

"Are you seeing anyone?"

I shake my head no, then I take a long drink of my whiskey.

"Not seeing anyone, no. How's it going for you? Any luck since the three amigos the other week?"

"Who was your last relationship?" she asks, ignoring my question.

I spin the tumbler around with my hand as I think about it. I've had a few mutual arrangements lately, none that would have been considered a relationship.

"Probably Venus Davenport." I see her brow furrow in confusion like she's never heard the name before. "The socialite. Dark hair, looks like—"

"Ahhh, the Kim K girl?"

I laugh. "So you do know who she is?"

She blushes. "Uh, not exactly. When I was researching you, I saw a few photos of you together from last year."

"Wait, was this before or after you gave me your number?"

"After. I wouldn't have approached you like that had I known who you were, you know that." She takes a sip of her martini. "So, why didn't it work out with you and Venus?"

"She wanted the fairy tale. I didn't."

"Have you ever wanted it?"

I don't hesitate with my response. "No."

"Why not?"

I shrug. "Never been a priority for me I guess, and never met anyone who made me want to change my mind."

She nods and sips her drink again.

"What about you? We've established you don't enjoy online dating. Any luck just meeting someone out and about?"

She groans and her head falls back a little. "No. I think I've officially sworn off online dating for now. I'd rather just take my chances with meeting someone naturally."

"I understand that, but what I don't understand is how it hasn't worked for you." She has a confused look on her face and I choose my words carefully. "I just mean as beautiful as you are and you're very warm and kind, charming"—she lifts a brow at me—"sexy as fuck." I know I'm venturing into dangerous territory, but I'm on my third whiskey of the night and throwing caution to the wind like it's nothing.

"Go on." That sexy grin of hers creeps into place as she swirls her skewer of olives around in her glass.

"I just mean I don't get how you haven't managed to find a man yet. Apart from your looks, you're incredibly engaging and likable."

She sighs. "Thank you but if I had to guess, I'm probably attracting the wrong types of guys, but I don't know why or how. I try to be nice and I'm not looking for just a hookup. I'm guessing that's a big part of the problem. That being said, maybe I should just go for a hookup or two before my virginity grows back."

I laugh and her eyes shoot from her drink to me. "Sorry, I know, boundaries."

"No, we're off the clock, we're friends, we can talk," I say against my better judgment and then, because I'm a glutton for punishment, I take it a step further. "How long has it been?"

Her laugh comes out in a huff as her eyes drop back to her glass.

"Two years," she says hurriedly before bringing the glass to her lips and finishing the martini.

"Fuck," I say without thinking. "Sorry."

She swallows and motions for the bartender to bring her another.

"No, fuck is absolutely right." She laughs. "What about you?"

"I'll take another too," I say to the bartender, holding up my empty glass.

Why am I having this conversation with her?

"About two months or so."

"Oh, wow." Her eyebrows shoot upward.

"Wow, what?"

"Just figured you were a weekly kind of guy." She smiles as her eyes nervously dart anywhere but mine.

"As in I have that many one-night stands?" Her face reddens. "Jesus, I'm not a twenty-year-old kid anymore who can't control it." We both laugh.

"Sorry, I don't know why I said that. I just thought you might have *friends with benefits* type arrangements."

"No offense taken. I did have an arrangement, but I've just been busy and unmotivated, I guess."

The bartender approaches with our drinks, saving me from having to expound on that conversation. I take a drink of the whiskey, savoring the burn before I turn to face her.

"I have an idea. Why don't I be your wingman?"

"My friends already offered, but I'm happy to let you step in as well when we get back."

"I mean right now, tonight."

"I'm not trying to hook up with a stranger in Vegas." Her eyes are big and round.

"I don't mean hook up. Just show me your moves. Maybe I can

help you analyze why you feel like you're not attracting the kind of man you want."

She thinks about it for a second. "Okay, Casanova," she says with a little giggle that might be coming from the martini she's sipping on. "So, where will you be?"

"I'll be right here. My back toward you, a space down so I can hear."

"Oh God, I'm nervous now." She looks up at me as I stand up from the stool. I look down at her full, pouty lips, reaching my hand out to gently grab the base of her chin with my thumb and forefinger.

"Don't be. You flirted just fine with me the night we met. Had me interested."

She blushes, then her eyes morph from scared to narrow. "Wait, if I managed to get your attention that night, then why are we doing this? You've seen my pickup game."

I chuckle. I was waiting for her to bring that up.

"Yeah, but Brontë, I told you that my thoughts that night weren't about getting to know you; my thoughts were only about taking you home and getting to know your sweet little pussy." I see her throat constrict as she swallows, her eyes fixated on mine.

"So unless you want to fuck the next man who buys you a drink, try to be on the lookout for their intentions. I'm not saying they won't want to fuck you—every man in here does—but see if they can get past it and not end the conversation with their room number or yours. It's not that you're putting out the one-night-stand aura; it's that you can't see through most of these guys' bullshit, including mine." I reach my thumb up and rub it across her bottom lip.

She lets out a nervous breath as I release her chin and give her a wink before turning away from her and stepping a few seats down the bar. I'm far enough away I don't seem like I'm with her, but close enough I'll hear her conversations.

Not even two minutes later the first guy approaches.

"Hey, you come here often?"

Strike one. Cheesy pickup line. Next.

Within two minutes she's made it clear to him she's not interested after he asks her for her number before even asking her name.

Contestant two is quick on that guy's heels. I'm guessing they know each other and had a bet on who could get her number first.

"That guy seemed like a tool," the second guy says, shaking his head as he sits down next to her. "Terry, pleasure to meet you," he says, reaching his hand toward her.

"Brontë, nice to meet you."

Okay, good start. Seems to be going well.

"So, I gotta ask because you are just incredibly beautiful. What are you doing here alone?"

She smiles coyly and thanks him for the compliment but says she's in town on business and just looking to relax tonight.

"Well, you're in luck because I happen to give the most amazing massages and my room has an incredible view."

Didn't last long. Next.

Several moments pass and the look Brontë gives me tells me she's about to give up when contestant number three steps up to the plate.

The small talk is nice, seems genuine.

"Derek, here on business from Chicago."

"Oh, I'm from Chicago too. Small world. Brontë, here on business as well."

I wait patiently for the inevitable invite up to his room or innuendo, but it doesn't come. They genuinely seem to be having a pleasant conversation. Brontë's sweet laugh echoes around me and I feel my stomach sour when I realize what I've done. I just told her to openly hit on random men while I sit back and watch. My stomach curdles at the way their conversation is flowing. I shake the thoughts of jealousy from my head, reminding myself that my only interest in her is physical and nothing more so who cares if she flirts with some other guy.

"So, would it be possible to get your number? I'd love to take you out when we're back in Chicago."

I can't stomach it a second longer. I spin around and walk up next to Brontë, reaching down to place my hand on the warm skin of her exposed thigh. She looks up at me, startled, and I lean down without hesitation, placing my lips against hers.

The kiss is soft and wet. I grip her inner thigh as I hook my other hand behind her neck and slip my tongue past her lips to tangle with hers. I break the kiss just as quickly, leaving her eyes heavy and confused.

"Sorry I kept you waiting, sweetheart." I look up at the young blond man sitting at the bar who is just as confused as Brontë.

"Uh, sorry I didn't mean—"

I just stare at him till he stumbles off his stool in his rush to leave.

"Why'd you run him off? He actually seemed really nice."

"Did he? Because I heard him ask for your number within what?" I look down at my watch. "Four minutes of meeting you?"

"So? He didn't ask me to go to his room."

"Yes, well, a man will sit with you here for hours, making small talk, getting to know you before he asks for your number and either he leaves, you leave, or the bar closes. Neither of you made a comment about needing to leave and the bar isn't closing. He knows if he can get your number within one drink, he can leave and go to the next bar where he'll find another woman to seduce and get her number or take her back to his room."

I see disgust fall across her face. "Seriously? Guys do that?"

"All the time, sweetheart."

"Do *you* do that?"

"I did when I was that age, yes." I reach down and push her hair off her shoulder as I lean against the bar. Her knees are touching my legs. It feels intimate. "You have to make them work for it, Brontë. I know you're not looking for a hookup and a man who wants more than that, a man who is interested in learning more about you will put in that work."

"And how do I do that?"

"Don't settle for a compliment or a free drink. Those things are nice, but anyone can offer that. A boy will offer you those things if he wants to fuck you; a man who's interested will show you why he's different, why he deserves you."

I pull the stool next to her closer and sit down. Her legs fall between mine.

"A man will put in the effort to make you feel like you're the only woman in the room. Like he can't take his eyes off you." She's leaning forward off her stool toward me. Her hand reaches out to casually rest on my thigh and I'm not even sure she recognizes that she's doing it.

"He'll put in the effort to woo you. To make you feel safe, like you can be vulnerable even though you just met him. Has a man ever made you feel desired, Brontë?"

She nods her head yes. "Yes. I mean, those three guys just did. They clearly saw me and wanted me."

I shake my head. "Not like that. I know you could get ten guys' numbers in ten minutes if you wanted to; you're beautiful and alluring. But those guys just want to fuck."

Her eyes darken as she drags them up my body and it's incredibly erotic. "But what if I want that too? What if I want a man who will fuck me?" She's trying to be bold, but she practically whispers the words like she's shy.

"A man *will* fuck you, honey. He'll satisfy every desire you have. He'll also hold your hand and make love to you. But those boys? They just want to fuck you with the focus of getting off, not fulfilling your needs." I lean forward, bringing us closer. "Have you ever been with a man like that, Brontë? A man who wants to please you?"

She curls her fingertips into my suit pants, lightly gripping the material. Her cheeks redden as she shakes her head. "No," she says softly.

"Don't be embarrassed, that's not your fault. But don't settle for the bare minimum from men, Brontë. You're much too special for that. A real man will pay attention to what turns you on, to how your body responds to his touch."

Her chest rises and falls rapidly. I can see her nipples harden beneath the silk of her blouse. I know I've already crossed all sorts of boundaries, but seeing her turned on like this, seeing her on edge is driving me crazy, and I have no intentions of turning back now.

"There will be no denying him because he will have you so turned on, so eager and ready to be pleased, that you'll beg for it."

Chapter 9

Brontë

"A real man will know exactly what it takes to have you dripping with desire, Brontë." He says my name and it sounds so tantalizing on the tip of his tongue. "He'll know how to toy and play with you so you're primed and ready."

His fingertips reach out and settle on my arm for a brief few seconds before he begins to move them, slowly dragging them up my arm as his eyes drop down to my lips that are now parted as I try to suck in enough air to quell the burning in my lungs.

"A real man will have you so turned on that by the time he slides into your soaking wet cunt—" The brashness of his words should shock me, but instead they only fuel the fire that's begun to burn inside me. "You'll be coming on his cock."

He reaches my neck with his featherlight touch, his hand coming around to rest against it as he drags his thumb softly against my throat.

I'm on the edge of my seat, leaning toward him like I'm wishing he'd do everything he just described to me right here, right now. I don't give a damn where we are or who's watching us. I look down at my hand that's balled into a fist, clutching his pant leg.

"Oh my God, I'm sorry." I release the material and reach for my martini, almost spilling it in the process before taking a large gulp that makes me cough.

Get it together!

He pulls a few hundreds from his pocket and tosses them on the bar top.

"Let's head upstairs, sweetheart, I think you've had enough lessons for one night."

My heart feels like it's about to beat out of my chest as we walk through the lobby of the hotel toward the elevator. Beckham's hand is at my back, guiding me through the throngs of rowdy Vegas partygoers. When we reach the elevator, he reaches around me, the warmth of his body pressed against mine as we await the car. The doors finally open, and we step inside where there are a few other couples.

He maneuvers me in front of him before settling his hands on my waist. I try to read his expression in the reflection of the mirrored wall in front of us, but I can't tell what he's thinking. His hands feel like they're going to burn through my skirt at any second.

How does he seem so unfazed by the conversation we just had?

I'm practically panting, already aching with need. I close my eyes and take in a deep breath, exhaling slowly as I attempt to calm my nerves. The car opens a few times, everyone finally exiting till it's just us, but he still doesn't move his hands from my hips till we reach our floor.

He presses against me, ushering me out into the hallway where we walk in silence, side by side till we reach our adjoining rooms.

I stop at my door that comes up first and turn to thank him for the night, but he grabs my arm and pulls me toward his door. He waves his keycard and swings the door open, holding it for me.

"How about a nightcap." It's not a question or suggestion, more of a demand.

I know I should be the responsible one here, but I don't want to be. I'm tired of always doing the right thing, the thing that's expected of me. I want to misbehave, to be naughty and adventurous for once.

I step inside his room, the smell of his cologne lingering from when he must have applied it earlier.

He follows behind me, flipping on a light before heading to the fully stocked bar in the far corner of the room.

"You like whiskey?"

"Sure." I smile, even though I've never actually drank it outside of a cocktail. Tonight is for doing things I wouldn't normally do, right? I'm in Vegas after all.

He pours us each a glass, then turns to drag two chairs next to each other so they overlook the massive window in the suite, the dancing lights of the strip far down below.

I take the tumbler he's extending toward me and bring it to my lips as he removes his suit jacket. He unbuttons another button on his Oxford shirt, his tie long gone after our meetings earlier. I'm fully engrossed in the way he's slowly and methodically rolling up the sleeves to reveal his tanned, muscular forearms.

Why are a man's forearms so hot? Such an innocuous body part to make a woman drool but damn, it works every time.

"What's going through that pretty head of yours? You haven't said a word since we left the bar."

My eyes snap upward to where he's staring at me. I bring the tumbler to my lips to take a sip, but the whiskey causes me to cough.

"Easy." He laughs, reaching for the glass, his fingers grazing mine as he places it on a small table near the chairs. "Sit," he commands, patting the seat next to him as he takes a seat.

"So tell me." He looks over at me as I slowly sink down in the chair, perched on the edge like I'm ready to jump up at any second and run for the door. "What"—he leans over and places his hand flat against my belly before pushing me backward so I'm fully sitting in the chair—"is going through that head of yours?"

It's not an overtly sexual move by any means but it's possessive, maybe a touch dominant. Beckham Archer doesn't wait for people to do something; he makes it happen.

The way he told me we were leaving the bar.

The way he grabbed my arm and brought me to his room.

The way he pushed me back in the chair just now, it's like he's already in control of me and I want to explore it more.

"I—I don't think I should say." I chew my bottom lip as a knowing smile forms on his.

"And why's that, Brontë?" The way he keeps saying my name, again possessive and in control. A power move I'm sure but it's working.

"It will certainly cross all sorts of boundaries and it would definitely break your rule."

He takes another sip of his whiskey. "Hmm, well, I don't recall saying we couldn't express what was on our minds."

"Tell me more."

"More what?"

"More ways a man would seduce me or please me."

He runs his hand over his jaw like he's contemplating if he should.

"Stand up."

I do as he says, standing in front of my chair. He reaches his hand out and grabs mine, guiding me to stand before him.

"Kneel."

I don't know what's happening and I want to ask questions but at the same time, I just want to feel. I fall down to my knees, folding my hands in my lap as I look up at him. He's sitting back in the chair, legs spread as he looks down at me. His blue eyes look dark against the dim light of the room.

"Good girl."

He finishes his whiskey, placing the empty glass on the table.

"Do you know why you're kneeling in front of me right now?"

I'm hoping it's for the obvious reason, but I just shake my head no.

"Because you want a man to control you, Brontë. You want a man to tell you what to do. You want a man to dominate you, to make you bend and break the rules. That excites you, doesn't it?"

My lips part but I don't answer.

"If I slide my fingers inside your panties right now, I guarantee you they'll be sticky with your desire, won't they?" I nod my head yes and he continues. "You liked hearing all those things I said to you downstairs, didn't you, you filthy girl?"

My pulse quickens as he sits up, leaning forward to tilt my chin upward with his thumb and forefinger.

"I'm giving you one chance, right now, to tell me what you want me to do to you tonight."

I open my mouth, then snap it shut as I contemplate what he just said.

Is he offering? Is he going to do it if I tell him or is this just another game?

"I—I want," I stutter before taking in a deep breath and squaring my shoulders. "I want you to fuck me like you described earlier. I want you to command me and take what you want from my body."

A delicious grin slowly spreads across his lips.

"Beg for it."

"You want me to—to beg?" I question, almost offended, but then I realize it's actually curiosity.

"Yes. You want this. That's why you're quickly bored of the dating apps, of the boys who so eagerly throw themselves at you, begging you for your number or to go home with them. You want a man who's going to make you work for it, to make you feel like you're doing something you shouldn't be doing."

I stare at him unblinking for several seconds before I scoot myself a little closer to him so his knees are on either side of my shoulders. It's like he has insight into my mind better than I do. He's right and he knows it; there's no use denying it. I thought something might be wrong with me when, after finding out who he was to me and my father, it didn't quell my desire for him. In fact, it made it burn hotter... if that's possible.

I reach for the buttons of my blouse, slowly undoing them one by one.

"Please, Mr. Archer," I say as I pull the blouse from my body, revealing my breasts in a sheer pale-pink bra and toss it to the floor, "use my body, make me feel good tonight."

I watch as his pupils dilate. I place my hands on his knees and pull myself upward to reach behind and unzip my skirt, letting it fall to the floor before kicking it to the side. I reach for the waist of my matching sheer panties, but he stops me.

"Don't." It's a one-word command. I obey, sinking back down to the floor and looking up at him as he slowly drags his fingertip across his bottom lip.

"Please," I say again, unsure what I'm supposed to do. "I don't want you to be a gentleman," I say, reaching my hands out to rest on his knees before slowly dragging them up his thighs.

"I have no interest in being a gentleman tonight." He leans forward and slowly wraps his hand around my throat, tugging me forward. "But before I take out several weeks' worth of pent-up sexual frustration on your tight little body, we need to get one thing clear. Tonight, stays here. What happens between us, is for us, nobody else. Do you understand?"

I nod and he tightens his grip on my throat, causing my airway to constrict.

"Yes, sir."

That grin is back, the one that does nothing to hide the intentions behind it. He leans forward. "My hand makes a nice necklace around your slender throat, doesn't it?" He lets his eyes fall from mine to where his fingers rest against my skin like he's admiring the view.

But then his eyes are back to mine and he drops his hand from my throat. He stands, reaching his hand down toward me. I take it and he helps me to my feet. Before I can steady myself, his hands are delving into my hair, pulling my lips to his.

He kisses me hungrily, like he's starving for my taste. I part my lips and his tongue snakes its way inside my mouth. He laps at my tongue with his own. I feel his hard length pressing firmly against me as he walks us back toward the bed.

Suddenly he's pushing at my shoulders till I fall back on the bed. My hair pools around my shoulders as I prop myself up on my elbows to look up at him.

"I have thought of nothing but this since I met you," he says as he methodically removes his watch before moving on to undo the buttons on his shirt. "You're soaked," he says, his eyes dropping down to the juncture of my thighs where my panties are indeed wet with my desire. He pulls his shirt down his arms, tossing it to the side, then he reaches for my ankles. He spreads my legs, planting my feet before leaning forward and running his nose right up my center.

"Ohh," I moan as he plants a kiss through my panties.

"Fuck," he groans, gripping my thighs tighter as he spreads me further apart, almost to the point of pain. He releases one leg, reaching up to pull my panties to the side. He looks up at me, his lips hovering above my slit. I can feel the warmth of his breath against my most intimate parts.

"Please," I say, my back arching as I try to scoot myself down to his tongue.

"You like to watch?" He doesn't give me time to answer before he drags his tongue up me in one long, slow stroke. I groan, my eyes fluttering as I try to keep myself upright, but it's no use. He continues to pleasure me with his tongue, switching between teasing my clit and kissing me.

"I need my tongue inside you." He grabs my waist and flips me to my stomach, spreading my thighs apart before pulling me up on my knees. "Chest down," he says, pressing his hand firmly in the center of my back till my face is in the sheets. He grips my waist, dragging me back to the edge of the bed before dropping to his knees and burying his face in me from behind.

It feels like only seconds before I'm coming, my legs shaking as I squeeze my eyes shut. He doesn't give me time to come down before he reaches over me, grabbing me by the throat again and pulling me upright so my back is against his chest. He turns my head so he can kiss me. His tongue swirls with mine as I hear the zipper of his pants come down and feel his hard cock press against my back. He breaks the kiss, his mouth at my ear.

"Are you ready for me to show you how a real man will fuck you, sweetheart?"

"Yes," I half moan as he undoes my bra, dragging it down my arms. He pulls me off the bed so I'm standing in front of him. His thumbs hook in my panties as he slowly drags them down my legs. Suddenly I feel nervous, and I reach my hands up to cross them over my bare breasts but it doesn't go unnoticed by him.

"Don't," he says, reaching around me to move my arms away from my body. He spins me around to face him. "Are you on birth control?" I nod. "I'm clean. I don't want anything between us, Brontë." He leans down and kisses my lips softly. "I want to feel your hot pussy against my bare cock, baby." He kisses me again. His lips cover mine, his tongue just barely touching mine.

"Lie back on the bed," he says, removing his pants and underwear to stand before me, gloriously naked. "Goddamn," he grunts as he takes his cock in hand and begins to stroke it as he looks down at me. "Your body is a fantasy."

I can't keep my eyes off his massive erection. It's thick and veiny, long and already wet with precum.

"You like what you see?"

I nod, my tongue darting out to wet my suddenly dry lips.

He crawls onto the bed, placing himself at my entrance. He drags the head between my folds, up then down and back up again.

"Mmm, even your pussy is beautiful. So warm and glistening, begging for me to stuff it with my cock." He stares down at me and oddly, I don't feel embarrassed or ashamed being so exposed to him. I feel sexy and desired, wanton and wild... just like he said I would.

"Please stuff me with your cock, Mr. Archer," I say, my voice breathy, filled with need. I'm begging and I'm not ashamed. I see the effect it has on him; his jaw ticks, his fiery gaze darting up to me as he grips the base of himself tighter.

"You think you're ready for me?" He slides his hand down my

thigh, sliding a finger inside me deep. He pulls it out, then slides back in, crooking it upward till I moan loudly. "I'd say you're ready."

He replaces his finger with his cock, inching inside me until he's sliding in and out of me at a pace that has me on edge. My back arches off the bed, my nails digging into the flesh of his biceps as his forearm presses firmly across my upper chest, pinning me to the bed.

"Oh, Miss Spencer," he groans. He moves his arm from my chest, his hand grabbing a fistful of my hair. He tugs on it slightly, causing my scalp to sting at the roots but it mixes with the pleasure, heightening it.

"What would your daddy say if he knew you were getting fucked by his best friend, hmm?" My eyes roll back in my head as my orgasm teases me. He's right; it is more exciting knowing we're doing something we shouldn't be doing.

"What would your friends say if they knew you liked getting your pussy stuffed by a man almost twice your age?"

His words are blunt and crass and they push me right over the edge. I scream and clutch at the sheets beneath me as he pumps himself in and out of me. My orgasm takes over, fireworks exploding behind my eyes.

A moment later he moans, releasing himself inside me. He rolls to his back, dragging me on top of him. We both lie panting in the darkness.

He drags his hand down my sweaty back, my cheek resting against his chest.

"I hope I didn't go too hard on you for round one."

"Round one?" I say, barely able to lift my head to look at him. "I'm exhausted." I laugh.

He tips my chin upward, his disheveled sex hair making him even more desirable. His voice is gravelly and low, a smirk on his lips.

"I've got the hottest twenty-four-year-old woman naked in my bed, begging me to fuck her... You think I'm going to stop after just once?"

Chapter 10

Beckham

I can still taste her on my tongue as we board our flight home. This morning wasn't awkward at all which surprised me. I figured after the harsh light of day, Brontë would avoid making eye contact with me, but it's actually the opposite.

"What?" She giggles, giving me a sassy head shake as she buckles herself into her seat.

"Didn't say a word."

"You didn't have to. You've got that look on your face."

"Look?" I ask, feigning innocence.

She rolls her eyes at me, frustrated I'm not playing along with her game. "You're annoying."

Brontë loves to be snarky, and I can't say I mind it. It's cute, but I also like to call her on it because it makes her blush.

I glance at my watch. "We've got eleven more minutes in Vegas. Care to show me what that mouth can do besides beg?"

I watch as her eyes dart to the side to see if the pilot heard me, a slight pink creeping slowly up her neck.

"You shy now?"

She pulls her bottom lip over her teeth. "No." She says the word softly as she uncrosses her legs. My eyes fall to where she has begun to gather the material of her dress in her hands as she spreads her legs a little further apart.

My head starts to angle downward, and I lean forward in my seat, my elbows resting on my knees as I realize what she's showing me.

"You're not wearing any panties?" My eyebrows shoot up because I am truly shocked. I know she likes to front being bold, but this is unexpected.

"Shhh!" She looks around again.

My mouth begins to water as my cock instantly shoots to attention. I fall to my knees and lunge for her, but she kicks her leg out just in time, planting her heel in my chest. I wrap my hand around her ankle as she slowly wags her finger at me.

"You little tease," I groan as the captain comes on the intercom and makes the final announcements before takeoff.

"Remember what *you* said," she says the word emphatically. "What happens here between us, stays here."

I nod and sit back in my chair, realizing she's right.

"Hand to God." I smile, even though my balls are screaming at me for release. "Back to being professional work associates. All the fun stays in Vegas."

This is going to be the longest fucking flight of my life.

———

It's been five agonizing days since our escapades in Las Vegas and I'm a wreck.

This plan to spend one night indulging in Brontë to get her out of my system has completely backfired.

Call me cocky but I thought for sure it would end up being a mistake for the opposite reason. That she would be the one to be hung up. The one I'd catch staring at me longingly, pining for something more. The one who would try to use any excuse to be close to me or make flirty comments about that night... but it's me, I'm the one doing all those things.

Truthfully, it kind of pisses me off she seems so unbothered by the whole thing. I heard her commenting to Trish from accounts payable today that she had a date lined up for this weekend already.

"Knock, knock. Hey, I have a few questions for you about Pierce. I've been trying to reconcile that account that I couldn't make sense of bu—"

"Not right now, Brontë," I mutter, not bothering to look up from my computer.

"Oookay," she says at my abrupt interruption. "Any chance you'll have some time later today or tomorrow before the weekend to go over it? I'd really like to draft up any remaining questions I have and send them over to their team before next week."

"I dunno, Brontë. Can't you just figure it out?" I feel flustered, out of my element, and I hate it. I let out an annoyed sigh and see the confusion on her face.

"Did something happen?"

I slam my computer shut a little harder than intended and it makes her jump.

"No, nothing I want to discuss with you." I stand up and grab my suit jacket and phone. "I'll be out tomorrow. We can talk about things next week."

I don't wait for a response from her. Instead, I march past her and straight to the elevator, sulking the entire way home.

Even after two grueling hours in the gym, I still feel like shit... even worse than I did earlier because I know Brontë didn't deserve for me to take out my frustrations on her, especially when I'm the one who instigated this.

I could have shut it down the moment she started asking if I would have taken her number if I didn't know who she was. I should have set her straight the night she crawled into my lap and kissed me, but I didn't want to... I still don't want to.

I'm not a dumb man. I've never let my dick make choices for me, especially ones that could destroy relationships, but I can't seem to shake this overwhelming desire for Brontë.

I spend the rest of my evening attempting to distract myself by flipping from one sports channel to the next, eventually calling it a night and crawling in bed, praying I wake up tomorrow a better man.

My alarm blares in my face at six a.m. Clearly, I forgot to remind myself last night that I was taking Friday off. I toss the covers back and slide my phone into my pocket, heading to the kitchen to kick this nagging headache that's settling in behind my eyes.

"Perfect," I mutter to myself as I rummage through my cabinet in search of Advil.

I grab my coffee and head to my living room to watch the news while I flip through email. A day off in my world is never really a day off. After several minutes of flipping through email, I shut my tablet off and reach for my phone, sipping on my coffee as I see a few text messages that must have come in last night after I went to bed.

Venus: *Hey, stranger (winky smiley face), haven't seen you in forever. Would love to chat and catch up if you have some free time. I'm still over in the Gold Coast. You know where to find me.*

I stare at the message, suddenly questioning if I should even reply after my night with Brontë. I flinch at that thought. Brontë and I aren't a couple. I need to make sure those kinds of ideas stay far removed from my brain.

Venus and I have had an on again, off again *relationship* for the last few years. She's a wonderful woman, but she wants more than I can give her. I've told her as much, which is why we broke up in the first place. Every now and then though, she ends a relationship with someone else and comes back to me, hoping I've changed my mind.

I'm about to toss my phone on the table when another text comes in that instantly has my heart in my throat. It's from Jonas. In all our years as friends, not once have I been scared to see his name come across my phone... till now. I try to mentally prepare myself on the off chance that somehow he found out about what the things I've done to his daughter, but it's no use. I slide the text open and instantly let out a sigh of relief.

Jonas: *Hey, Chantelle wanted me to remind you about Brontë's birthday party tomorrow. She said skipping it isn't an option. Be there. Don't make me be the bad guy and defend you when you don't show up.*

My relief is short-lived when I realize that not only am I going to spend my weekend hanging out with the one woman I'm not supposed to be hung up on, but her entire fucking family will be there as well and I have to look her dad in the eyes.

"You're a fucking idiot, Beckham."

I type out a response and hit send.

Me: *Only if it's an open bar. I'll be there.*

I don't know what I hoped to accomplish with a day off, but it's turned out to be a whole lot of nothing. Did I really expect one afternoon away from constant temptation by her mere existence was going to do anything?

The only thought that has been consistently playing through my mind tonight is Brontë telling Trish about her date.

I pace back and forth in my bedroom, glancing at my watch. It's just after six which means Brontë should be home from work. I have no idea what time her date will be, but maybe if I stop by her place now, I can catch her before she leaves.

I head to my closet and start pulling out different shirts, suddenly very aware of what I'm wearing.

What am I planning to do once I get to her place? What am I going to tell her?

Hey, I think I'm pretty fucking hung up on you and can't seem to get you out of my head. By the way, fuck this date, come home with me.

"Shit!" I toss the two shirts in my hands on the floor in frustration and walk out of the closet. I decide on a shower instead, hoping that maybe it will clear my head. Then I come up with what I think is a pretty convincing plan.

Maybe if I go over to her place, I could use it as a chance to apologize for being rude to her yesterday. Then I could segue into asking about her plans for the night and when she mentions the date, I could use it as a chance to remind her about not falling for these fuckboys' attempts to just take her home.

I get dressed and give myself a third glance in the mirror as I finish with a spray of cologne before heading out to drive over to her apartment.

I park down the street from her building, sitting in my car for several minutes, deciding if I seem desperate or crazy. I don't want to linger on it too long because I think I already know the answer to that. Both.

I have a clear view of her building. I shut the car off and open the door, stepping out just as I see the front door open and Brontë step outside with two other women. I sink back down in my car as the three women laugh and talk as they take a few steps in the opposite direction before Brontë stops and then quickly looks down into her purse like she's searching for something.

I squint at the other two women. I can't be certain, but I think they were the ones that were with her the night we met. Suddenly Brontë pulls something that looks like her cell out of her purse, holding it up as if to say she has it, then they turn and start walking down the sidewalk again.

I'm about to shut my door and head home when I wonder why she's heading out with her friends instead of on her date. Was she telling Trish that in the hopes I would overhear and get jealous? Did he cancel on her? Maybe her friends are going to go with her and hide out in case it goes south and she needs an escape plan. I've heard of women doing that.

Against my better judgment as a forty-five-year-old man, I get out of my car and make my way down the sidewalk to follow them.

They don't go far, only a few blocks, and then enter an already rowdy-looking dive bar named O'Malley's with giant corny gold letters across the top in a Gaelic-looking font and a four-leaf clover.

I wait several minutes to walk inside, keeping my head down as I head for a dark corner in the back.

"What can I getcha, sugar?" A short woman with black hair approaches my table.

"Guinness." I smile, clearly inspired by the Irish setting.

"Tab?" she asks and I nod, handing her my card before she walks back toward the bar.

It smells sticky in here with a touch of mold. Not my kind of place and honestly, it doesn't seem like Brontë's either. I scoot further back into the corner as I search the room for her, spotting her almost immediately.

It's only now I get to fully take in her outfit. She's wearing a pale-pink top that hangs off both shoulders, sitting just above a long white skirt that has small matching flowers. She turns and I notice a slit that runs all the way up her mid-thigh. She looks delectable. Like an easy-going Sunday morning.

Her blond hair flows down her back in soft curls, swept to one side like she brushed her fingers through it at some point and tossed it to the side. She laughs unapologetically at something one of her friends says and it makes my stomach clench.

She's far too good for me. What the fuck am I doing?

I contemplate closing my tab and walking out before I even get my beer, but my waitress appears and places it on the table just as I reach for my wallet.

"Thank you." I grab the glass and down half of it in one go. I tell myself I get five more minutes before I have to leave out the back and head home, but then I see a young man approach her.

She smiles, holding out her hand as she introduces herself. She points over her shoulder at her two friends, introducing them as well. Then she follows him over to his table where she sits down and casually talks to him.

It's innocent enough. They are clearly just getting to know one another when a waitress brings over a tray of shots. It's clear by the expression on her face that she doesn't want it, but with the guy's persistence she ends up taking it.

I shake my head, curling my fist into my hands because I know what the fuck he's trying to do. I drum my fingers on the table, watching intently as the night carries on. I don't know how long I've been sitting here, but I've finished my second beer and the bar is now so loud it's giving me a headache.

The music is loud, thudding in my chest as several sweaty couples grind on each other in the center of the floor. I watch as the man stands up, extending his hand toward Brontë. She looks up at him, then slides her hand into his as he leads her out onto the dance floor.

I grip the glass in my hand so tight I'm shocked I don't shatter it. I want to leave. I can't stomach the sight of his hands on her waist as his body grinds against hers. It's awkward and clunky; the kid clearly has no rhythm, but I'm not sure that's the point. His intentions are obviously to feel her up as his hands begin to wander over her body.

She can't possibly be enjoying this. He reaches around and grabs her ass and I see her hands shoot behind her to pull them back up to her waist. I lean forward in my chair, my blood pressure through the roof. Then he slides his hands up her body to cradle her face as he pulls her in for a kiss.

I stand up so fast I bump the table and the glass teeters back and forth. I shoot my hand out and catch it just as it tumbles off the table. When I look back up, Brontë is nowhere in sight, but the man she was with is heading right toward me with his buddy next to him.

"Dude, that girl is so fucking fine, bro." His friend elbows him in the ribs as they walk toward the exit to my right.

"Just wait," he says, turning to face his friend as they step outside to the alley, "she'll be begging me to take her home after a few more shots. Like candy from a baby."

They both burst into laughter. I shoot my hand out to grab the door before it fully closes and follow them outside. Neither of them notice me as they undo their flies to take a piss against the back wall of the bar.

"You think she'll come back to our place then, like for real? I'll make sure I'm out of your way."

"Hell yeah, dude, she'll be so wasted she won't know where the hell she is anyway."

I walk up behind them and kick the one that was with Brontë in the back of the leg right where his knee meets his shin. It buckles and he stumbles, getting piss all over his jeans.

"What the fuck, bro? Watch it!" he shouts as he stuffs himself back in his jeans and looks down at the wet streaks.

I stand there with my hands in my pockets as I stare at both of them.

"Aw, man." He attempts to wipe away the urine but it does nothing. "You fucking dick!" he shouts, looking up at me. He lunges toward me with a cocked-back fist, but I step to the side which only angers him more. He pulls his fist back again. This time I swerve and he lands the punch square into the brick wall.

"My hand!" he screams, cradling it with his other hand. "You fucking broke my hand." His face is bright red as his friend scrambles to help him, but I push him away.

I grab the kid by the shirt, kicking his legs out from under him so that his face is inches away from his own piss on the ground.

"Don't you ever fucking speak to her again, you understand me? If I see you or that pencil dick little weasel with you around here again, I'll make sure that neither of you ever reproduce."

He's full-on crying now, tears and snot mixing together on his face as I let him fall to the ground. He continues to moan about his hand as his friend runs to his aid.

I step back into the bar, motioning for the waitress to settle my tab and debating on my next move. What I want to do is grab Brontë and drag her back to her apartment and teach her a lesson about guys like that, but I know that's part of her age, going out to shitty bars and dancing. If I did drag her out of here, especially in front of her friends, she would only resent me, just like she does her father, and that's the last thing I want.

Instead, I slip out the back and walk the few blocks back to my car, reality hitting me that this is why a twenty-four-year-old is just a fun one-night stand, nothing that you can build on because we want two completely different things.

I climb in my car and put it in drive, pulling out into traffic. That's when it hits me... Shouldn't this be what I want? A man who has never desired the happily ever after with a wife and kids in the suburbs. Shouldn't I be loving the idea of a hot hookup now and then with no strings attached and no feelings?

Suddenly the uncomfortable realization hits me and settles into my stomach. That's not what I want at all with Brontë Spencer.

I want more.

I want all of her.

Chapter 11

Brontë

"Happy birthday!"

Silas and Jenson run into my arms, barely letting me make it through the front door of their house.

"Thank you, boys!" I take turns hugging each of them, swinging Jenson around a few times.

"We got you a present," Silas says matter-of-factly.

"Oh, how exciting!" I crouch down to meet them at eye level. "Let me guess," I say, tapping my chin like I'm thinking hard. "Is it a dinosaur egg?"

"No!" Jenson shouts.

"Oh!" I clap my hands together. "It's a transformer, isn't it!"

Silas rolls his eyes in exasperation, clearly already too old for my silly games.

"No silly." Jenson props both hands on his hips as he steps nose to nose with me. "Optimus Prime is too big!" His hands dart out over his head.

"Well, you boys have stumped me then. I'm all out of guesses."

"Mom, can she open it now?" Jenson asks Chantelle as he jumps up and down in excitement.

"She will open it later with her other presents."

"Awww, why not now?" he says, his lower lip pooching out.

"After cake, Jenson; you know this. Happy birthday, Brontë." Chantelle turns to me and pulls me in for a warm hug.

"Thank you. You really didn't need to go through all the trouble of this." I motion toward the beautiful balloon arch and the six-foot-wide banner that hangs in their atrium.

"Nonsense. I know you're only ten years younger, but you're the only daughter I have whom I get to spoil with pretty stuff like this instead of baseball and dinosaurs." She whispers the last part, throwing me a wink.

"There's the birthday girl!" My dad walks around the corner, arms spread wide as he pulls me in for a hug. "Come here."

"Thanks, Dad." He loops his arm around my shoulders as we make our way toward the kitchen.

"You need to see this cake your stepmom had made for you. You're going to flip."

We walk into the kitchen and I gasp when I see the five-tier cake on the counter. The base icing is a pale pink, my favorite color, with a cascading waterfall of beautiful daisies, my favorite flower.

"Your father said you loved daisies; I hope that's still the case?" Chantelle looks at me questioningly, and I nod.

"You remembered?" I look over at my dad who's admiring the cake, his arm still around my shoulders.

"Of course I remembered. I know I wasn't present, Brontë. I've got so much to make up for, but I remember so many things about you." He says the words in a hushed tone, almost as if he's saying them to himself. When he turns to look at me, I see tears in his eyes.

"Can we just eat it now already?" Silas interrupts with an exasperated tone, making us all laugh. "It just seems silly to wait until later. There's enough for us to eat some now and some later." He has one hand on his hip, the other flipped palm up for emphasis.

"No. You boys follow Mrs. Ludlow and go put your swim trunks on. You promised me a cannonball contest." Chantelle turns Silas around by his shoulders and swats him playfully on the behind. "I bet your sister wants to help me judge so make sure you boys try your hardest."

"A cannonball contest? How fun!" I clap and grab Silas' hand, Jenson running up to grab my other hand. "I'll help the boys change. I'm going to put my suit on too," I say as I take them upstairs.

After we change, I bring the boys back downstairs and we peek around the corner of the French doors that lead out to the pool. Chantelle is reclining in her chair, her long legs outstretched, a pair of cat eye sunglasses perched high on her nose. She looks like a throwback to one of those fifties bombshells with her big floppy black-and-white hat.

"Okay, so remember what we talked about? Your mom is out there in her chair so let's go surprise her. On the count of three we'll run out and shout 'cannonball' and jump in, okay?"

"Got it," Silas says, giving me an enthusiastic double thumbs-up which Jenson watches him do, then copies.

We tiptoe to the door, the boys giggling the entire time. I pull it open, grabbing their hands as we step outside, still out of view of their mom.

"One, two, three..." I whisper, then we sprint around the corner and straight for the pool.

"Cannonball!" we all three shout as we jump into the pool, sending water splashing and Chantelle squealing.

"Success!" Silas says, high-fiving me, then attempting with Jenson who completely misses his hand.

"You are a bad influence." Chantelle laughs, wiping the spray of water from her sunglasses.

The boys and I continue our cannonball contest, Chantelle giving us each tens.

"I'm going to sit out a few rounds," I say, climbing out of the pool, already exhausted. "I'll sit up here and judge with your mom."

The boys don't show any signs of slowing. They continue to jump one after the other, swimming to the edge and climbing out to do it all over again.

"My God," I groan, leaning back into the chair next to Chantelle. "I already feel fifty and I'm only halfway there."

"Wait till you push a baby or two out. You'll feel like you can't even laugh or sneeze anymore." She laughs and shakes her head. "Worth it though... even though they have endless energy and love to bring bugs and snakes and toads into the house unannounced."

I look over at her and raise my eyebrows. "Bugs? No, thanks."

"Oh, did I tell you about our new kittens?"

"You have kittens?"

"Two," she replies, holding up her finger with an annoyed look on her face. "The boys found them somewhere. They said they wandered into our backyard. We've been searching for the mom but no luck."

"Where are they? You guys keeping them?"

She sighs. "I told the boys they could keep them, but they have to learn to feed them and scoop litter. That will *not* be passed off to Mrs. Ludlow." She says it sternly as if she's speaking to the boys. "We have them in one of the guest bedrooms right now that has an en suite. You can go up and play with them if you want."

"Aw, I will for sure. I've been debating on adopting one, but I don't think I'm home enough, especially not with the new job."

"How is that going?" She turns to look at me, sipping her lemonade.

I shrug, reminding myself to play it cool and not act too eager. "It's good. I got to travel with Beckham to Las Vegas for some meetings so that was pretty cool."

"Beckham, huh?" She looks at me over her glasses.

"Er—Mr. Archer. He actually insisted I call him Beckham." I can feel my face growing red. "Anyway, he's involving me in more day-to-day stuff so that's been cool. I get to flex my finance degree which feels satisfying since I paid for it."

"Well, I'm glad to hear that. I know your father will be as well.

He's been worried about you, but I told him to relax, she's extremely capable and can handle it." She winks at me.

"Thank you. I think he still thinks I'm that little seven-year-old girl."

"I think you're right. Plus, he's a father; they always worry about their little girls." She reaches over and squeezes my hand. "And if Beckham is ever out of line, don't be afraid to remind him who your father is."

I choke as I try to swallow, sputtering and coughing. "What do you mean?" I finally manage to get out.

"Oh, if he's just too hard on you. These billionaire types are a different breed. I know the type; I'm married to one." She laughs and I feel myself relaxing, realizing she's just making a general statement and not something more specific. "They can be a little too big for their britches now and then. That's why it's good for us ladies to remind them who keeps the tempo."

"He's been great so far."

"Speaking of," she says, looking at her watch, "he's supposed to be here by now."

"Who? Beckham?" I shoot out of my chair, suddenly very aware that I'm in a bikini.

Why the hell would I be nervous for him to see me in a two-piece? He's literally had his face practically buried inside me.

I blush at the memory, then physically shake my head to try and refocus away from those memories.

"Yes, Beckham. Are you okay?" She eyes me, confused by my overreaction.

"Yeah, yes, I'm okay. I, uh, just didn't realize he was coming here. For my birthday?"

"I thought it might be nice for your dad to have his friend here so we can sip champagne and gossip. Did I overstep inviting your boss? I guess I didn't think about it like that at the time. I'm so sorry."

"No." I wave away her concern, the two lines between her brows disappearing. "It's perfectly okay. Not an issue at all." I feel panic grip my chest. How the hell am I going to play it cool when I'm half-naked and my hot-as-hell boss is here, especially after all the naughty things he did to me?

"Who's ready for Marco Polo?" I shout, plugging my nose and taking a running start before cannonballing into the pool again. The boys squeal in delight as I close my eyes and begin to search for them.

"Marco!" I shout, hearing Jenson giggle to my right as he whispers polo. I lunge toward him, but he gets away.

We spend the next several minutes playing, each of us taking turns as Marco. "Your turn again," Silas says, pointing toward me.

"Marco!" I shout, but neither of the boys answer. "Marco!" I repeat, but again, no answer, just distant giggles.

"I hear youuuuu," I say, lunging forward but there's nobody there.

"Marco!" I say again, this time feeling the edge of the pool as I reach my hand out, only it's not the edge of the pool, it's someone's shoes.

I open my eyes, my hand resting gently on a pair of loafers. I turn my head upward, shielding my gaze from the sun as I look up, staring straight up the body of Beckham.

"Polo," he says in that low sexy voice with a smirk on his face.

"Guess you're it." I go to grab his leg to pull him into the pool, but he steps backward, just out my reach.

"Someone doesn't like to play fair."

"I think we both know I have a penchant for breaking the rules."

We stare at each other for a moment before the shout of one of the boys brings my attention back to what we were doing. I look over my shoulder, seeing Silas and Jenson in a splash fight and I turn back to Beckham, but it's not his eyes I catch. It's Chantelle.

She's sitting back in her chair, her sunglasses pulled down toward the tip of her nose as she studies us both. Beckham must notice that I'm looking past him and slowly turns around to greet her.

"Hello, beautiful." He smiles toward her as he walks over to where she's sunbathing, bending down to kiss her on the cheek. "You look like you're having a rough day," he jokes and I swear I see her blush.

Good to know he has that effect on most... if not all women.

"Jonas is inside, getting the meat ready for the grill if you'd like to join him."

"I'll go find him," he says, shoving his hand into the pocket of his navy golf shorts. He's wearing a white polo that stretches across his chest, his biceps threatening to stretch out the seams of his sleeves. A pair of classic tortoiseshell Wayfarers are perched on the bridge of his nose and that signature lock of dirty-blond hair flops down over his forehead.

The man's body would look good in a damn potato sack, I think to myself as I watch him walk away, his firm ass reminding me what it felt like to grip as he thrust deep inside me.

I ignore the look on Chantelle's face and turn back to continue my game with my brothers. I'm trying to stay focused, but I find myself constantly looking over my shoulder, attempting to catch a glimpse of Beckham again.

"Okay, boys"—Chantelle stands near the edge of the pool— "let's go inside and shower off so you can get ready for the cookout."

"Awww, Mom. Just five more minutes," Silas groans.

"Did you not want cake then?" Their mother puts on her stern face as if to say, *if I have to tell you twice, you won't get any.*

At the mention of cake, both boys doggy paddle to the edge of the pool and climb out in record time, racing each other toward the house.

"Dry off first, boys!" Chantelle says, grabbing their towels and running past them. "Oh, I almost forgot," she turns and half shouts back to me, "I got you a birthday pool float. It's in the pool house." She points toward the building in the back before chasing the boys into the house.

I climb out of the pool and walk over to the pool house where there is indeed an adorable hot-pink flamingo pool float. I smile and grab it, bringing it with me back to the pool where I slowly lower myself down onto it.

I lean back, letting the warmth of the sun lull me almost to sleep. It's so peaceful, floating aimlessly in the pool as I close my eyes and relax. I have no idea how long I've been out here when I hear the familiar toe-curling sound of Beckham's rich voice.

"Happy birthday, Brontë."

My heart feels like it skips a beat, but I play it cool. In fact, I don't even bother opening my eyes. I simply smile and let my head fall back an inch further.

"Thank you, Mr. Archer."

He chuckles. I can hear the smirk on his face as weird as that sounds. "Back to Mr. Archer, is it?"

I shrug nonchalantly when I feel a spray of water across my face. I flinch and remove my sunglasses.

"I asked you a question," he says, crouched down next to the water.

"What the hell?" I don't attempt to hide my annoyance at him. "Around my family, yes, you're Mr. Archer. We are merely boss and employee… or friend of my father in this current situation since it's out of the office. I thought we were attempting to regain some professionalism after Vegas anyway? Remember, the fun stays there."

I push my float over to the ladder and climb out. I squeeze out my hair, letting the water run onto the cement beneath my feet.

Beckham's eyes are hidden behind his sunglasses, but if I had to guess, he just dragged them up and down my body. He stands, shoving his hands in his pockets.

"You have fun last night?" His tone is clipped.

"Yes, I did. Why? Did you?" I ask curiously.

"How was your date?"

"Date?" I ask, confused, shaking my head. "I didn't have a date."

"I overheard you tell Trish you did."

"Oh, yeah, I was supposed to, but the guy canceled on me last minute so I just went out with Taylor and Sylvia." I am suddenly very aware of my half-nakedness as I reach for my towel and wrap it around my body.

"So you just danced with a complete stranger and let him feel you up and kiss you?"

My head snaps up so fast. "You saw me last night?" He doesn't answer, his lips set in a hard, thin line. "What were you doing at O'Malley's?" I narrow my gaze at him and take a step closer to him.

"I came over to talk to you about something and you came out of your building with your friends as I arrived."

My mouth falls open. "You fucking followed me?" I want to shove him into the pool, but I know that will cause a kind of commotion that will bring my family outside. Nervously, I glance over my shoulder to make sure nobody can hear us, but we're the only ones outside.

"I hadn't planned on it, but you're welcome I did, considering that piece of shit you were with was planning on getting you drunk and taking you back to his place. I mean, come on, Brontë, did you learn absolutely nothing from our talk in Vegas about these boys? Hmm?" He reaches out to hook his finger under my chin, but I push his hand away.

My cheeks flush with anger as I point a finger in his chest. "I am not yours to protect or follow. I think you need to leave." I don't wait for an answer. Instead, I turn and walk toward the house. "And don't follow me this time," I say over my shoulder, but he doesn't seem to hear me, or if he did, he doesn't care as he marches after me, his toes on my heels.

I walk through the French doors that lead into the kitchen, my family gathered around the massive granite island that's filled with food.

"Hey, I was just about to head out with these steaks, burgers, and dogs. Grab a beer and help me grill," my dad says to Beckham as I round the island, grabbing my bag and making a beeline toward the stairs.

"I'll join everyone outside soon. I just want to change and meet the kittens really quick," I half shout as I take the stairs two at a time. I head down the hallway, finding an empty guest room to change in. I close the door behind me, resting against it as my heart thuds loudly in my chest.

"Brontë." Beckham taps lightly on the door behind me as he turns the handle and presses against it. "Let me in."

I don't know why, I know I'm asking for trouble, but I step away from the door and let him come inside. He closes it behind him, his eyes no longer hidden behind his glasses.

"Let me just say that I didn't intend on following you last night." He runs his hand through his disheveled hair. "I truly came over to talk to you. I know I don't even have a right to do that, but I was worried about you."

"Worried about me? Why?"

"Because I thought you had a date and after the way things went down between us in Vegas, I thought that I not only owed you an apology for my behavior, but that I should warn you away from men like me."

I let out a laugh that comes out in a huff. "That's rich coming from you. And trust me, you don't have to worry about me going after men like you." I can see my words sting as he visibly flinches. "You made it abundantly clear by your behavior toward me in the office that Vegas was a mistake for you. Whatever. That's fine if you feel that way, but to punish me by lashing out at me and treating me unprofessionally afterward was childish."

I go to step past him, but his arm shoots out to grab my elbow.

"You think I don't know that?" He grits the words through his teeth. "You think I like feeling this way? Knowing that I can never have you even though I can't close my eyes without seeing you behind them." He tightens his grip on my arm as he tugs me closer to him. "You think I enjoy the burning pit of jealousy I feel when I see another man's hands on you like I did last night? The way he touched your ass? The way his lips tasted yours like mine did?"

I struggle to hold on to my anger as I see his stoic facade slip away. I want to tell him that I want more, that I hate the idea of another man's hands or lips on my body also, but I don't know what's being exchanged between us right now and I refuse to be seen by him as just another regret.

"I can't even take a single fucking breath without thinking of you." His lips inch closer to mine, my resolve slipping as the towel wrapped around me slowly slides down my body.

He doesn't hesitate now. He spins me around to face him, his hands diving into my damp hair as his lips find mine. The kiss is hungry, possessive, demanding. He isn't asking, he's taking, and my mouth opens to let him in.

"Stop," I say suddenly, pressing against his chest to separate myself from him. "No—you can't just do this. You can't use me, then act like I'm worthless, then get jealous when you made it clear I was a one-time thrill for you."

"I didn't mean to make you feel worthless, Brontë; that's the last thing I wanted." He hangs his head. When he lifts it again, his eyes are soft. He steps closer to me again, his fingers slowly sliding up my arm, leaving a path of goosebumps in their wake.

"You are amazing and wonderful, more than a man like me deserves." He walks me backward till the window in the room is at my back. His other hand reaches up to slide up my other arm till his hands meet at my neck. "You are an enigma, a fever dream of everything I fantasize about." He leans forward slowly, kissing the corner of my lips. "Delicious and forbidden."

I close my eyes as he continues to speak, his words and featherlight kisses causing my head to swim. He spins me around to face the window, reaching around me to part the curtains so we're looking down at where my family is gathered around the massive built-in grill.

"Tell me you don't feel it too." His breath is warm against my neck as he leans down to whisper in my ear. "Tell me you don't lie in bed at night touching yourself, imagining it's my fingers, my tongue on your warm skin." His hands glide down my exposed body till he reaches my hands.

"Grab the window frame," he says, lifting my hands and placing them against the white molding around the window. "Don't move them," he commands before turning my face toward him and kissing me hungrily. "Understand?"

"Yes," I half moan as he reaches beneath my bikini top and cups my bare breasts. My eyes flutter closed as he rolls my nipples between his fingertips, then pinches them hard. "Ow!"

"Be quiet," he says, pinching me again, harder. My body responds, need pulling deep in my lower belly as he unapologetically commands me.

"Oh, honey." His voice is thick and deep in my ear as his fingers slide down my belly, into my panties and right between my folds. "You're already soaking wet for me."

I close my eyes, biting down on my bottom lip as my fingers dig into the window frame.

"You like being used by me. You act like you don't, but you know it makes your tight little pussy quiver at the thought of me taking what I want from you." He teases me a little more before sliding two fingers all the way inside me.

"Ohhhh." I can't stifle the moan that falls from my lips as he begins to fuck me with his fingers.

"That's right, baby. Look at you about to come on my fingers while your entire family is just right down there. They have no idea just how filthy you are, do they?" His lips are at my ear, his fingers sliding in and out of me from behind now while his other finger dances across my clit.

"Just remember this next time some boy at a bar wants to buy you a shot or grind up on your body. Can he make you feel like this, Bron-të?" His strokes are long and slow, keeping me teetering on the edge and it's driving me wild. "Answer me," he says, stilling his movements.

"N-n-no," I manage to choke out as he resumes his movements. I can feel anticipation building in my body, about to explode. Tingles are moving from my toes up my legs.

"That's right, sweetheart. Now, relax and come on my fingers so I can taste you." He barely finishes the statement before my orgasm finally finds release. My legs shake as waves of pleasure roll through me.

Beckham's thumbs are in the waistband of my bikini bottoms, dragging them down my thighs as he falls to his knees.

"I promise this will be quick; I just need to lick you clean." Seconds later his hands are splayed against both of my ass cheeks as he buries his face in my pussy, devouring me till I'm shaking, coming on his tongue in under a minute.

———

LIGHTNING BUGS DANCE ACROSS THE BACK PATIO, JENSON AND Silas chasing them as they run off their sugar high from the cake earlier. I never got a chance to meet the kittens when I went upstairs to change but after cake, the boys officially introduced them to me and showed me their favorite toys which we played with for over an hour.

After my little rendezvous with Beckham earlier, the afternoon went off without a hitch. We enjoyed the cookout and he left shortly after, taking a piece of cake for the road. If my family had any inclination about what happened between us upstairs, they certainly didn't act like it.

"So, sweetie, how does it feel to be a quarter of a century old?" My dad walks outside and places his hands on the back of my chair.

"Well, when you put it that way—old." I laugh as Chantelle playfully smacks his arm.

"I hope you had a wonderful day today." She looks at me questioningly and I smile and nod.

"I did. I had a great time. Thank you both so much."

"Listen, I know it's late and you'll be heading home soon, but I need to talk to you about something."

I look up at my dad as he speaks, his expression serious and my stomach suddenly flip-flops into a knotted mess.

"Okay," I say, placing my nearly empty water glass on the table and standing to follow him inside. I look over my shoulder at Chantelle who offers me a supportive smile, but it does little to ease my anxiety.

"Have a seat." He gestures as he sits down behind his desk. He spins around, opening a painting on the wall like a door to reveal a built-in safe like you see in thriller or spy movies. He types in a code, removing a single file before closing it again and sitting down.

"There's something I've been waiting to tell you about until today, your twenty-fifth birthday."

I feel like I'm on the verge of throwing up. Suddenly, I get the insane idea that he's about to tell me his best friend is really my dad and not him. Panic seizes my chest and I'm about to freak out when he slides the folder across the desk toward me.

"Your mother and I created a trust for you that you gain full access to on your twenty-fifth birthday."

Relief washes over me as I try to comprehend what he just said.

"A trust?"

"When you were little, I paid child support and alimony to your mother. With each year as my net worth grew, I started contributing more. She said it was way too much and with her job, she was able to provide for you for the most part. I told her back then that we should set up a trust for you so that's what we did. We both contributed to it over the years and your mother even had her life insurance policy go into the trust for you."

I feel tears prick my eyes. Talking about my mom still makes me emotional, especially when I realize that even in death, she was so selfless, more concerned about me than her own failing health.

"So what does that mean for me?" I ask as I pick up the folder from his desk.

"It means that you have absolute freedom to do whatever you want with your life."

I furrow my brow and open the folder, scanning over the documents when my eyes see the trust total. I feel them bug out of my head as I audibly gasp.

This can't be right.

"Fifty million dollars?"

Chapter 12

Beckham

"Sir, there's a Brontë Spencer here to see you. Should I send her up?"

I smile as my doorman mentions Brontë's name. What a lovely and unexpected surprise.

"Yes, Ritchie, send her up. Thank you."

I half sprint to the bathroom, double-checking my hair and swishing around some mouthwash before walking back to the entryway just as the elevator opens up to my penthouse.

"How did you and my father become friends?" she asks as she walks toward me, a folder clutched against her chest just like when we first officially met in my office.

"Good evening to you too, Brontë." I smile as I walk toward her.

Truthfully, I've been a scared shitless mess since her birthday party on Saturday. Being that it's Sunday evening and I hadn't heard from her, I fully expected to pretend once again on Monday morning that nothing happened between us.

"Sorry." She squeezes her eyes shut and shakes her head. "I know you weren't expecting me, but I really need to talk to you about something."

"Yeah, absolutely. You want a glass of wine?"

She shakes her head, then chews her bottom lip for a second. "Actually, on second thought, yes, please."

I walk over to the bar and find a Malbec I've been eyeing. "Red?"

"Hmm? Oh, yeah, that's fine." She waves nervously as she opens the folder in her hands and studies it.

"Got the winning lottery numbers in it?" I pour us each a glass and hand her one, but she doesn't seem to hear my question.

"So anyway, how did you meet my dad?" She takes the glass from me and sips it as we walk toward the barstools and take a seat.

"I guess I assumed you knew how we met but I'm happy to share. About ten years ago he reached out to me, to my foundation actually. He wanted to make a rather large donation but wanted it to remain anonymous. When he told the donation coordinator the amount, she immediately called me. We have donation thresholds. Once a donor reaches a certain amount, usually anything over a million, I personally call them and talk about why they want to donate, how we will use the funds and so on."

"How much did my dad donate?"

I laugh. "Twenty million."

"Twenty million?" Her eyes grow large. "Jonas Ramsay? You're sure it was my father who donated twenty million dollars to charity?" She laughs and shakes her head.

"Now that I think about it"—I spin the wineglass between my fingers—"ten years ago would be right around the time you changed your last name." She looks up at me from her glass. "Your father told me. Maybe it was his way of paying penance?"

She nods her head, taking a healthy gulp of wine.

"Maybe. I guess that would make sense. He knows how much charity and nonprofits mean to me and—or did—mean to my mom."

"So that's how we met. Of course I knew who your father was, everyone does, but I'd never formally met him. I invited him for a round of golf at my club to discuss the foundation and his donation and we ended up setting up a weekly game. The rest is history. Why do you ask?"

She shrugs but there's clearly something on her brain. "I guess I wondered how someone as charitable and involved in giving back to his community like you ended up friends with... well, he just isn't as nice as you."

I laugh. "No, he's not but that's one of the things I like about him. Being that he's a decade older than me, I was still in my thirties when I met him and he taught me some invaluable lessons. He taught me about being firm in my decisions and not second-guessing my gut. He also taught me about how to not completely fuck up in business and how to always be prepared for something to go sideways. But most importantly, he taught me the value of time."

"Meaning?"

"He told me it was okay to be selfish with how I spent my time and with whom. He told me back then on that golf course and several times since. '*Beckham, you can always make more money. You can always make more friends. You can always buy more stuff, but you can never get more time. Time is the great equalizer among men.*' That stuck with me and made me realize that he's right; it's okay to be protective with how we spend our time because no matter how hard I work or how many deals I win, it won't give me more time on this earth. When it's my time, it's my time."

"That's interesting, pretty profound actually."

I reach over and tuck her hair behind her ear. "That's why I said that maybe he was paying penance with that donation. Obviously, money will never change how he treated you and your mother, but giving that money to families in need maybe made him feel some sort of relief from his guilt of losing so much time with you... even if it was only for a second." She nuzzles her cheek against the palm of my hand for a moment, her warm smile instantly making the pace of my heart kick up a few beats. "All that to say, what do you need to talk to me about?"

She doesn't say anything, just pushes the folder she's been gripping across the counter toward me. Confused, I pick it up and flip it open, scanning it briefly. It's a trust in her name, that's very clear. I drop my gaze down to the bottom where I see the dollar figure.

"Wow." I whistle and shut the folder, placing it back on the counter. "Is this your way of putting in your notice?" I smile and it makes her laugh.

"No, this is my way of telling you I need your advice."

"I'm flattered but I would suggest you reach out to my personal finance guy. I can give you his card."

She shakes her head. "When my dad explained all of this to me last night, where the money came from and whatnot, he didn't even ask me what my plan was... He just told me what he *felt* I should do." She raises her hands as if to defend herself already. "I know, he's obviously extremely smart, being that he's a gazillionaire, but he doesn't care about what I want to do with the money. He feels I should use the bulk of it to create some sort of sustainable, passive income that will grow in time and set me and my future generations up for success. When I asked him about donating some of it, I couldn't even finish my sentence before he shut it down. He told me I could donate some of it, but that he and my mom didn't work as hard as they did for me to just piss it all away."

Her face contorts with the last statement and I understand that Jonas has a way of not mincing words. If anyone can be so blunt it's hurtful, it's Jonas.

"I'm sure he didn't mean that it would be pissing it away if you gave some to charity. He's probably just worried that you'll give it all away and not create a future for yourself."

"Doubtful." She rolls her eyes. "It's just—it's not fair and it's such a double standard that he can donate twenty million to your foundation, but if I tried that, he'd freak out and tell me I'm pissing it away?"

"Brontë, when he donated that amount to my charity, he was already a billionaire several times over. Twenty million was a drop in the bucket to him."

"Exactly, he should have given more!"

"I'm just saying he already had a future established for him and his family and future generations, including you, when he made that donation. If you wanted to donate that amount, it's almost fifty percent of your net worth."

"If he already has his future generations set up for success that would include me then, right?" I nod in agreement. "Then why the hell does he care what I do with *this* money? When he dies, he'll just be passing everything along to his kids anyway."

"And will you take that money and keep it or donate it?"

"Donate it," she says without missing a beat.

I laugh. "And I bet you anything, he knows that. So take this money now, set yourself and others up for success so that when you get a much larger inheritance from him someday, you can donate every damn penny if you want."

I can see the wheels turning. "Honestly, I get that he wants me to set myself up for success, but I also know that I can easily do that with half of this trust. What I would love to do more than anything is set up my own nonprofit. One that would pay the people who work there actual livable wages." Her eyes light up as she talks.

"You know, when I was waiting tables through grad school, I interviewed at this organization for inner city kids that ended up offering me my dream job, but I couldn't take it because it would have been a fifty percent pay cut from being a waitress which was already scraping the bottom of the barrel with my school schedule and they didn't offer health insurance. It broke my heart."

I reach out and grab her hand, intertwining our fingers together.

"Imagine getting that offer now. You could take that job and not worry about anything because you have the money in savings to do so."

"But I'll never burn through fifty million; I just won't. Even with inflation and buying a house, I prefer to live small."

"I understand, but hear me out. I agree with your father in this sense. Keep even a fifth of that money for yourself. You can work with a financial advisor to find the best investments for you; maybe that's just the stock market or a mix of real estate. And the rest, you can easily donate several million to different existing nonprofits and then use part of it to help startups. There's a ton of young entrepreneurs out there who are dying to change the world for the better, but they just don't have the capital or know the right investors."

Her eyes light up and a smile spreads across her face.

"Imagine meeting young people like you who have innovative ideas that could help others, benefit our community and our planet, feed and clothe the homeless, help animals, or whatever it might be, and you could cut them a check to make that dream a reality all while collecting a dividend check every quarter when they become profitable. Or someday even cashing out your shares if you need to. In the meantime, you can create that nonprofit you want and start building it up."

"See, this is why I knew I wanted to talk to you about this. You get it."

"I don't know about that but I'm happy to offer any input and listen as you talk through things."

She nudges my shoulder. "This is why I like you so much." She smiles and I feel that butterfly in my stomach again.

"Yeah? You like me?"

"Mm-hmm. We're like-minded." She points at her eyes, her fingers in a *V* before pointing them toward mine.

The air hangs heavy between us. I think we're flirting; it certainly feels like it and I like it. In my past relationships or flings, there were never these kinds of moments. Moments that aren't overtly sexual but feel more intimate than any physical interaction we've had.

"I appreciate your honesty and feedback tonight. Means a lot that I can trust you."

"You trust me?" I can't hide the smile on my face.

"I do," she says and our eyes lock. "Hey..." She hesitates as if she's second-guessing what she's about to say.

"Yes?"

"Would you be willing to talk to my dad with me about all this—what we talked about with the trust?"

"Of course." I smile.

I can feel the rhythm of my breathing increasing as she leans in a little closer to me and the tension builds.

"It's getting late." Brontë's words are barely above a whisper as her gaze falls from my eyes to my lips.

"Yes, it is," I murmur, reaching my hand out to run my thumb over her plump bottom lip. "You better get home before the big bad wolf eats you alive."

She giggles, her tongue darting out and touching the tip of my thumb, sending a bolt of electricity to my cock. In an instant, my desires go from flirty and partly chivalrous to downright filthy and possessive.

"I should walk you to the elevator right now."

"Or what?"

"I shouldn't say it; it wouldn't be appropriate."

"Why not? We're not at work." I intake a sharp breath as her tongue grazes my thumb again, this time on purpose.

I want to say what I'm thinking. I want to be blunt, to scare her.

"Or I'm going to have you on your knees in my bedroom with your hands tied behind your back and a riding crop turning that alabaster skin of your tempting little ass pink."

I fully expect her face to turn red or for her lips to fall open, aghast at my blunt imagery, but she squares her shoulders, then shrugs.

"Sounds like a hollow threat," she says defiantly, and it only makes my desires stronger.

I grab the edge of her stool and jerk it, her hands darting out to steady herself as I bring her body between my outstretched legs.

"Look at me," I say as I grab her chin. "You can tease me all you want, Brontë, but if that's all it's going to be and you don't plan on indulging me at some point, you better cut it out because I've told you once before, I'm not the kind of man you want to play with."

Her eyes dart back and forth as she searches my expression. "I thought I had indulged you in Vegas."

"And you think because of that you get a free pass to drive me absolutely wild?" I let my hand fall from her chin to her throat, my fingers wrapping around it delicately.

"Is that what I'm doing?" Gone is that timid woman who stumbled in my office a few weeks ago. "I thought this was forbidden, Beckham? I thought going behind daddy's back was too much for you?"

I can't hide my laugh. She's pushing my buttons knowing full well what she's doing. She wants me to break. She wants me to be so consumed with desire I throw the rules out the window and take her like I did yesterday at her birthday party.

"Are you topping from the bottom, young lady?" I squeeze my fingers tighter and I feel her throat constrict as she swallows nervously. "Or is that what this is for you? A chance to act out, rebel, and get back at your father by fucking his best friend?"

I lean in, running my tongue slowly up her bare neck, nipping at her earlobe.

"Does it turn you on to know that you have this kind of control over me? That no matter how hard I try, I can't seem to resist you? Is that what you're trying to do to me? To get me to break and bend you over this countertop so I can bury my cock in your sweet, wet pussy?"

"Maybe," she says calmly, her eyes growing heavy with lust. "I want *you* to beg for it."

Chapter 13

Brontë

"Good night, Mr. Archer."

I smile sweetly and wave as the elevator door closes between us. I won't lie, getting him so turned on he was seconds from losing it was more fun than I expected, but walking away without allowing him to deliver on his threats will make for a long, lonely night.

I wanted to. I wanted to beg him to take me, but something about the delayed gratification of knowing that he'll be thinking of nothing but me all night makes me feel powerful.

My Uber is already waiting for me when I exit his building. It's only a ten-minute ride to my neighborhood but it's a little too dark and late for me to be walking home alone in the city.

"Thank you. Have a good night."

I shut the car door and dig through my pocket for my key ring, finding them and letting myself into my building. I check my mail, then walk through the lobby toward the elevator as I sort through a few mailers and my bank statement.

"Brontë?"

I snap my head up when I hear my name and spin around to see Chantelle over by the front desk in the lobby.

"Hey, Chantelle, what are you doing here? Is everything okay?" I panic, suddenly worried something has happened to my father or my brothers.

"No, no, everything is okay." She smiles and walks over to me, giving me a kiss on the cheek. "Do you have a few minutes?"

"Yeah, absolutely." I punch the elevator call button and the doors open immediately, taking us up to my floor.

"Do you want some tea or wine?" I shut the door behind us and place my folder on the counter, pointing toward my small kitchen.

My apartment isn't large. It's a small one-bedroom, one-bath, but it's plenty of space for just me. I even lucked out and got an in-unit washer and dryer.

"No, I won't keep you long. In fact, I'll just get straight to the point."

I walk to the fridge to grab myself a bottle of water as she perches her purse on my countertop, her fingers wrapping around the bamboo handle.

"I don't think what you're doing with Beckham is a good idea."

I freeze, my hand outstretched halfway to the water bottle. I tell myself not to whip my head around in shock; it'll only give me away. Instead, I clear my throat and reach for the bottle, closing the fridge behind me as I unscrew the cap and take a long, welcome drink of the cool water.

"What do you mean?" I attempt to play coy but I can already tell she can see through it, just like she saw through my sad attempts to act unbothered around him at her house.

"Brontë," she says, her shoulders dropping just as I let out a sigh.

"It's not what you think."

"It's not?" She crooks a suspicious, yet perfectly shaped eyebrow at me.

"Well, I mean, it is but it's just—we've only fo—"

"Ah—" She holds up her hand. "I do not need or want to hear

details. I just noticed something at your party this weekend and I felt as your stepmother," she says it slowly, eyeing me, "I should warn you and say my piece."

"Warn me?" My stomach suddenly feels tight. "Warn me about what?"

"About Beckham, sweetheart." Her expression is sympathetic or maybe it's pity like she's had to give this warning to others in the past. "He's not a bad man, but he's not Prince Charming. He's never going to give you a happily ever after."

"Oh." The tension in my belly slowly dissipates. "I know that. I'm not looking for that. Maybe someday." I shrug, bringing the water to my lips for another drink.

"Well, if you are going to pursue something with him, outside of flirting or whatever it is you two have told yourself this is, you need to tell your father."

"No." I shake my head vigorously. "Wait, did you say something to him?"

"To your father? No. I wanted to come to you first and frankly, it's not my place to tell him. It's yours and Beckham's."

"I don't think it's necessary to tell my dad. It was just—" I wave my hand because in all honesty, I have no idea what it *just* was. I thought it would just be a flirty conversation we had, or maybe that one hot kiss, and then it was that one night in Vegas, but after the way we flirted tonight and he didn't mention once that we *shouldn't do this,* I truly have no idea where we stand.

"I don't say this to be mean, Brontë." She reaches her hand across the counter for mine. "If it was just a drunken mistake or it is *just* flirting, that's one thing, but if this thing turns into a fling, a weekend thing, an exciting whatever because it's forbidden... Feelings will manifest; they always do. Either you'll fall for him or him for you and someone will get hurt. If I had to put money on it, I'd say it will end up being you."

"Has..." I swallow down the dryness in my throat. "Has he done this before? Beckham, I mean? Does he go after younger women and break their hearts?"

She furrows her brow. "Honestly, I don't think so. I've never seen him do it and your father has never mentioned it. I've met two women he's dated; both were longer relationships. The most recent one... she was, she was the one who got hurt. She wanted it all with him but he didn't. I just don't want to see that happen to you. Like I said earlier, he's not a bad man. He doesn't have a reputation for being a player but —well, he's kind of like George Clooney, always insisted he has no interest in kids or marriage, and I think women always assume they'll be the one to change his mind but end up with a broken heart instead."

I nod my head slowly, pondering her warning and thinking about what this would mean if my dad did find out because we slipped up.

"And after how hard you and your father have worked and still do work to rebuild your relationship, the last thing you want is a brand-new complication thrown into the mix. I won't say you owe your father respect because I know it's a very complicated relationship between you both, but Beckham doesn't and if he wants to pursue this with you, he needs to tell him."

"I understand and thank you for your honesty." I suddenly feel guilty that I even put her in this situation to begin with. "And I'm sorry you had to come over here and talk to me. I should have been smarter."

"Well, for what it's worth, your father is none the wiser. He is a pretty oblivious man sometimes for being so smart. It took him about five solid months of heavy flirting from *me* for him to realize I was interested in him." She laughs and flings her purse over her shoulder, turning to head toward my door.

"Hey, can I ask you something?"

"Of course." She spins back around to look at me.

"Do you have a good relationship with your father?" She cocks her head, I'm sure wondering why I'm asking, but she answers anyway.

"I do, yes. He's back in Meridian, Idaho, with my mom. They've been married forty-nine years this year." She smiles. "Why do you ask?"

"Just curious."

"Are you worried you won't find a meaningful relationship because of how your childhood was?"

I can't hold back my laugh. "Do you always see everything so clearly?"

"I'm a mom, I catch on. But I've also been in your shoes. I fell for a man who was twenty years older than me and I was terrified of what my father would say, what my friends and everyone else would think. Especially because Jonas was a billionaire. I thought for sure everyone would see me as the gold-digging succubus who was only interested in him for his money."

"Who says I'm falling for him?"

"Your eyes."

I play nervously with the now-empty water bottle in my hand.

"I barely even know him." I bite back the tears that threaten to fall. "It's so silly. I literally tried giving him my number at a bar the night of my graduation party, before I even knew who he was. Who knows, maybe we were meant to be, but life is cruel and has other plans." I'm now laughing but the tears have begun to fall and I'm wiping them away furiously as I nervously chatter on. "Why can't I just go after guys my own age, ya know? Or why can't they actually be the kind of men I'm interested in?"

Chantelle steps forward and pulls me in for a hug. We stand there for a few moments as she rubs my back and I let out the pent-up tears I've been holding back.

"I just don't want to be a head case that only goes after men old enough to be my father because of my daddy issues."

"Hey." She pulls back, her palms pressed against my cheeks. "You and your father are working through things. Don't think that all your attraction toward older men is rooted in an issue. You're addressing those issues; you're healing from your past... You just need to be gracious with yourself."

"I'm trying but then I end up doing something silly like flirt with my dad's best friend." I roll my eyes at myself.

"I need to get home but, Brontë, don't be so hard on yourself. I'm not saying that there's no chance something could actually develop between you and Beckham; I'm just telling you that before it does turn into *something,* he needs to be honest with your father about his intentions. Beckham's a good man but I also don't want you throwing away a chance at marriage and kids and all that because you're blinded by the attraction of someone older and successful." She squeezes my hands in hers. "Just listen to your heart. It won't steer you wrong."

We say our goodbyes and I'm left with no more clarity than when she arrived on how I should proceed with things.

I walk to my bathroom where I stand in an overly hot shower for far too long, my fingers and toes like prunes when I finally emerge, playing out every scenario in my head and the possible outcomes.

I try to convince myself that flirting and fooling around is necessary to get out of the infatuation, honeymoon stage and see if there are any real feelings and emotions beneath all that, but in order to get that far, I'm risking so much on the off chance that one of us develops feelings and the other doesn't.

———

"THIS CAN'T BE RIGHT."

I flip back and forth between the reports given to me by Pierce Investments, trying to reconcile the random withdrawals I'm seeing coming out of the employee investment account.

I pick up the phone and call Gretchen, the woman I've been doing most of my conversing with regarding files and documents.

"Hey, Gretchen, it's Brontë again," I say apologetically. "I'm sorry but can you double-check for me that I have all of the reports for cash flow?"

"Hey, Brontë, no worries. Yes, give me just a moment; let me put you on a brief hold."

I wait patiently for a few moments before she comes back on the line.

"Yup, that's everything. Why, what's up?"

"I just can't make sense of some withdrawals I'm seeing."

"For which account?"

"The employee investment account. I see the deposits going into the account and I've matched them with individual employee ID numbers so I know they're contributing directly from their checks pre-tax, but I can't make sense of the random withdrawals. They're not on a schedule and they're all varying amounts."

"Oh, sorry," she says, "I wish I could be of more help but I'm just the messenger on a lot of this stuff. Let me make a note for someone in accounting to get back to you. Does that work?"

I shuffle through a few more files. "Actually, let me try to go through things one more time. I very well could be missing something. I'm going to reorganize this paperwork, then go through it again. If I'm still confused, I'll shoot you over an email to have someone call me."

"Okay, sounds good. Good luck!" She offers me a chipper goodbye and hangs up.

After three more hours of trying to reconcile these numbers, I give up and gather what I've found so far and head to Beckham's office after double-checking his calendar that he's not busy.

I knock on the door that's halfway open and walk inside to see Beckham looking more handsome than usual. It's late in the day, probably close to half of the company has gone home, but Beckham's tie is straight, his sleeves down and his vest fully buttoned.

"Hey, got a minute?"

"For you? Always." He winks at me and a ribbon of warmth

unfurls through my abdomen at the way he so effortlessly makes me all warm and gooey inside.

"Okay, I have gone over these cash in and cash out reports for hours, but I cannot make sense of these seven transactions."

I drop the pile of papers on his desk, placing them in order as I read off which each report is.

"Here you can see that these numbers go with employees, it's their ID number. I can see that each ID number has the same exact deduction each month into this account here." I reach for the second report. "So all these employees are individually contributing different amounts, but each amount for each employee is the same each month. It's an investment account that Pierce set up where employees will donate a percentage pre-tax, and then Pierce does the investing for them."

"Makes sense." Beckham nods, following along.

"I have tracked all of the deposits to this account, but what I can't figure out is, there has been seven different deductions from the investment account to an offshore account. The deductions are varied in amounts and dates. It's not a quarterly or even monthly transaction."

His brows furrow as he studies the paper I handed him.

"Did you ask their accounting team to explain?"

I shake my head. "Not yet. I had hoped it was just an error on my part so I told Gretchen to hold off on having one of them reach out to me until after I could go through everything again."

"Well, looks like you're still unsure so just have them call you." He hands the report back to me.

"That's why I came in here. I wanted to ask you what this company is?" I point to the stock symbol next to one of the withdrawals. "I've seen it next to all of the withdrawals and on several other reports."

Beckham looks at me funny. "Are you serious?"

"Yes," I say confused.

"That's SITS, Systems Information Technology Services. That's

Pierce's parent company, it's one of your father's companies, under his wide umbrella of Ramsay Consulting."

"Wait." I shake my head as if that will help the information I just received somehow settle into place and make sense. "I knew my father owned Pierce, but I didn't realize SITS was one of his subsidiaries too. How did I miss that? On other documents it lists Pierce directly under Ramsay Consulting."

"I'm sure it was just an oversight from their legal department. Maybe some old forms or something."

"Maybe but that still doesn't make sense why SITS would be taking out these withdrawals from an employee investment account." I shuffle through the papers, looking for anything I might have missed that's right in front of me. "Also, where is this account that these withdrawals are being deposited into? I looked up the routing number and it's registered as an offshore account."

Beckham stands and slides his suit coat over his arms before walking toward his en suite bathroom to check his reflection over.

Where the hell is he going that he's so concerned with how he looks? Or worse, who is he meeting?

I push those thoughts from my head. One thing at a time.

"What are you insinuating, Brontë?"

"I think that Pierce is stealing from their employees."

Beckham's hands still on the back of his head as he smooths out his hair. He turns around slowly to look at me.

"You better have solid proof of something like that before you go making accusations, especially during acquisition talks."

I square my shoulders. "I do have solid proof, don't I?" I point to the report in my hand.

"No, you have some unexplained accounting error. You need to work with their finance department in grueling detail, asking every possible question before you go burning a bridge with Pierce." His tone is serious, his eyes wide as he crosses his arms over his chest. "You really think your father would allow that to happen? I know he's not involved with the day-to-day of Pierce, but they still have to report their earnings and losses. So does SITS."

"Maybe he's too far removed or maybe their reporting is wrong. If a company is going to steal from their employees, they're going to do a damn good job of covering it up, especially if they're going to risk it being revealed during a merger. Or maybe," I say a little too confidently, "he's very aware of it and knows that by selling Pierce to his best friend, it will get overlooked."

I can see the anger spread across his face. His eyebrows shoot upward, his jaw clenches, and his eyes narrow as a red flush spreads up his neck.

"Now you're accusing me of being willing to overlook fraud based on a personal relationship?"

Shit, that's not what I meant, but I shot my mouth off.

"Well, no, not you per se, but..." I try to backpedal. "My dad can be shady and we both know that. He has a history of making some not so moral decisions and maybe he's taking advantage of your friendsh—"

He holds up his finger and I snap my mouth shut.

"Brontë, I have an appointment I need to get to, but I'm going to be brutally honest with you right now. Don't bring your personal past with your father into this company and your job. That is between the two of you and for what it's worth, he is a changed man. I know he's wronged you, hurt you beyond belief, and he has to work damn hard to rebuild that trust and relationship with you, but I won't have you projecting your issues onto my relationship with him. Understood?"

My initial, emotional reaction is to tell him to go to hell, but I take a deep breath and realize that he's absolutely right.

"You're right," I say slowly, his face softening with my admission. "I'm sorry. I did let my past with him cloud my judgment, but I do want to speak with him about this once I get confirmation from Pierce's financial team that this is, in fact, all of the reports."

He shakes his head. "Tomorrow, get clarification from Pierce.

Then I'll speak to your father about it once you've confirmed with them."

"Seriously?"

He gets that look on his face again. The one that says, *question my authority again and face the consequences.*

I roll my eyes. "You hired me for my expertise in forensic accounting. The least you can do is trust me to have a civil conversation with him about what I've found."

He closes the distance between us so fast I don't even have time to react. He presses his hand flat against my chest, walking us back two steps till my ass hits his desk, his hand traveling up my neck to my hair where he grabs a handful of it, tugging it gently enough that it doesn't hurt but hard enough it sends a message. My neck is tilted back, my chin upward so that I'm looking at him. His body is pressed against me, his cock rigid against my thigh.

"I'm only going to say this once, sweetheart. You work for me; therefore, you answer to me. I don't care if we're in the boardroom or the bedroom. If I'm giving you orders to give me a report, answer the phone, or suck my cock, you obey me."

His words are harsh, but they set my body ablaze. I don't even want to know the psychology behind why I enjoy when he bosses me around like this because I'm sure if I do, I'll run for the hills, and I'm not ready to walk away from this fantasy yet.

"And what if I don't obey you, Mr. Archer?"

I swear his eye twitches at my defiance. He tightens his grip on my hair, yanking harder, my scalp burning. He spins me around, bending me over his desk and placing his forearm forcefully against my back so that my chest and cheek are flat against the surface. My skirt is being lifted up over my ass and I don't need to see what he's doing to know what's coming. A second later, the whooshing sound of his hand flying through the air followed by the loud smack of his hand against the bare flesh of my ass fills the room.

"Ow!" I yelp and attempt to stand up, but he pushes against my back harder.

"Stay still," he commands, bringing his hand back and smacking the other cheek just as hard.

He releases his arm from me, pulling my skirt back down and helping me to stand back up.

"Next time"—he cups my cheeks—"it'll be the riding crop and I can promise you it won't be just two times. It will sting much worse than my hand."

"Then why do it?" I ask softly.

"Because I'm the boss and there are consequences to not obeying me. I want you to be a good girl for me, sweetheart. Can you do that?" I nod slowly and he leans forward, kissing me softly. "Good girl."

He helps me gather my papers and walks me toward his door, shutting off the lights on the way.

"Now go home and take a nice bath, enjoy a glass of wine." We're standing alone outside the elevator.

"Are you heading home?" I ask but he doesn't answer me.

"Tonight, when you pull your little nightie up and see my red handprints on your sweet little ass cheeks, I want you to think of me. I want you to tuck yourself in bed and slide these fingers"—he holds up my hand and plants a kiss on the tip of my fingers—"into that delicious cunt of yours and come all over them for me."

"You know you could just come over and do it for me." I bat my eyelashes at him, hoping that my sad attempt at seduction will work but it doesn't.

"Tempting but I have a meeting I can't miss."

He plants a kiss on my forehead and steps into the elevator, punching the button for the garage floor.

"I'll expect an answer tomorrow on how many times you made yourself come tonight." He winks at me just as the doors begin to close. "That's an order, sweetheart, so remember what happens when you disobey."

Chapter 14

Beckham

I'm beyond sexually frustrated but something about using Brontë for a quick release before meeting up with my ex for dinner just feels wrong.

Brontë and I haven't had a conversation about what *we* are, but I don't think it's really necessary. *We* aren't anything... We're either a dirty little secret or a huge mistake just waiting to implode.

We both know that whatever this thing is between us will be short-lived and just an exciting little story for her someday, once she's left my company and moved on with her life. A pit forms in my stomach as I think through those thoughts. Something about her far beyond her physical beauty pulls me to her, like an invisible string tying us together. But what are my options here? Let myself fall for her and tell her only to have her laugh and tell me it was just a fling? Or worse, that she never saw me as anything more than a way to get back at her dad.

I hate that I'll just be a memory in her life someday, but I hate even more the idea that she would ever see me as a regret.

I check my watch before pulling my car into traffic. I have fifteen minutes before I'm late to dinner. I step on it, driving a little more recklessly than I'd like but I make it. I step out, handing the keys to my Rolls-Royce Wraith to a very eager-looking attendant and head inside.

"Evening, Mr. Archer," the host says with a warm smile. "Your party is already seated. Right this way, please."

I follow him through the dimly lit restaurant to a private table, shaking a few hands and reciprocating a few head nods along the way. It's pretty impossible for me to go anywhere anymore without some associate stopping me for a quick chat or a piece of advice.

"Your table, sir," the host gestures to where Venus is sitting patiently.

"Thank you."

"Long time, no see." She smiles as I bend down to kiss her gently on the cheek.

"Likewise, Venus. You look beautiful as always." I take a seat and reach for my water, attempting to bide my time so I don't just come out and ask why the hell she insisted on meeting with me.

"So how's business?"

"It's business," I reply, knowing she doesn't really care. Venus was never good with small talk or the day-to-day inconveniences that me owning and running a company entailed. Business bored her, even if it did allow her to live an exceptionally posh life on her father's dime.

"And your social life?" She hooks a perfectly manicured eyebrow at me.

"It's social." I smile, motioning for a waiter.

"Evening, sir. Your waiter will be out in ju—"

"Just need a scotch on the rocks in the meantime, please," I say, interrupting the young man who nods. "Macallan, please."

"Right away, sir. And anything for you, ma'am?"

Venus smiles and gently shakes her head.

"So who is she?"

"Who is who?"

Venus gives me a look, one I've seen a dozen times while we were together.

"You know, you're not as clever as you think you are."

I laugh and a new waiter returns with the scotch which I gladly welcome considering the territory we're heading into. He introduces himself and tells us the specials, handing us some menus with a promise of returning in a few moments.

"There are only two reasons you would refuse to meet with me for so long, let alone ignore my texts and calls. One is you're dead, which clearly"—she holds out her hand toward me, dragging it up and down—"you're not. Or... it's another woman. One you either haven't yet told about me or don't plan on telling about me."

I savor the burn of the scotch as it lingers on my tongue before numbing my throat on the way down. And for some reason, either the liquid courage or the reality that I don't want to hide how I feel about Brontë, I tell her.

"She does know about you."

She tries to remain stoic, unbothered, but I see the tendon in her throat tense when I say those words.

"Everything?"

"Everything, meaning?"

"That you wanted to marry me at one point."

I down the rest of the scotch and remind myself I drove so I need to cut myself off right now.

"I never wanted to marry you, Venus, you know that."

"Ouch." She smiles and shrugs one bare shoulder. "You really know how to make a woman feel all warm and nostalgic on a trip down memory lane."

"*You* were the one who wanted to get married and you blamed me for the relationship falling apart because of it when I was honest and open with you from day one about my lack of desire for marriage and a family." I can feel myself growing frustrated by the direction this conversation has turned.

"Do you love her?"

"Why did you call me here, Venus?" I ignore her question, a tension headache forming at the edges of my temples. I really don't know why I agreed to meet with her tonight in the first place. Maybe to get her to stop texting and calling me. Maybe because some part of me was mildly curious about what reason she could possibly come up with now to try and convince me to give us another chance.

"Was it just to do this again? Hmm?" I lean forward, resting my elbows on the table. "Another postmortem about our relationship?"

"I'm pregnant."

Not at all the answer I was expecting but I feel relief instantly wash over me. I didn't want to have to remind her of all the reasons we weren't good together. It's never easy and it certainly makes me feel like shit to make a woman cry.

"Congrats!" I raise my water glass toward her, but that's when I notice what looks like tears at the edges of her eyes. She doesn't seem happy like I thought she would.

"Thank you." She sniffs, then dabs her napkin at the corner of each eye. "Congrats to you too."

I tilt my head in confusion, the expression on her face mirroring my own.

"It's yours," she says as if I should have deduced that on my own. Her hands fall to rest on a small, swollen belly that I'm just now noticing.

"M—Mine? No. How?" She lets out a slight laugh in the form of a huff. "I know how babies are made, Venus; you know what I'm asking. You had an IUD and I always pu—" I glance around, then lower my voice. "I always pulled out."

She shrugs. "I guess one got through somehow. That's all it takes, Becks."

"Don't call me that; you know I don't like it." It's petty but she does know I can't stand the little nickname she gave me. I've asked her time and time again not to call me that. "How far along are you?"

"Just shy of four months."

"We ended things just over three months ago."

"Yes, I was a few weeks pregnant then. I just didn't know it."

"I get how it works," I say, holding up my hand in frustration. "I'm just talking through things." I lean back in my chair, running my hand over my jaw. My stomach feels like there's soup sloshing around in it.

"Apologies for the wait, did you ha—"

"We're not staying," I say to the waiter. "You can bring me the check."

"Uh, okay. Will do." The young man spins on his heel and walks away.

"Really? Can't even feed your baby?" She pouts, rubbing her belly.

"Don't do that." I narrow my gaze at her. Venus was always good at manipulation, even if it was small or deserved on my part. She has a knack for tossing guilt around like it's dollar bills. "You have to give me a minute to process this, Venus. It's not just an accident; it's life-changing and fifteen minutes ago I thought my life was going in a completely different direction."

"Well, you better figure it out, Beckham, because this baby is in our lives."

"I'm aware of that but you just waltz in here and tell me you're pregnant and it's mine, and I'm just supposed to believe it and say what? Let's be a family?"

"You think I'm lying? That I would fake a pregnancy?" She's angry now.

"I didn't say that. Clearly, you're pregnant."

"But you think I'm lying that it's yours?" I don't respond this time and it doesn't go unnoticed. "Why would I need to lie about you being the father? I don't need your money; my family has more than you."

I stare at her, not sure how to respond because I don't want to hurt her or upset her, but I don't believe her unless she allows for a paternity test. During our time together, there were two instances that never sat right with me. She managed to explain them both away and I had no proof that she'd been unfaithful, so I chose to forgive her and move on.

But in all our years of on and off again, we never had a single pregnancy scare and when we broke up, she hadn't mentioned missing a period. In fact, she once joked that she was one of the only women who still had regular periods you could set your watch by while on an IUD.

"If this child is mine—"

"If?"

"Yes, if. I will be there one hundred percent. I will be the best father and love that child, but before I can commit that to you, I want a paternity test."

"Are you fucking serious?" She raises her voice as she lifts her hands, then lets them fall to the table, the silverware clanging together loudly.

"Venus, don't make a scene, please." I know I shouldn't have said it, but it was on my tongue and out of my mouth before I could shut the hell up. In my defense, Venus loves to make a scene and right on schedule, she stands up, grabs her half-empty glass of water, and tosses it right in my face.

"You can go to hell, Becks." She says that nickname again, emphasizing it with a hiss at the end before grabbing her purse and storming out of the restaurant just as the shocked waiter returns with the check.

———

"ABSOLUTELY NOT. BRONTË IS CONFUSED, I'M SURE."

I shrug and take the papers back from Jonas who sits across from my desk.

"I said the same thing to her, but she insists that she has triple-checked all of the reports, bank accounts, financials, etc. from Pierce and she cannot make heads nor tails of these withdrawals."

"And she thinks I had something to do with it?"

I shake my head. "No, I just told her that as the parent company, I would discuss it with you."

"I'm sure it's just a misunderstanding, but whatever it is, it should be addressed with Jack and Bryan over at Pierce. You know how these things work, Beckham. I don't have time to be involved in the day-to-day of my subsidiaries."

"I understand, Jonas. I'll give them a call this afternoon."

"And Beckham"—he points a finger at me—"don't go in with both guns blazing. I don't need you flushing this deal down the drain because of your ego."

I plaster on a fake smile and raise my hands in capitulation.

"Speaking of Brontë, how's she doing? Any progress on convincing her to stay in our world of finance?"

I appreciate that Jonas wants his daughter to follow in his footsteps, but he needs to allow her to find herself and her passion. I'm tempted to say as much but after my dinner with Venus last night, my brain is already scrambled and barely focusing on the task at hand. Mix in very little sleep and a few nightmares and I'm barely able to make it through another few hours of work.

"She's doing well. I think she's really enjoying getting into the weeds on this Pierce acquisition. She's really growing confidence in her decisions; she's a quick learner too." I smile, reflecting back on a few conversations we've had where I attempt to explain something but she's finishing my sentences, already completely aware.

"Does she have a boyfriend?"

"What?" His question takes me by surprise, pulling me out of my own thoughts and putting me right on edge. "Boyfriend?"

"Yeah, wasn't sure if you've noticed anyone picking her up or taking her to lunch. Maybe one of these little arrogant shits you've got working for you." He laughs, his throaty, almost gurgle of a laugh as he leans back and crosses his ankle over his knee.

"Oh, not that I've noticed but it's hard to say. I don't see her much outside of meetings and the birthday party of course."

Shit. Why the fuck did I bring that up right now?

"Yes, her birthday party. She seemed to have a good time." He laughs like he's remembering something. "I gotta say, it's great having her back in my life. Seeing her playing with the boys in the pool was something I never thought I'd get to experience, or them. I know you don't want kids, but damn, they will make you realize what's important in your life and the lengths at which you'll go to protect them."

Silence settles between us as he picks at a piece of lint on his exposed sock.

"Well, thanks for your time, Jonas. I'll let you get back to work so I can give the boys at Pierce a call." I stand and extend my hand out toward him which he shakes and pats my shoulder.

"Anytime, Beckham. Keep me informed on that issue. Like I said, I'm sure it's just a little mistake on Brontë's part."

He gives me a wink that for some reason leaves me a little unsettled and has me questioning for one tiny second if he, in fact, does know what the issue is and like Brontë alluded to, might expect me to just sweep it under the rug as his friend.

I'm about to give Jack, the CEO of Pierce, a call when I see a text from Venus.

Venus: *I have my next ultrasound on Wednesday next week. 10am at East Side Women's Health. You should be there.*

I pinch the bridge of my nose, another tension headache threatening to take over. I lean back in my chair, keeping my eyes closed as I practice a few yoga breaths. I'm just starting to get into it when I hear a knock on my office door and Brontë steps inside.

"Hey, sorry to interrupt, but did you happen to speak with my father about the inconsistencies in the Pierce financial records?"

"I did," I say, sitting up and straightening my tie.

"And?"

"And it's nothing." I see her countenance fall. "Before you start, I am going to call Jack and Bryan at Pierce and get their take on it. For all we know, it's just a misunderstanding."

"But it's not a misunderstanding. It's fraud. I've outlined that very clearly to you."

146

"Brontë." I try to calm my very frazzled nerves. "I said I'm going to call them."

"These employees have worked hard and dedicated their lives to this company, and they're being fucked over. This needs to be taken seriously."

She's clearly angry, frustrated too, and I let her just rant, hoping if she gets it out of her system, she'll let me actually handle it like I said I would.

"Everyone thinks it's just a simple mistake or misunderstanding on my part because I'm young and inexperienced but that's bullshit. I have done the research and fact-checking. I've done the due diligence, and I can feel it in my gut that these reports aren't right." She shakes the papers in her right hand as she speaks.

"I said I'll handle it, Brontë." I keep my voice calm as she talks over me.

My temper is building, I can feel it. It's not that I don't believe her; in fact, I'm starting to really believe she's the one who's right in all this. I'm sure someone is lying but with the bomb dropped on me last night with Venus and the fact that either my best friend Jonas or the leadership at a company I'm possibly about to buy is lying to me has me about to fucking explode.

"Of course my dad is going to deny anything if he's involved, or maybe, like I said before, he's not the man you thi—"

"Enough!" I shout, shooting up out of my chair and slamming both of my hands down on my desktop. "I said I'd fucking handle it, Brontë, so let me fucking handle it!" I spit the words out like they're venom, my face probably red with anger by the look of shock on her face.

"Now, please," I say calmly as I sit back down, the palms of my hands stinging. "Leave so that I can call Jack and Bryan."

Without another word she spins on her heel and marches out of my office, slamming my door on the way out.

I know I need to calm down first, but I dial Jack's number anyway and he answers on the second ring.

"Mr. Archer, to what do I owe the pleasure?" His joyful tone somehow puts me in an even shittier mood.

How dare this motherfucker try to pull one over on me, then act like everything is okay.

"Afraid it won't be pleasurable, Jack."

"Oh?"

"We've been going through your financials extensively and no matter which way we look at it, no matter the explanations we get from your accounting department, we cannot make these withdrawals from your employee investment accounts make sense."

"Okaaay, interesting. This is the first I'm hearing of it. Walk me through it. What's the issue?"

I explain in detail what Brontë has now explained to me several times.

"Oh, hmm, I'm sure it's just a mis—"

"Not a misunderstanding, Jack," I cut him off, my tone clipped. "Don't do me the disservice of insulting my intelligence or Brontë's. Get with your accounting department and get your damn records sorted or this deal is off."

"Whoa, whoa, Beckham. There's no need to react emotionally in all this and call off a deal. I'm sure we can get it figured out on my end."

"You better. And so you know, Jonas is aware of the situation. He has no idea what the error is either, but you can bet your ass that if he finds out who fucked up, they're gone."

"You spoke with Jonas?" I can hear the tension in his voice.

"Of course."

"And he didn't know anything about it?" He pauses. "Interesting."

"What are you insinuating, Jack?" I don't like the direction this conversation is going.

"I'm not insinuating anything, Mr. Archer, but I can tell you that I know my people and they wouldn't be skimming from the books.

We aren't the only ones with access to those accounts; parent companies have access as well."

"I don't like to beat around the bush, Jack. In fact, I'm a pretty straightforward man, so let me put it to you this way. I don't give a rat's ass if it's you or Jonas himself who is robbing your employees of their retirement. I'll find out who it is, and I'll not only have their job, but they'll never work in this industry again, and you can be damn sure they'll face federal charges. So do us both a favor and get your ducks in a fucking row or I walk."

I hit the button to end the call, really missing a good old-fashioned desk phone receiver that could be slammed down for theatrical effect.

I tap my foot nervously against the inside of my desk. It's pushing six so Brontë is already gone, I'm sure. I owe her an apology. This is the second time I've snapped at her with no explanation and taken out my anger on her.

I walk out of my office, toward her desk, but it's already empty. I glance at my watch again, double checking the time. I turn to walk back to my office when the elevator door dings. When the door opens, a tall, rather bony man steps out, his gray tux almost hanging from his body.

Miles Davenport, Venus' father.

"Miles, what can I do for you?" I ask, squaring my shoulders, my stance wide. I'm not inviting this prick into my office.

"You know why I'm here."

I shrug. "No, I don't actually."

He takes a few steps forward, pointing his knobby finger at me. "Listen here, you little shit. I never liked you. You're arrogant and you're nothing but trouble for my daughter. But you better do the right thing. You better step up and be a father to her baby."

"Or what? Are you threatening me, Miles? You know," I say, stepping forward as I look down at him. After the argument with Brontë and the talk with Jack, I am in no fucking mood. "You really don't want to do that."

"So you're just going to be a deadbeat father, you asshole? I will ruin you! I will own this compa—"

"This does not concern you, Miles, so get the fuck out of my office. If you want to stick your nose where it doesn't belong, start with your daughter. Go have a talk with her about who she's been letting stick it in her."

His hands ball into fists, his nostrils flaring, and I'm not sure if he's about to have a stroke or attack me. I leave him like that, uninterested in talking about this.

When I get to my office, I slam the door and pick my phone back up, scrolling through it till I find Brontë's name to give her a call, but I decide in person is probably better. I go back to my messages. There are no new texts from Venus.

The pit in my stomach slowly comes back. It's not that I don't plan on going to that ultrasound, I do. I just need time to calm down and mentally check out before I respond to her. Even though I know there's no way I'll find out if the baby is actually mine or not before next week, on the off chance that it is mine, I don't want to regret missing out on these moments.

I let my mind wander to what it will be like as a father. Sunday afternoons playing ball in the park. A stroll down by the lake to look at the boats. My heart aches. Not because I don't want those moments, but because for the first time in my life, I do, but not with Venus.

I picture Brontë carrying my child instead and the sour feeling slowly unfurls into excitement but is quickly stifled by guilt. This unborn baby didn't ask to be born and I shouldn't be miserable about it just because it's not with the right woman. I try to think through how it could work with all of us. If I'm honest with Brontë, explain that Venus just showed up and told me about this and tell her that I want to make things work between her and me, would she try?

I tap my foot faster, thinking through the other side of it. What if she doesn't want kids? What if the thought of being the stepmom to someone else's baby, scared that Venus and I will someday find ourselves back in each other's arms because it's easier that way, is too much?

Brontë is barely twenty-five, just starting out in her career with huge goals of running her own nonprofit. She doesn't need a middle-aged man saddled with an unexpected baby and an ex who still wants to work things out. The least I can do tonight is to go over to her place and apologize to her about earlier. I'm not sure dropping the Venus and baby bomb on her is right yet. Not until I know the truth about the paternity and not until she and I talk about what we are and where this is going.

I push all the negative thoughts from my head, shrugging on my suit coat and grabbing my phone off my desk to go make things right with her.

I try to ignore the fact that at the end of a long, stressful day, the only thing that calms me, the only thing that brings peace to my soul no matter the situation, is the thought of holding her in my arms... because that terrifies me more than anything.

Chapter 15

Brontë

I pull open the door to my apartment, Beckham leaning partially against my doorway.

His hair is mussed, his tie loosened, and there's a bottle of wine in his hand and a pathetic attempt of a smile on his full lips.

"Hey," he says. "I owe you an apology."

"Yes, you do." I can't hide the smile that threatens to break across my lips so I step aside and open the door wider, motioning for him to come inside.

He steps through the doorway, his imposing figure making my open concept kitchen and living room suddenly feel incredibly small.

He looks around the room. "I like your place."

"Yeah? Not exactly a penthouse." I take the wine from his hand as he leans down to untie his shoes, kicking them to the side of my door. It's a mundane action, something we do as humans every day, but for some reason it strikes me as intimate.

"Penthouses are overrated."

"How so?"

I stand on my tiptoes to reach my wineglasses when I feel him standing right behind me. His hand rests softly against the exposed skin of my waist from my outstretched arm, his other reaching up to grab the glasses for me, placing them on the counter next to us.

"They're cold and lonely, high above the rest of the world. They make you believe you're keeping the rest of the world out, but in reality, you're keeping yourself locked in." He looks down at me as I spin around to face him, but his eyes aren't focused on me. Even though he's looking down at me, it's like he's looking through me. "Like a very expensive prison."

"If given the chance, I think most would take your penthouse over my place any day."

"I like your place. It's warm and welcoming." He doesn't put any distance between us. His arms rest on my waist as he looks around, his eyes settling on the few framed photos of my mother and me and then to the various little candles and knickknacks that I've collected over the years. He smiles and looks back down at me. "It's you."

We stand so close, and even though it's the end of the day, I can still smell his cologne. It's very subtle but it's there. I want to bury my face in his neck and never leave the warmth and comfort of his chest, but Chantelle's words about one of us developing feelings and getting hurt echo in my brain.

"I'm sorry," he says gently, his fingers brushing down my cheek. "I was angry and frustrated and I took it out on you and that was wrong."

"Were you angry at me?"

He shakes his head. "No, darling. I was angry at the situation with Pierce. I don't appreciate being lied to or dicked around."

I'm gripping his shirt as his hands slide into my hair, tilting my head just enough so that his lips angle perfectly over mine. The kiss is sweet and warm, his lips covering mine. I want more but he breaks it, stepping away to grab the wine.

"Corkscrew?"

I open the drawer to the right of us and retrieve it. I hand it to him and he grabs it, along with my hand and looks at me.

"Am I forgiven?"

I shrug. "Maybe. You might have to do some more groveling later, which could include some serious lip service."

"I'm always happy to offer lip service. It should probably take place from my knees, don't you think?" He winks at me and it shoots right to my core. I want to grab the wine from his hand and tell him we can drink it later, but he looks like he could use it, and honestly, I really love just talking to him.

"So, I spoke with your father about the financial records, and I called Jack."

"What happened?"

"Your father says he has no idea what's going on and I do believe him. I know you might feel differently, but I'm going off my gut here and it's telling me he's not lying. He has no reason to skim from employees and he certainly wouldn't risk his empire and reputation for a few hundred thousand."

I nod. "That is true and makes more sense than where I was going with it. What about Jack? I mean, could it be him or maybe it's just a regular accountant in the organization who's found a way to hide their scam?"

"If I had to guess, that's probably more accurate. Jack played coy, even had the audacity to insinuate that Jonas might know more than he's leading on."

"Are you serious?" My eyebrows practically jump off my forehead as I grab our glasses and Beckham pours the wine.

"I told him that I didn't care who was doing it; I'm going to not only find out who it is but I'm going to fucking destroy them and make sure they face charges. How fucked do you have to be to steal from your own employees? I told him to get his shit sorted or I'm pulling the deal."

I reach out and grab a fistful of his shirt, attempting to pull him toward me but pulling myself forward instead. My chest hits his, our wine sloshing over the glasses, but I don't care. I kiss him hard and deep.

"Fuck me, baby. You really love taking me by surprise, don't you?"

"Sorry." I blush, placing my glass on the counter and reaching for a towel to clean up the mess I made.

Beckham grabs the towel from my hand and tosses it aside. His hands go to my waist and he hoists me onto the counter with almost zero effort.

"Don't ever apologize for taking what you want."

His hands are back in my hair, mine gripping his shirt. We're all lips and tongues and frenzied passion like we both can't get enough. Like we know there's an expiration date on us.

"You drive me crazy," I murmur against his lips, my confession slipping out. I've tried my hardest not to reveal to him that this isn't just lust. It's deeper. There are feelings brewing, but I can't risk admitting it because I know it will be the final nail in the coffin if I do.

"It's just money and power, baby," he teases, dragging his tongue down my neck as his hands find my breasts.

"It's more than that," I say, bringing my hands up to his face. His eyes scan mine.

"What is it then?"

"You." We stare at each other before I continue. I search his face for signs that he's not interested in talking, but they're not there. His eyes are asking me to continue so I do. "You're charming and sexy, obviously, but you're also compassionate and caring; you're kind and take the time to be interested in people. And yes, the way you command a room or situation is a huge turn-on. I love that you're willing to walk away from something that could net you millions if it means doing the right thing."

I wait for him to crack a joke out of discomfort or make a sexual remark to bring it back to the foundation of our relationship, but he does neither.

"You're not like anyone I've ever met." He rests his forehead against mine and it's a moment of intense vulnerability for both of us.

"You don't give a fuck about the money or cars or what your wealth can get you, do you?"

I shake my head no.

"Sometimes I wonder..." His words trail off as he gets lost in thought.

I want to ask him to continue but I'm afraid it will break the spell. He stands between my thighs, staring at me, searching for something, but I don't know what. His hands and eyes both drop down to my waist, his fingers encircling me as his thumbs rub back and forth over my lower belly.

"You are so beautiful, so perfect." His words are a whisper. He's clearly lost in another world. I want to ask him if something happened between him and my dad or what else is on his mind that's making him so confused, but instead, I reach out and cup his cheeks, making him look at me.

"Take me to bed, Mr. Archer."

I don't have to tell him twice. He slides me off the counter, my legs wrapping around his waist as he walks us down the hall to my bedroom, but he's impatient. He stops halfway down the hall, pressing me against the wall as he pulls at my blouse, popping a few buttons off in the process.

"I'll buy you a new one," he says against my neck as he trails his warm tongue down my neck to my breasts. He bites the top of my breasts, his one hand reaching up to pull down the cups of my bra as he thrusts himself against me to keep me pinned in place. "I'll buy you whatever you want; just never take this from me."

An alarm bell goes off in my head. I know I should stop this right now, but I don't want to.

He knows the money means nothing to me; he knows that it would never keep me, but if I had to guess, it's the only version of intimacy or feelings that he's known in his relationships.

"I can't get enough," he murmurs, kissing and biting my nipples. His hand slides up my neck to grip my jaw from the underside, tilting my head back and upward to give him better access.

"I need more," I groan as he releases my face and looks up at me, his eyes burning with desire. He pulls me from the wall and slides me down his body, walking us the rest of the way to my room.

The room is only illuminated by moonlight and the single street-light that shines through my window.

"Come here." He grabs my hand, pulling me back to him the moment we cross the threshold. His hands are back in my hair, his lips on mine as he kisses me like it's going to be the last time.

Gone is the filthy-talking, dominant businessman, replaced with passion, need, and longing. He unbuttons the rest of my blouse, sliding it down my arms without breaking our kiss. Next, he reaches around and unhooks my bra, letting it to fall to the floor. He kisses each bare breast, his hands reaching down to unzip my skirt, sliding it and my panties down my thighs so that I'm left standing before him fully naked.

He kicks my clothes to the side, taking a seat on the edge of my bed to look at me. I feel awkward for a second, standing there naked, neither of us talking, but the way he's looking at me suddenly makes me feel confident, sexy.

"What's on your mind?" I finally ask as I step closer to him and run my hands through his silky locks.

He smirks. "You."

"Well," I say, climbing into his lap to straddle him, "I'm right here. What are you going to do with me, Mr. Archer?"

"Tease you," he whispers, leaning forward to kiss my shoulder. "Taste you." He kisses me again. "Devour you"—another kiss—"please you"—another—"worship you." He continues with this process, kissing, biting, and licking me all over as he tells me the ways he plans to explore my body.

As he undresses, I half expect him to tie my hands with his tie or spank me with his belt, but he does neither. He takes his time with me, trailing kisses over every inch of my body, his tongue dancing between my folds and around my clit as he brings me to orgasm once and then slides his fingers inside me to make me come again.

It's not rushed or aggressive; it's slow and languid, my pleasure building between each release slowly. I reach my hand down between us, wrapping my fingers around his rigid cock; they don't come close to touching. I stroke him, a hiss falling from his lips.

"I want to taste you," I say in his ear, gently biting his earlobe.

I don't wait for permission. I slide down his body, taking his cock in my hand as I swirl my tongue around the tip. A bead of precum hits my tongue and I close my eyes, savoring his taste as I wrap my lips around him.

He groans, his head falling back as he props himself up on his elbows to look down his body to watch me. His thick thighs are tense beneath me. I look up his body, his chiseled abs flexing as his hand comes down to settle on the back of my head.

"Ohhh, sweetheart," he moans, and it makes me even wetter. I love the way he calls me little terms of endearment but especially when we're being intimate. Is it the daddy issues? Probably but I don't let myself linger too much on the thought.

I'm getting into a rhythm when I feel his hands under my arms and he's lifting me off him, rolling me to the side as he gets off the bed and stands.

"Fuck!" he shouts, his hands behind his head as he paces next to the bed. His cock is standing straight up, bouncing with the movement as his chest rises and falls rapidly.

"Did I do—"

"No." He half laughs, looking down his body. He drags his hand down his chest to grip himself as he looks at me. "You did nothing wrong, baby." He steps to me, his hand reaching down to cup my jaw as he drags his thumb over my lip. "I was just about to come and I didn't want to finish down your throat."

"Oh?" I can't hide the disappointment in my voice.

"Trust me, I want to. I'll give you the chance soon, but tonight is about you."

He crawls back up my body, positioning himself at my entrance as he slowly presses forward. He eases himself in and out of me, an inch at a time until finally, his length is fully inside me. His tongue is in my mouth, his hands holding mine as he looks down at me. A lock of his hair hangs down over his forehead, his eyes burning into mine as his body says things to me that his lips can't.

It feels different. It is different. This isn't sex or fucking or hooking up. We're making love and we both know it. The air is thick, heavy with desire and unspoken emotion. Our bodies move together like they were made for each other.

I've never felt like this with anyone. I've never had my body respond to someone so effortlessly with zero inhibitions. It feels like in this moment he could tell me he loves me, wants a life with me, and I wouldn't think twice; I'd say I want the same.

But do I? Do I want a life with a man that truthfully, I barely know? A man who's old enough be my father... A man that if I did pursue something with, could potentially be the end of my relationship with my own father.

I push the thoughts from my head again, living in the moment between us as we both reach our release together. It feels like the orgasm takes over my body, reaching every possible nerve ending, sending my emotions and sensations into overdrive.

"You're going to be the death of me and I'm not sure I'd even fight it."

Beckham kisses my sweaty forehead as he rolls me to his chest, settling onto his back. I lie half dazed across his body, his warm skin pressed against my cheek as I drag my nails over his belly.

We lay in silence for several moments. Beckham mirrors my movements with his hand on my back, the tips of his fingers tracing inanimate objects, causing little shivers to run down my spine.

"So," he says, finally breaking the silence.

"So?" I say, smiling up at him as I lift my head a little.

"Have you thought any more about your trust?"

I sigh and absentmindedly make little circles on his chest. "Not too much honestly. It all feels a little overwhelming."

He props himself up, one arm crooked behind his head as he looks at me.

"Talk to me about it."

I shrug. "I want to do what you and I talked about. I want to use a big part of it to start a nonprofit and to fund startups. I also want to donate a big chunk. I've at least made a list of about a dozen or so groups I want to donate to first."

"That's a huge start, sweetie. Why are you feeling overwhelmed?"

"I dunno. I guess for as much as I love volunteering and I've always dreamed of starting my own nonprofit, I don't actually know where to even start. I also don't know where to find startups that need investors. I know I just need to do the research and work."

"I actually happen to know a guy who not only started his own foundation, but he's still actively on the board and is very business savvy. Some would even say he's a bit of a financial genius. Hell, he also happens to have an endless supply of contacts and connections that could get you set up with more startups needing investors than you know what to do with." He gives me a little wink and it makes me giggle.

"I know. I just don't want you to think I'm using you or not willing to put in the work myself. Plus, you've got a multibillion-dollar empire to run. Who says you have time for some twenty-five-year-old with a measly fifty million."

He jackknifes upward, grabbing both my sides with his hands, causing me to crumple into a fit of giggles.

"You're a little smart-ass, you know that."

"Stop!" I laugh. "I'm going to pee!" I squeal and convulse until he finally relents.

He leans over me as I catch my breath. His eyes still soft, a genuine smile pulls at one corner of his mouth as he brushes my unruly hair away from my face.

"I'm not worried you're using me, Brontë. I'd like to be an asset to you, to help you out. I'm very honored that you trusted me in the first place to come to me about it all."

"Well, it's clear what value you bring to this equation, being a mentor at work, now being my financial guru and life coach..." I hesitate to finish the question, but I do anyway. "So what do I bring to the equation, a midlife crisis piece of ass?" I laugh, hoping my sarcasm hides my true feelings.

"Is that what this is? A midlife crisis?" His brows furrow a bit, but I can't tell if he's just pretending to be offended to not hurt my feelings.

"Or my daddy issues. My need to rebel and relive out those angsty teenage years that I didn't get to do." I giggle and poke his chest playfully. "Either way it's probably some sort of mix of it all, a manifestation of our desire for the forbidden." I bounce my eyebrows up and down, but he doesn't join in on my playfulness.

"Have you told anyone about us?"

Us.

The word rings in my ears for a moment and I feel a tinge of panic grip my throat. Does he think I have? Is he worried I'm out here writing our names together in cursive on my notebook or sending salacious texts to my friends about our rendezvous?

"No!" I say emphatically, my hand going to my chest in astonishment. "No, I haven't told a soul."

"Not even Sylvia or Taylor?" The *V* between his brows deepens and I shake my head no.

"No. Have you said anything to anyone?"

A knot forms in my stomach at the thought of this getting out and back to my father. Then I remember my talk with Chantelle. Technically, I didn't tell her anything—she wouldn't let me—but I didn't tell her otherwise either. I contemplate bringing that up, but I know it will only worry him; however, I know Chantelle won't tell my dad.

"No," he says softly but something about the way his eyes look away from me when he answers, makes me second-guess his honesty. I'm tempted to mention it when I realize that the fact I had a conversation with my stepmom about us is also a gray area so I have no leg to stand on.

I wonder who he would possibly tell. Maybe an old friend at the club? That doesn't seem right; he'd be too worried it would get back to my dad. Also, I just can't see Beckham confiding in anyone... unless he told Chantelle and she made it seem like she figured it out on her own. Then, for some strange reason, Venus pops into my head.

My stomach curdles and my heart aches at the thought of him confiding in her about me, *us*. Jealousy surges through me and I want to ask him if they're still friends, if they ever talk or hang out. Hell, they could still be hooking up and I wouldn't know. Do I want to know?

"Hey, what's going through your head?"

I look up and smile. "Nothing," I lie, not wanting to sour the mood after tonight's lovemaking.

"I should probably get going," he says, sitting up further and swinging his legs over the edge of the bed.

He reaches for his clothes, but I shoot my hand out to still his movements.

"Stay?" I say half as a question, half as a plea.

He hesitates, his eyes looking from mine to his hand, then back to me. He scoots back into bed, pulling the covers up and holding them open, patting the spot next to him. I smile and crawl into the spot, cuddling into his chest as he pulls the covers up over us.

I fall into a deep, dreamless sleep, all thoughts of *what if* and *maybe we shouldn't* pushed to the outer recesses of my mind. Because I know that someday, probably soon, this little fantasy world we're living in will come to an end.

When I wake the next morning to the blare of my alarm on my nightstand, I silence it and stretch my arms overhead, rolling over to find an empty space where Beckham slept. I sit up and see a small note, scribbled with his handwriting.

Good morning, beautiful,

Apologies for slipping out early without a goodbye, but I have an early meeting and needed to run home before work. Take your time coming in to the office. Just know I woke with a smile on my face.

XO,

Beckham

I smile, a warmth spreading through my body as I recall last night. The way he held me, the way he looked at me like he was trying to memorize every facet of my being. I grab the pillow he slept on and inhale the slight, lingering scent of him.

I slide out of bed and grab my robe, heading to my kitchen for coffee with phone in hand. I slide it open to my group chat that has several messages as I wait for the coffee to brew.

"What the hell?" I mutter as I see exclamation points and out of context comments from my friends that don't make any sense.

Sylvia: *Looks like some serious tea you need to spill, Miss Spencer!*

Taylor: *Damn, to be a fly on the wall in that restaurant.*

I scroll up to find what they're referring to. It's an article Taylor sent, dated just one day ago with a headline that makes my heart plummet, accompanied by a picture of Beckham and Venus at dinner.

Financial Billionaire Beckham Archer and Socialite Venus Davenport Make a Splash at Heated Dinner!

Chapter 16

Beckham

Holding Brontë in my arms last night felt like a dream, one I didn't want to wake up from but one I knew I had to because it's not real.

Hearing her refer to herself as my midlife crisis physically hurt last night. I know it's my fault; I've led her to believe that's all she is to me and truthfully, I don't plan on convincing her otherwise.

Apart from the obvious reason that we're risking so much being together, I know that she deserves more. She deserves a man her age who can give her a happily ever after. She deserves someone whom she doesn't have to explain or hide.

I lean back in my chair after finishing up my meeting with my executives when Brontë opens my office door and steps inside, closing it behind her.

"Good morning." I smile but she doesn't respond; she just walks slowly toward my desk.

She has a sheepish look on her face, but my gaze doesn't linger there. No, I'm too focused on her tits that are practically spilling out of her shirt. She's left three buttons undone, a red lace bra peeking through. It matches the bright-red pencil skirt she's wearing that hugs her full hips tightly.

"Do you have a few minutes, sir?" Her tone is breathy.

"I do. What can I help you with, Miss Spencer?"

She reaches my desk, placing her fingertips on the surface.

"We have a problem, sir."

"We do?"

"Mm-hmm." It almost sounds like a moan the way she says it. She reaches up, removing the clip that's holding her hair on her head, and it tumbles in loose waves down her shoulders. She shakes it out seductively and I feel myself twitch against my leg.

"You see, last night was good, wonderful, but I didn't get my fill." She drags her finger down between her breasts and back up again, my eyes following the movements.

"Is that right?"

"You were sweet and tender, so attentive to my needs, but I think —" She reaches for a button and pops it open. "I need a little reminder about how powerful you are." She bites her bottom lip as she pops open another button.

My fingers dig into my armrests, preventing me from diving across this desk and ripping another blouse from her body. But I like this game. I don't know where it's coming from, but I'll gladly play.

"Of course you do, sweetheart." I lean back in my chair, attempting to remain calm and casual. "You do like it filthy, don't you?"

She nods her head.

"Do you need to be reminded that I'm in charge, Brontë?"

"Yes."

"Do you want me to use that tight little cunt of yours on this desk?"

Her breath hitches and she stumbles with her reply.

"Y-yes."

"Then come over here right now before I have to make you."

165

She gets a devious little grin on her face and slowly shakes her head no.

"Make me."

I can't hide my shock. I laugh. "Say that again?"

"Make. Me." She says the words louder this time, a burst of confidence shining through.

"Hmm, I thought that this"—I say opening my bottom drawer slowly—"might come in handy with your little attitude around here." I pull out the riding crop, laying it across my desk.

"You just happen to have that?"

I stand up and straighten my tie. "Happen to? No. I brought it especially for you, sweetheart."

I take one step around the desk toward her, and she tries to dart away, but I reach out and catch her hand. I yank her toward me, immediately bending her over my desk.

"What did I tell you, Brontë?"

She giggles and I grab her other arm and pin them to her back.

"Answer me." I grip her hands with one of mine, the other coming to wrap around her throat so I can bend her head back. I'm leaning over her as she's arched, her ass pressing against my erection as I bring my lips to her ear.

"I told you I would punish you if you disobeyed me, didn't I?"

"Yes." Her words are strained; she's loving this. She wants me to punish her. To use her.

I yank her skirt open, grabbing a handful of her ass, my cock growing hard instantly. I reach over her, grabbing the riding crop and dragging it slowly over her bare ass. She squirms and I tap it against her. It stings and she jumps.

"Stay still." I don't give her time to respond; I raise the crop back and bring it down swiftly against her flesh. Instantly, it reddens.

"Ow!" she yelps and I do it again on the other cheek.

I groan, grabbing her ass again, wanting to lean down and bite a mouthful, but instead I release her. She looks over her shoulder at me, confused as I walk back to my chair and sit down.

"I know you want me to fuck you, but you have to be punished." I lean down and open my bottom drawer, reaching inside to pull out a toy I also bought to use on her. I place it on the desk and her eyes fall to it.

"I thought you just punished me."

"That was just a taste, baby girl. Now I want to savor it. And no," I say before she can even ask, "it's never been used and I bought it after our first time together. I knew you'd need to be punished and I knew I would want to watch you fuck yourself with this toy on my desk."

Her eyes grow wide as she reaches out and picks it up.

"You want to please me, don't you, Brontë?" She nods. "Then get your ass over here and sit on my fucking desk so I can watch you fuck yourself. Don't make me tell you again."

She obeys this time, walking around to me. I motion for her to turn around and she does so I can unzip her skirt. I remove it, along with her matching red thong, and spin her back around to face me so I can remove her top and bra as well.

"Leave the shoes on." I smile as she stands in front of me, stark naked with a dildo in her hand.

I help her onto the desk, placing a heeled foot on either side of me on the armrests.

"Now, that is a mouthwatering sight." I grit my teeth, my mouth pooling with saliva at the sight of her spread in front of me, her pink pussy staring back at me, begging to be eaten.

"Are you wet, sweetheart?" I don't wait for her to answer. I grab the dildo and spit on it, then hand it back to her.

She drags it slowly down her body, then back up, slipping it between her lips and into her mouth a few times as she maintains eye contact with me. The next time she drags it down, she starts to tease herself with it, before placing it at her entrance and pressing it inside.

"Ohhh," she moans, her eyes rolling back in her head as she slides it in and out, already slick with her juices. I watch her stretch to accommodate it and my cock pulses, begging for attention, but I don't give in.

"That's right, sweetie. Fuck that tight little pussy for me."

I can't hold off on touching her. I reach out, placing my hands on the inside of her knees, then slowly dragging them up her thighs. She responds, her groans growing louder as her legs begin to shake.

"Look at you, stuffed with a dildo on my desk, about ready to come. Are you about to come, baby?"

"Y—yes, yes, yes." She pants over and over, the word growing louder as she gets closer. She's there, her head falls back, she tries to clench her thighs together, but I stop her. I reach out and grab the toy, pulling it from her before she can finish.

"What the hell?" she snaps, sitting up, still panting and confused as I smile at her.

"I told you, you're being punished. You've been a naughty girl."

"You asshole." She lunges to grab the toy from me but I catch her hand.

"Open your mouth." She stares at me. "Are you going to make me say it again?"

She opens her mouth and I slide the toy between her lips.

"Taste yourself."

I tease her and she indulges me, sucking on the toy until I can't take it any longer and I pull it from her mouth.

"I want the real thing," she teases with a pouty gaze, her eyes dropping down to my lap as her tongue comes out to lick her lip.

"Yeah?" I say, reaching down to unzip my pants. I reach inside and wrap my hand around my cock that's begging for release. I pull myself free and stroke up and down my shaft as she watches me intently.

"Maybe I just finish myself off and make you watch?"

"Please," she says sweetly, and it almost makes me blow early.

"On your knees," I command and this time I don't have to tell her twice. She scrambles down from the desk, settling onto her knees as she looks up at me, her lips slightly parted.

"That's right, sweetheart. You're right where you belong, aren't you—on your knees, begging to suck me off."

I reach behind her head and pull her forward till her lips are on my tip. She doesn't hesitate as she wraps her hand and lips around my cock and begins to suck me like her life depends on it. She twists her hands up and down my shaft in time with her mouth bobbing up and down.

"I have fantasized so many times about seeing your mouth on my cock." I grit the words out. I look down at where her mouth is wrapped around me, her lips puffy, her wide eyes looking up at me.

"Fuuuuck," I groan, my hands diving into her hair as I grip her head. I hold her head in place, my hips coming up to fuck her face as my movements grow erratic. My heart feels like it's about to rip through my chest. My legs stiffen and my chest burns as I shoot my load into her mouth, a string of inaudible sounds coming from me as my entire body finds release.

I look down, her lips still wrapped around me when I hear someone shouting my name in the hallway.

"Beckham, you goddamn son of a bitch!"

I pull my cock from Brontë's lips, my cum spilling down her chin as I stuff myself back into my pants and grab her clothes from the floor.

"Under the desk!" I whisper, pushing her backward.

"Who is that?" she says as a loud pounding echoes through my office and the door handle begins to turn.

"Your father," I say as a look of shock settles over her face and I finish zipping myself back up.

"It's open!" I say, standing up, straightening my tie and running my hands through my hair. I grab my water bottle, hoping I can mask my breathlessness with drinking.

Jonas Ramsay doesn't seem to notice as my door flies open and he barges in, a wagging finger already pointed in my face.

"What the hell were you thinking?" he shouts and I fully expect him to lunge across this desk and beat the living shit out of me.

"I can explain," I say with my hands in the air. I can explain, but I don't want to and I'm damn sure he doesn't want to hear about how me and his daughter ended up as fuck buddies.

"You better because I thought we had trust. Where's Brontë?" he says, looking over his shoulder toward the hallway. "Tell her to get me a coffee, would ya?"

"She's, uh, she's volunteering today," I say, a bit confused. Maybe he hasn't found out about us. Shit, now I don't know what I'm explaining.

He rolls his eyes and sits down heavily in the chair in front of my desk.

"You better have a damn good reason you not only threatened Jack Niles over at Pierce but also insinuated to him that I knew about this little accounting error going around or possibly had something to do with it."

Relief washes over me and I release my breath.

"First of all, I never insinuated shit; he did. I told him that you had nothing to do with it and he said maybe I should double-check that theory. Second, I'll threaten him and anyone else who attempts to sell me shit based on fraud. We are both way too smart and way too successful to be beholden to some mediocre financial firm that thinks they can pull the wool over our eyes."

"Goddammit, Beckham." He sighs and leans back in the chair. "What are we going to do about this? I don't want the company. I know you could turn them around; they're worth fighting for. We need to get to the bottom of this nonsense now before the SEC gets involved."

I shake my head. "Honestly, Jonas, if it is fraud, the SEC will get involved. I want whoever is doing this to be punished and brought up on charges and you should too. You don't want our names tied to someone else's dirty laundry."

"True," he mutters. "Let's set up a meeting with Jack and Bryan. We'll go over everything and get this sorted so we can get things moving forward again."

"I think that sounds like a good idea." I feel a pinch on my ankle. "Shit!" I jerk my leg back and Jonas eyes me. "Sorry, sock must have pulled a leg hair."

"Well, sorry to barge in here like this. You want to grab an early lunch?"

I stand and walk toward him. "I can't, buddy. Sorry. Got a full day. Rain check?"

"Sounds good," he says, and I walk him to the door, closing it behind him after we say goodbye.

A second later Brontë is emerging from beneath my desk, half-dressed. She must have somehow shimmied into her clothes while I was speaking to her father.

"That was—" I don't finish the thought because she's clearly upset. Her hair is a mess. She's carrying her shoes, and her shirt is only half-buttoned and untucked.

"Hey," I say, reaching for her, but she jerks her arm away and walks past me.

"Hey!" I say again more firmly as I grab her arm and place my other hand against the door so she can't open it. "I know that was uncomfortable, but what's going on? Talk to me."

"Seriously?" She steps out of my grasp, her expression going from anger to hurt. "You shoved me under your desk while my mouth was full of your cum. Talk about humiliating and feeling like a cheap fucking whore."

"Whoa. I have never called you that nor wanted to call you that. What was I supposed to do? It was your father, Brontë. Do you want him to find out?"

She rolls her eyes and shakes her head, crossing her arms as her shoes dangle from one hand.

"I thought that's what got you off honestly, sneaking around behind Daddy's back. You freaked out last night when I asked if you'd told anyone; you made it seem like that was the last thing you'd want, someone to find out about this."

"Don't put that all on me. You made it clear multiple times you didn't want my father to find out either. You said it, this"—she motions between us—"wasn't worth coming between my father and me and it wasn't worth you risking your friendship with him."

"I—not like this. You really want him to find out while my dick is in your mouth?" I regret the words as soon as I say them. I see her flinch.

She looks down at the floor and it hits me that the fun has seemed to run out for her. Maybe that's what this morning was, a last-ditch effort to bring back the spice and excitement by fucking in my office.

"I guess this just solidifies why it was all a mistake in the first place."

Her head snaps up and her eyes meet mine.

"So we're done then? This is it?" The anger is back and I'm thoroughly confused.

"Brontë, what the hell is this? I can't keep up with it anymore. You either want me because I'm your dad's best friend, I'm too old for you, I'm forbidden, or a dirty secret you can tell your friends about."

"Is this about Venus?"

"What?" I ask, confused.

"I saw the headline."

"What are you talking about?" My stomach tightens.

"My friends sent me an article that showed you two having dinner the other night. Apparently, she threw a drink in your face?"

Fuck.

I nod. "She did but no, this has nothing to do with her. She's just a friend now, someone I'm helping out with something."

She laughs, clearly not believing me.

"A friend? You must be doing one helluva job *helping* her if she threw water in your face."

"Well, clearly, I'm being a really bad friend to a lot of people right now because I can't seem to keep from pissing everyone off."

Her anger subsides a little and I reach for her. "Brontë, I'm sorry about the desk thing. I didn't know what to do and I didn't mean to treat you like you meant nothing."

"It's fine," she says, clearly not fine, "but why didn't you tell him that I should be involved in that meeting with you, him, and the guys from Pierce? I've been the one doing all the heavy lifting with this acquisition. I found the fraud and it's like you guys are acting like it's a big boys' club, like because I'm young and new, I can't have any input in a meeting or conversation with them about it."

I hang my head. Yup, I screwed up again.

"I just—I just wanted to get him out of the office, Brontë. I feel like I'm trying to juggle all this shit and it's not working."

"You know what's really shitty about all this?" Her expression tells me I'm not going to like what she's about to say. "You have no problem whipping out your dick for me to suck in your office, but you won't stick your neck out for me for one single meeting where I can present what I found."

She stares at me, then without another word she opens my office door and leaves.

Chapter 17

Brontë

I get that Beckham is confused because I am too.

I thought I wanted a fling, something totally out of my good girl comfort zone that would just be a summer fling or even a one-night stand. But here I am, crying on my couch over a man I have no business having feelings for while I scrape the bottom of a pint of Ben & Jerry's.

I toss the empty container on the coffee table and reach for my phone for what feels like the hundredth time. Still no texts or missed calls from him.

I contemplate calling Sylvia and having her come over so I can vent, but as a mom to a young child, she can't just drop everything every time I get my heart broken or make bad life choices.

I could call Taylor. I know she'd be more than happy to listen to this hot mess of a situation I've gotten myself into but I decide against it. I'm not sure if I'm embarrassed or just not ready to hear *I told you so* from my friends a bunch of times... not that they would shove it in my face but they'd tell me that I need to put my big girl panties on and move on. Something I'm not sure I'm ready to hear or do.

Instead, I send a text to Chantelle, the one person who actually knows what I'm going through and will offer me legitimate advice.

Me: *Hey, any chance you're free for lunch tomorrow? Could seriously use some advice.*

She responds almost immediately.

Chantelle: *Of course. I'll meet you outside your office at noon.*

———

"As much as I enjoy our social time, I'm pretty certain you don't need advice on a new possible hairstyle or outfit." Chantelle gives me a sympathetic smile as our waiter places our water on the table along with our menus.

"Yeah, not exactly."

"Beckham?"

I nod, taking a sip of the water.

"Oh boy. Maybe I should have opted for an afternoon wine."

"I feel so confused and he does too, I think."

"What do you mean?" she asks.

"So, as you know and mentioned, he's not the forever type. I never told him I was looking for marriage or kids. I wasn't positive I wanted those things either, but lately, the other night specifically, it almost felt like he wanted more with me."

"Wow, that is not what I was expecting."

"Right? He was asking me about if I'd told anyone about us and I told him no. I realize that you caught on but I didn't actually tell you so I just failed to mention that you know. Anyway, he almost seemed distant and weird after I made a comment about it. His expression seemed, I dunno, disappointed maybe?"

The waiter reappears and we both order a chicken Caesar salad.

"So how did that conversation end?"

"Well, there's more to it. I made a comment about me basically being his midlife crisis and he once again seemed agitated by that comment."

She laughs. "I can see why a man like him wouldn't like that comment."

"Really? I thought for sure that's how he saw me. As just a young piece of ass."

She snorts, water almost coming out her nose. "You didn't say *that*, did you?"

I nod. "Ummm, maybe. I told him that he contributed so much to the relationship, as a mentor, boss, friend, etc. We talked about my ideas for the trust and—"

She holds up her hands to stop me.

"Brontë, first let me just say this. Beckham isn't a stupid or reckless man. That's why I came to you in the first place. The fact that he's willing to risk his relationship with your father to be with you, tells me right away this isn't just a hookup or 'hot piece of ass.' I thought you knew that when we spoke about this."

"I—I didn't think about it like that, no."

"If you had stopped me and said it was simply flirting, then I wouldn't have given you that warning, but the fact that you have known each other for a few months now and something has continued to build between you too, the man has feelings for you."

I feel my heart flutter and I know it shouldn't. I shouldn't want that.

"I—" I hesitate, my eyes dropping down to where my fingers are twirling the paper wrapper from my straw around each other. "I think I have feelings for him too."

She reaches over and touches my hand lightly.

"He said *us* the other night. It took me by surprise and then the way he"—I feel myself blush—"sorry if this is oversharing, but it felt like we made love. It was so different than any other time. It was like our bodies said all the things we know we shouldn't say." I can feel warmth spreading through my body as images of that night flood my brain.

"Has he said anything to you about telling your dad?"

I shake my head. "No, because I've made it clear to him that I don't want my dad finding out and honestly, with his mixed signals, I don't know if it's worth it to even attempt to tell him and risk blowing everything up."

"What mixed signals are you seeing?" she asks just as our waiter brings out our salads.

"Thank you," we both say in unison.

"He's clearly into me physically and we talk a lot about what we're passionate about, what drives us, but with work stuff, I'm sure you've heard about some issues that have arisen with the Pierce acquisition?"

"No." She smiles. "I stay out of any business talk. I learned long ago that Jonas will rant for hours if I open that can of worms. He'll discuss things but he doesn't tend to go into anything major. Our therapist told him it's unfair to dump all that on me."

"Well, Beckham has allowed me to do a lot of the due diligence and reconciliation of financial records with Pierce and I found some *discrepancies*, you could say. After a lot of back and forth with their financial team and expressing my concerns multiple times to Beckham, he went to my father and Pierce about it, instead of allowing me to be involved. Now, they're all having this meeting that I'm not even invited to even though I found the fraud. It's frustrating. I wish he would stick his neck out for me more when it comes to that. He has defended my honor, you could say, to this sleazebag that is their head of sales but this, this is huge. I deserve to be in those meetings."

I can feel myself getting flustered. I drop my fork and rub my temples.

"Sorry, I just feel like an idiot. You must think I deserve this."

"No, never," she says sympathetically. "Listen, if you both have feelings for each other, it is worth it to talk about it. Be honest with each other, even if it's uncomfortable. You'd rather live with rejection than regret, trust me. I went through something similar with your father, you know?"

"I didn't know."

"I was the cliché young secretary whom the boss started flirting with, although I was the one who started the flirting. It went on for months. He thought I was just young and not actually into him. We traveled for work together once and things, well, they went too far," she says and I appreciate the discretion considering it's my father. "We both did the whole *we shouldn't have done that, it won't happen again* song and dance for a while before it happened again and then again. I was too scared to tell him I was falling for him because like you, I thought it would mess things up and I'd rather forever be his secret little hookup, than lose him by telling him how I truly felt."

"What changed? What made you decide to tell him?"

She shrugs. "Nothing changed. I just decided that what I felt for him was worth telling him. If you both agreed that this would be a one-time thing, something that you both know for whatever reason absolutely cannot go further than physical, I would understand wanting to keep your feelings to yourself. If you can walk away right now, tell him that yes, we should stop and you can still work together and move on, then do it. Don't keep fooling around because feelings will only grow stronger and someday, I guarantee you, your father will find out. But if you think it's worth it, tell him how you feel and see if he feels the same and if he's willing to talk to your father with you."

"Oh God," I groan, downing half my glass of water at the thought of telling my dad I'm falling in love with his best friend. "How bad do you think it will be?"

I cringe when I see the expression on her face.

"It won't be easy, that's for sure."

"How did your parents handle it when you told them how old my dad was?"

"Oh boy." She laughs, sitting back in her seat. "It wasn't good, I'll be honest. My parents thought they did something wrong. They thought if they had raised me better, I wouldn't go after a man twenty-plus years older than me. But I asked them to give him one chance and they did."

"And now? They like him?"

She rolls her eyes. "Yes. He and my dad are great friends. Which is wonderful and I love it truly, but I guess I didn't expect that every time my dad called, he'd be talking to my husband instead of me."

"That's so great." I feel relief wash over me. "Do you think it could be like that with Beckham and me?"

"I'd like to think so. I think where you might run into more of an issue is, your father knows Beckham. He trusts him, and guys have that silly bro code about dating each other's sisters or whatever, even when they're this age. But it could also play to your advantage. Jonas trusts and respects Beckham; he knows he's a good man which is why I keep reiterating that whatever you two decide, you need to do it quick and make sure you tell him before he finds out on his own or there's a good chance there's no coming back from that."

I sigh as her words sink in. I do feel some relief that she thinks there's actually a chance we could make it work but also that she thinks he has feelings for me. It's giving me the confidence I need to just be honest with him about how I feel.

"Hey, something else I'm curious about that I could use your advice on regarding my dad."

"Please don't tell me you're pregnant." She rests her hand dramatically against her chest and it makes me laugh.

"No! It's about the money from the trust."

"Phew!" She jokingly runs her hand over her brow.

"I—I want to use the bulk of the money to start a nonprofit and run it. I don't want to pursue a career in the financial world." She nods and I keep going. "Beckham listened to my goals and helped me map out a really strategic plan where I could use a portion to invest in startup companies so that it would yield dividends once profitable so, an income stream, plus I will invest some for my future but most of it, I want to donate to other organizations and my own foundation."

"That's wonderful, Brontë. You truly are an amazing woman; your mother would be so proud."

I smile. "Thank you, that means so much but... is Dad going to be disappointed in me? I know he used to get frustrated with my mom about her donating and volunteering and he told me not to be *silly* with the trust when he told me about it at the birthday party."

Her brows knit together. "I didn't realize he said *that* to you. I would have spoken to him about that."

"I get it in the sense that he has built this massive empire so he's extremely smart and knows how easy it is to lose money with bad investments or changes in the market, but the reality is, I can take the risk. I'm not putting all my eggs in one basket and being reckless. I just don't want him to be disappointed in me. With Mom being gone, I just want to make at least someone proud." I try to hold back the tears, but one tumbles silently down my cheek and splats on the table next to my plate.

"Oh, sweetie." Chantelle scoots her chair back and walks over to hug me. "I know I'm not your mom and I'll never replace Nadine, but I'm proud of you. And listen, your father, he can be brash; we both know that, but at the end of the day, he's just worried about you. As a parent, we want certain things for our kids. We don't want them to go through struggles or hardships and sometimes we get blinded by our own age and experiences so we want to warn them against making any possible mistake, but that's not how life works and he knows that. The bottom line is, as much as he might talk about something being silly, it's hurtful and rude and I will set that old man straight, but he only wants you to be happy. He only wants the best for you."

I reach up to touch her arm that's wrapped around me.

"Thanks, Chantelle. Hey, maybe I could just knock it all out together, you know? Hey, Dad, I'm in love with your best friend and I'm not going to work in finance. Two birds, one stone." I laugh.

"Oh boy, let's not give the man a heart attack." She sits back down in her chair. "Don't be afraid to be honest with people, Brontë, but more importantly, don't be afraid to be honest with yourself. Your dad is a different person than he was a decade or two ago. That doesn't absolve his behavior by any means and you are perfectly valid in your concerns and feelings regarding him, but if I could offer any little bit of feedback, it's to give him a chance to prove that. Just talk to him."

I leave our lunch feeling confident, reassured, and ready to go over to Beckham's tonight and lay it all out.

———

I adjust my shirt nervously in the elevator at Beckham's penthouse. I didn't even bother changing out of my sleeveless black blouse and matching skirt from the office today.

Work was tense to say the least. Both of us kept our interactions to a minimum, clearly feeling like we're walking on eggshells, unsure how to proceed or what to say after the argument in his office yesterday.

I was a little surprised that Ritchie let me up without calling Beckham first. Hopefully it doesn't get him in any trouble, but I can't focus on that issue very long because the elevator doors open and Beckham is standing in his foyer with another woman.

"Brontë? What are you doing here?" His face is a mix of shock and panic and that's when the woman next to him turns around and I realize it's Venus.

"Uh, I, uh, I'll come back another time. I'm sorry. I just wanted to talk for a moment, but it can wait. Sorry." I turn to leave, but Venus' voice makes me stop in my tracks.

"It's her, isn't it?"

I turn back around and look at her as she looks at Beckham with a smirk on her face.

"She's the one that you've been seeing? The reason you wouldn't return my calls and texts?"

My stomach feels like a pool of acid, burning and churning inside me.

"Venus, don't," Beckham says, his hand curling into a fist of frustration.

"You told her?" I ask, confused, and his eyes flash to mine, then to the floor. "You told me you didn't tell anyone about us."

"I didn't tell her who; I just told her that I was seeing someone."

"When?" I ask but I already know the answer. "At that dinner?"

"Yes."

"Is that why you threw water in his face, because he's seeing me?" I feel jealousy rear its ugly head again and the need to be territorial.

"No." She laughs. "I did that because"—she slowly turns her head from me to look at Beckham with an almost maniacal smile on her face—"she doesn't know, does she?"

My body starts to feel shaky. Her hands slowly come up to cup her lower belly and that's when I see the bump. It's small, but it's there.

"Well," she says with a huge smile, "since we're all divulging secrets and you're seeing the father of my baby, I guess you should know that I'm pregnant."

I stand perfectly still, then for some reason, I burst into laughter.

"You're kidding, right?"

She gives me the fakest, sympathetic smile and head shake I've ever seen as Beckham brings his hands up to his face.

A cool flush settles over my body as I realize that she's serious and clearly, this isn't brand-new information to Beckham. He knew and kept it from me.

I stumble as I try to turn around, my foot getting hooked on the other, and I almost fall before catching myself. I punch the button to call the elevator.

"Brontë, wait. She's lying. I have no idea if that is actually my child or not. She's refusing to take a paternity test and I swear—we never—"

I hold up my hand to silence him, bile burning my throat as my stomach churns.

"You knew"—I hiccup, tears running down my face—"and you came over to my apartment the next night and ma... made—" I feel like I can't get the words out of my mouth.

I don't finish the sentence. When the elevator opens, I step inside and hit the button. The last thing I see before the doors close is Beckham, pleading with me to stay.

I clutch my own body. I feel like I'm going to vomit and it's all so strange because we've never expressed our feelings for each other.

We've never talked about a future.

We never said we were exclusive or in a relationship or anything.

We've never even discussed when we'd hook up again because I thought I was protecting myself by not acknowledging my feelings.

Yet here I am, leaving his penthouse with a broken heart and no hope of a future with a man I thought I could trust... a man I did trust.

Chapter 18

Beckham

"She's a little young, even for you, don't you think, Beckham?"

I pound against the elevator door, white-hot anger burning through my veins at the sound of her sickly-sweet voice.

"Why the fuck did you do that?" I shout at the top of my lungs, my voice booming through the marble entryway and bouncing off the elevator doors.

"Because she's right; *you* should have done it already. You owe the woman you're fucking an explanation as to why you're going to be a father suddenly, don't you think?"

I spin around, Venus' expression revealing she's startled at my outburst, but I don't care. I'm sick of this woman fucking with me for no reason.

"I know, we both know," I correct myself as I slowly walk toward her, "that that baby isn't mine."

"You don't know actually and there's something else you don't know." She has an arrogant look on her face, one that tells me I'm really not going to like what she says next. "I didn't have an IUD the last few weeks we were together."

184

"What?" I shake my head in confusion, certain I just misheard her.

"It expired. I'd had it for five years and when the doctor asked if I wanted a new one put in, I opted not to."

"Is there a reason why you thought it was okay to gamble with someone else's future like that without telling them?" My fingers are curled into the palms of my hand so tight I'm surprised I haven't drawn blood.

Her face morphs from cocky and smug to angry in a flash.

"What about my future, Beckham? What about what I wanted?" she shouts. "Everything in our relationship was about you!" She jabs her finger toward me, tears stinging her eyes.

"What are you talking about, Venus? I told you from day one I had no intentions of ever becoming a father or a husband and you took that choice away from me because you're selfish! If you wanted those things, why did you stay? Why did you beg me to stay when I left?"

We're both angry, shouting, crying, but I can see it's not going to accomplish anything. I feel defeated. I thought there was a good chance that she was lying about this child being mine, but now, I don't think she is. I fall to knees, my head in my hands.

"How could you do this to me? I finally met the woman I want those things with, and you robbed me of having them with her."

"I'm thirty-eight, Beckham. My chance at being a mother was fleeing fast so I did what I had to do."

She walks up to me, running her hand through my hair as she looks down at me.

"I didn't purposely do this. Yes, I took a chance on removing my IUD, but you're right, you were always so careful. I didn't think it would happen, but that one drunken night we reconciled after breaking up and then getting together for the last time, it happened. Look at me, Beckham."

I look up at her; she's standing over me, both her hands on either side of my face now.

"I know this isn't what we planned and I know it isn't what you wanted, but we can do this. We can be a family. We were great together; can't you see that?"

"I don't love you, Venus. I love her."

"I know you think you do, sweetheart, but she won't give you what I can, what I already have." She touches her belly softly. "You'll get over her, you always do, and you'll come back to me."

I push her hands away from me and stand up, disgust settling over my face that I don't even attempt to hide.

"I will never love you, Venus. I never could because what you did is unforgivable. I'm in love with Brontë and nothing you say or do will ever change that."

"How can you love her? You barely know her. I gave you every part of me and it still wasn't enough!"

I see so much hurt when I look in her eyes and for as much as I hate her in this instant, I don't want her hurting. I don't want her to still pine for me or wish for what could have been.

"Venus, I'm sorry, truly I am. I never meant to lead you on or hurt you in any way. That's why I tried to be as transparent as possible with you about what kind of future I saw for myself and us. That's why I never talked about someday when we're old, or what a family would be like with us. I thought that you wanted the same things as me because you told me you did. You also led me to believe that what I could offer you was enough."

She stares at me, unblinking, like she doesn't know what to do or say.

"I'm sorry I shouted. I know that in your condition, the last thing you need is any undue stress. I meant what I said at the restaurant; I will step up and be a father. I won't resent you or this baby, but it's going to take time for me to work through it. To trust you, to be happy or excited about it. I'm sorry if that makes me sound like a complete asshole, and to be honest, I feel like a piece of shit that I'm not feeling those things right now."

"Will you go with me to the twenty-week scan? The doctor says we can find out the sex."

I shove my hands in my pockets. "Yes. I'll go with you."

————

It's been an agonizing week of every day attempting to have some semblance of normalcy between Brontë and me.

"Morning." I offer a smile in the break room as she makes her morning coffee.

"Morning," she says without looking up at me from her phone.

I glance around; it's just the two of us.

"Brontë, can we please just talk?"

"I'm really not interested," she says, her eyes still glued to the phone.

"Just let me expla—"

"Please," she says dogmatically, cutting me off. "Just let me focus and do my job. I'm very stressed about the meeting with Pierce and my father today. I just want to move on from all of this and get this situation figured out and resolved so the acquisition can move forward."

"I understand."

She nods and grabs her coffee, her heels clicking against the tile floor as she walks toward the door. She stops in the doorway, looking over at me.

"And thank you," she says, "for including me in the meeting today."

I nod and she exits.

Two hours later, we're seated across from each other in one of the conference rooms with her father Jonas, Jack Niles, and Bryan Winthrop.

It takes every ounce of my being not to stare at Brontë, her beautiful blond hair framing her face like an angelic halo. The sun shines through the windows behind me, highlighting her sparkling blue eyes. I glance back down at my hands, then back to her, hoping that I'm not being too obvious with her father sitting next to me.

It physically hurts my heart to see her so downcast. I can see her smile that she flashes as she shakes the men's hands, but it doesn't reach her eyes. It's empty, hollow. That glow she normally has, has dulled and it's all my fault. I want nothing more than to fall at her feet and beg her for forgiveness. To make her feel loved and happy again. To bring back that sparkle in her eye but I know the damage has been done and it's far too late.

"Gentleman," I say with a nod. "Thank you for meeting with us today. As we all are well aware, Brontë here has pointed out some pretty serious discrepancies in your financial records, and there doesn't seem to be any sort of reconciliation between accounts, cash flow, credits, debits, etc. Now we've had a lot of back and forth and I know we all want this acquisition to move forward so we need to get this resolved today." I point to the table for emphasis. "Or this is the last time I threaten to walk."

Jack and Bryan look at one another, Jack nodding to Bryan who has a very serious look on his face. He pulls out his iPad, opening the screen, and sliding it across the table to us.

"Seems like we found the source of the problem."

Brontë's ears perk up and she grabs the iPad, bringing it closer as she scrolls through whatever she's looking at. Slowly, a smile spreads across her face.

"I knew it was fraud," she says confidently and hands the iPad over to me.

"After some internal investigation and pretty intense interrogation, we found out that Chad Bellview, our president of sales, was behind it, along with one of our accounts payable interns whom he had manipulated after a sexual affair had started between them."

Brontë's eyes bug out of her head.

"That dickless shitbag?" I can't hold back my laughter and Jonas' head snaps to the right to look at me as Brontë giggles. Jack, who I haven't seen make a single facial expression since meeting him, can't hold back and even cracks a slight smile at my comment.

"We have fired him immediately, along with the intern, and are pursuing legal action. We are also working to make restitution to our employees," Bryan says.

"I knew I didn't like that guy, apart from being a sexist prick. I guess the silver lining is, it was someone I would have fired immediately after the acquisition went through."

"You've always been a fantastic judge of character, Beckham," Jonas says, clapping my shoulder.

"All right, now that we've established who was doing it, you men need to work to get your ducks in a row at Pierce. For now, the acquisition is paused until this is resolved. I won't have my name or Jonas' involved in this any more than it already is." I stand up and button my suit jacket, shaking Jack and Bryan's hands before ushering them out of my conference room.

———

I leave work early, heading straight over to the women's clinic where Venus mentioned she's having her twenty-week scan. I sit in the car outside, trying to gather up any ounce of excitement I can, but it's just not there.

"You okay?" I hear her muffled voice outside my window as she taps gently against the glass. I smile half-heartedly and open the door, walking inside the building with her.

I stare at the monitor as the doctor moves the wand around Venus' swollen belly. I can't make sense of what I'm seeing but seconds later I hear a loud, rapid whooshing sound that fills the room.

"And that is your baby girl's heartbeat. Sitting perfectly right at one hundred forty beats per minute."

"Baby girl," Venus gasps, reaching her hand out and grabbing mine, tears in her eyes as she looks from the monitor to me. I squeeze her hand with both of mine, looking at the monitor, but no matter how hard I try, I feel nothing.

I listen to the doctor, but it sounds like everything is just echoing around me. I nod and smile; I hold Venus' hand, but I feel so empty, so broken.

Am I broken? How can I be hearing my baby's heartbeat and feel nothing? What kind of man am I? What kind of father could I ever hope to be?

I sit in my car in silence for several minutes after the appointment. Venus waves goodbye as she leaves, and I contemplate driving around for a few hours. The last place I want to be is home alone.

I reach for my phone and decide to try one last time. I find Brontë's name and give her a call.

"Hello?" Even her voice sounds empty.

"Hey."

Silence.

"I know you already told me a dozen times, but I can't—I need to see you, please. I just want to talk."

"Why? What is left to say?"

"You were my best friend; I miss talking to you. Confiding in you. I don't know what else to do, Brontë." I'm pleading. It's pathetic but I don't care.

"I'm down by the lake. Montrose Beach."

"I'll be there shortly and thank you."

I hang up and fly through traffic, my heart feeling like it's about to beat out of my chest at the thought of being able to talk to her again.

When I get there, she's sitting all alone on a bench, the sun slowly setting behind her. I take a seat on the bench silently, both of us staring out at the water for several minutes.

"I just went to the twenty-week ultrasound today with Venus." She doesn't respond but I can feel Brontë tense beside me. "She's having a girl."

"You're having a girl," she corrects and it makes my stomach flip.

"I..." I hang my head. "I feel like a piece of shit. I felt nothing when I looked at that monitor. I felt nothing when I heard the heart-beat. I felt nothing when she told me I was going to be a father."

"You were blindsided. For someone who has never wanted children, I can imagine it will take a while for you to get to a point where you are excited and happy."

"You think it will happen?"

She nods. "Even if it takes till delivery day. I think once you look at her, hold her, you'll know and you'll feel it. If she is yours, that is." She looks over at me. "Are you still doing the paternity test?"

I shrug. "I'm not sure there's a point to do so anymore." Her brows furrow in confusion. "After you left, she confessed that the last month we were together, she didn't have an IUD in."

"What?" Her expression mirrors mine when I found out.

"Yeah, that was my response. Apparently, it expired and she didn't have a new one put in because she said she was getting older and her chance at becoming a mother was diminishing."

"So she traps you?"

"I know, it's fucked. She said that the night it happened—" I cringe mentioning it and I see Brontë's eyes drop from me down to the ground. "We broke up and got back together a few times, always around arguments regarding her wanting more than I was willing to give. She said that the last time we got back together before we permanently broke up, we had a drunken night together where I wasn't *careful*, but truthfully, I don't remember that. I don't know if it was because of the alcohol I don't remember or because it didn't happen."

"So you still have doubts that she's yours?"

I rub my hand over my jaw, the scruff of not shaving for two days rough against my palm. "I guess I do."

"Did she say she wants to try and work it out with you? Be with you now?"

I look at her and nod my head yes.

"Beckham." I look over at her. "You have to demand a paternity test. You can't possibly go into something this life-altering and not do your due diligence. You're so thorough with doing that in business, but this, you just shrug off and believe her? A woman who lied to you about contraceptives and then attempts to manipulate you into being with her?"

"This probably makes me even shittier, but I fear that if it does come back as my child, I'll just look like a deadbeat trying to get out of responsibility. And what if my daughter finds that out someday? That I denied her and demanded the courts to prove she was mine? What kind of relationship would I have with her?"

She reaches out and gently places her hand on mine. "Coming from someone who had a deadbeat dad who came back into my life, she'd forgive you."

I let her words sink in as I stare down at her hand on mine. I reach over and take it, holding it with both of mine, dwarfing her tiny fingers. I bring it to my lips, planting several small kisses against her cool skin.

"Is there any hope?" I look over at her, the wind blowing a few tendrils of her hair around her face. "Any chance that we can be together again?"

She looks at me, her eyes filled with tears already, and she slowly shakes her head no.

"I can't," she whispers.

"Why?" I want to beg and plead.

"Because I don't want a fling." She slowly removes her hand from mine. "I don't want a secret hookup on your desk or in your car. I want more. I want it all. I want a relationship with you and happily ever after, and I know you can't offer me that. I fell, wholeheartedly, Beckham. I loved you and I know I shouldn't have, but I'm not sorry and I only have myself to blame."

My eyes shoot up to hers and I reach out and grab her hand again.

"You *loved* me? As in did? You don't love me anymore?" My heart feels like it's cracking, crumbling inside my hollow chest and it's going to kill me.

"Please," she says, her lower lip trembling as she shakes her head. "Please don't make me answer that if you're no longer mine."

"I understand. I won't press the issue again."

I release her hand slowly as she walks away, taking my heart with her.

Chapter 19

Brontë

I wanted him to run after me, to chase me down and tell me that he was still mine.

Still? Was he ever really mine? No.

I don't know what I'm feeling right now besides numb. I can't be angry at him for telling Venus about us when I never told him that Chantelle knows and that I confided in her after she found out. I also can't be angry at him for not telling me that he found out Venus was pregnant with what could be his child. I can't imagine trying to process that kind of information and it happened long before I was even in the picture.

But the biggest reason I can't be mad at any of it is because I was the one who told him it was just *having fun*. I wanted it to be just that, but my heart got in the way and now I'm paying the price just like Chantelle said would happen.

I wonder what would have happened if I told him that yes, I was still in love with him. Or yes, there is a chance that we could be together again, but in what capacity? What does *be together* mean to him? Sneaking around? Hookups with no future? And how would you balance all of that with a new baby and co-parenting?

My head spins with the mental gymnastics of trying to make it work. The reality is, maybe if we loved each other enough, we could have made it work but I can't ask him to fit me into his life now that he has a baby on the way.

My heart aches at the thought that someday soon, he'll be cradling his baby daughter and it won't be with me. Kids and marriage haven't been at the forefront of my mind, but maybe that's because I hadn't met the right person. My mom used to tell me that she never thought she wanted children. She was focused solely on a career until she fell in love with my dad and it made her want a family with him. I get that now.

"Oh, Mom. I wish you were here." I stare up at the sky as I wait for the walk symbol to flash, an idea popping into my head.

I pull my phone out and find my dad's name, hitting the call button.

"Hello? This is a lovely surprise." My dad's melodic voice puts a smile on my face.

"Hey, Dad. Why do you always act like you haven't heard from me in weeks?" I laugh, wiping away a few remaining tears that still cling to my cheeks.

"Well, you're a busy woman, always kicking ass at work and volunteering. I'm just grateful you make time for your old man."

"I'm calling because I wanted to spend more time with you actually."

"Oh?" His voice goes up an octave.

"Would you want to take the Porsche out this weekend? I thought we could pack a picnic, catch up, and maybe... go visit Mom's grave?" The other end goes silent. "Dad?"

"I'm here. I just... I would love that, sweetie. Thank you." There's a hint of emotion in his voice, but he coughs it away.

"Great. I'll stop by your house on Saturday. We can pack lunch at your house and then leave from there?"

"Sounds great, B."

I hang up the phone just as I make it back to my building. I put myself on autopilot, stripping out of my clothes and running a bath with lavender Epsom salt and some oils Sylvia bought me that I always forget to use.

I bring my glass of white wine, a book, and find an easy listening jazz Spotify playlist on my phone and drown out the sad, lonely thoughts in my head that are telling me to jump up, run across town to Beckham, and tell him I take it back.

———

"Top up or down?"

"Seriously? We can't take the Porsche 911 Carrera Cabriole out and *not* put the top down; it would be a sin." I smile and my dad claps, rubbing his hands together like a kid in a candy store.

"That's what I was hoping you'd say, but your stepmother always complains about the wind messing up her hair."

"Top will be down, but I get first dibs driving."

"Deal."

We pack our picnic basket and say goodbye to my brothers who whine and cry that they can't come with us. I climb into the driver's seat and navigate to Lake Shore Drive where I let her loose.

It feels magical to have the sun on my face and the wind whipping past us. I look over at my dad, who's smiling so wide his cheeks are covering half of his eyes.

"Mom would have liked this," I say loudly so he can hear me over the wind.

He reaches over and squeezes my knee, something he's done since I can remember. It's his little way of reassuring me.

While Mom and Dad didn't get along, my mom loved my dad's penchant for fast cars. She used to sneak me out to go drive his Porsche when I was little. It probably wasn't the safest thing for a toddler, but for twenty minutes or so, she and I would pretend to be off on some grand adventure together.

We make our way to Hollywood Beach north of the city to have our picnic. We lay out a blanket and I unpack the gourmet lunch Chantelle insisted on packing for us.

"Damn, when did picnics start including caviar and fig jam?" I hold up the two containers.

"That's Chantelle, always goes above and beyond."

"She also knows your expensive taste," I tease.

We eat for a bit, enjoying the cool breeze off the lake and watching a man and his dog playing Frisbee in the surf.

"So how are you feeling about work? I was very impressed with your work on the fraud situation with Pierce."

"Work is okay, it's work." I shrug. "I was actually a little worried if you even knew that I was the one who found it." I look up at him. "You just didn't seem too concerned about including me in the talks and meetings with Pierce to resolve it."

"I'm sorry, sweetie. It wasn't my intention to exclude you. You are an incredibly and exceptionally bright woman and I don't say that just because you're my daughter. I've told Beckham as much half a dozen times. I just screwed up honestly, no excuse. I can still be a little bullheaded about business sometimes and I think this was one of those situations."

"I appreciate you clarifying. I wanted to make you proud." I say it a little sheepishly, like I feel silly still trying to get my dad's approval as a twenty-five-year-old woman.

"You did—do! I am incredibly proud of you and to be able to call you my daughter. I'm serious, ask Beckham, I'm always singing your praises."

"Thanks."

"Speaking of him, any idea what's gotten into him lately?"

I take a bite of my baguette and shrug.

"He's been a real pain in the ass lately. Grumpy and pissed off about something. If he doesn't get it together soon, I'm canceling our golf game tomorrow."

"Hadn't noticed," I say around a mouthful of bread.

Of course I've noticed and of course I know what's going on with him... He's about to be a father to a very unplanned and unexpected baby.

"I, uh..." I wipe my face with my napkin and take a quick sip of my soda. "I had hoped to talk to you today about the job situation and the trust."

He looks at me, waiting for me to go on.

"I'm sorry, I'm really nervous." My voice catches in my throat and my dad reaches his hand out to me. "I want to establish my own nonprofit with part of the trust. I also want to donate a decent portion of it to at least a dozen different other organizations that I've worked with, and I'd also like to use some of it to invest in startups by people who don't have the capital or the connections." I say it all in one breath. "Oh, and the remainder I want to work with a financial advisor to invest for myself for my retirement and possible children someday."

I sit with my spine stiff, scared to move or look at my dad. His hand is still on mine and he slowly removes it.

"Why were you nervous?" he finally asks quietly.

"I know that you and I haven't always seen eye to eye about how Mom and I wanted to spend our money and time and like I said earlier, I want you to be proud of me but I can't..." I feel myself tearing up and I choke back the tears. "I can't not pursue my dreams and goals, Dad. I can't stay working in an industry that, even if I'm good at it, it sucks the life out of me. I need my soul fed; I want to feel inspired by what I do and give back."

There's no use fighting the tears any longer. It's a mix of everything I've been bottling up over the last few weeks, months, years even. I hang my head, the tears turning into sobs as my body aches with the release.

My dad doesn't say a word; he just pulls me into his arms and holds me while I let it all go. Beckham, anger, doubt, fear... my tears pull it from my body.

"Brontë, I do worry about you. I worry about your happiness and your heart; I worry about your ambitions and goals, but I never worry that you won't accomplish them. I worry that you'll be too scared to see your full potential. No matter what you choose, I'm your father, and I want you to be happy. I want you to be fulfilled. You and I aren't the same person and while I might give you my fatherly and unsolicited business advice, you don't have to take it for me to be proud of you... ever."

"You're not angry or disappointed?"

"Oh, no, honey. I hate that I made you feel that way. I know I'm blunt and often speak my mind way too freely—your stepmom tells me that often. I speak with passion and I can see how it would seem like it was my way or the highway. You've always been a free spirit, just like your mom. Truthfully, as much as I wanted you to work in my world so that we could work together, run Ramsay Consulting together someday, I don't want to see you giving up your dreams like your mother did. She would kill me if I let you do that."

"What do you mean? What dreams did Mom give up?"

"She was just like you. She dreamed of opening her own charity someday, probably something for animals. You know how your mom liked cats." We both laugh, remembering how Dad always joked that Mom *never met a stray.*

"I-I had no idea. I mean, she instilled in me my love of volunteering, but she said she loved accounting; she made it seem like her dream job. What happened?"

He points to himself. "Me. I ruined it. When I left, she had to go get a job that paid well and had benefits. She wanted to show you that she could do it on her own; she wanted to support you two. That's why she started the trust, to put the alimony and child support in it for you someday."

I feel my heart break for her. I had no idea.

"She didn't want you to know because she worried you would think it was your fault that she went back into finance." He grabs my hand again. "On the same vein of sharing secrets, something you don't know is your mother and I made up in the years leading up to her death."

I jerk my head up. "What?"

"She and I were good friends, always were better friends than spouses. She reached out and told me that she was dying and she wanted me to promise her that I would fix things with you, no matter the cost."

"Why didn't she tell me?"

"She was worried you'd be hurt or angry at her for forgiving me for what I did to you both. She said you weren't ready to forgive me yet and she didn't want to force you into it because she was dying."

I feel so confused and sad. So many things I'm finding out about my mom that I just wish I could sit and talk with her about.

"You know she still made me take her out in my Porsche with the top down just like we did today down Lake Shore. She'd smile and close her eyes, holding her hands up in the air like she was flying."

I watch as a single tear slides down my dad's face as he describes the scene. He looks out over the lake, and I know that he has so many unsaid things, so many unfinished memories with her... so many regrets.

"If you could do it all over or if you could have Mom back for one day, what would you say to her?"

He looks at me, then back to the water.

"I'd tell her I'm sorry. I'd tell her that she was an amazing woman who deserved the world and I failed her. I'd tell her that she raised an amazing woman and that she should be damn proud of who you are. I'd tell her all those little things I held back, all those times she looked nice or made me laugh or made me happy."

He scoots back and sits right beside me, sliding his arm around my shoulders and bringing me closer. I rest my head on his shoulder.

"I'm not a good example, Brontë, but one thing I can tell you, don't live life with regrets. Tell the person you love them. Say the thing you're too scared to say. Go after the goals and dreams you think you can't accomplish or don't deserve or can't make work because at the end of this life, you don't want to be left holding on to the *what-ifs*. They'll just be a pile of regret weighing you down."

I don't know what I expected today or how I expected our conversation to go, but it was nothing like this. I feel closer to my dad, more than ever. We pack up our lunch and take the final drive to Mom's grave just north of the city.

When we finally pull back into my dad's driveway and shut the car off, he reaches over and squeezes my knee again.

"Promise me something, B?"

"Yeah?"

"From here on out, let's be open and honest with each other, okay? Nothing will come between us ever again."

Chapter 20

Beckham

I stare down at the third tumbler of whiskey in my hand.

Rain pelts the windows of my living room as I slump down in my chair, looking out over the city. The lights look fuzzy from the droplets hitting the windows and running down the glass into each other.

I wonder where Brontë is. What she's doing. If she's smiling and laughing through the pain or if she's a complete wreck like me. Her words about getting a paternity test have been swimming through my mind all day.

I wish I had a father in a situation like this. One I could call and explain everything to. One who wouldn't judge or condemn but listen and offer me advice man to man, even if it's the kind of advice I don't want to hear.

The Elvis record I've had on repeat all night begins to skip and I walk over to change it, opting for Ray Charles' *Genius + Soul=Jazz* album.

My phone buzzes in my pocket and I pull it out to see that my lawyer, Alton Feldstein, is calling me. I slide the answer button across the screen.

"Hello?"

"Hey, Beckham. Sorry to call so late but I wanted to let you know that we got the approval to move forward with purchasing the lot next to the Archer Foundation. Figured you'd want to hear the good news as soon as possible."

"Thanks, Alt, appreciate the update." I try to sound as sober as possible but my tongue feels heavy in my mouth. It is good news. I've been looking to acquire an empty parking lot next to the foundation for about a year now with hopes to expand.

"You okay, buddy? Sound a little down and out."

"Yeah, I'm okay," I lie.

I've known Alton since undergrad. We were both members of the rowing team at Yale and when he went to law school and I went to grad school, we kept in touch and remained friends over the years. The moment he passed the bar and opened his law firm, I was his first client. Now his firm is the largest in Chicago and one of the most sought-after for new graduates to get their foot in the door.

"I've known you a long time, man. Who is she?"

I laugh. "You bastard, how the hell do you always know?"

"I'm a lawyer; I read people for a living."

"I thought you scammed people for a living," I tease.

"Want me to stop by and help you finish that bottle of whiskey you're probably already halfway through? I'm still at the office, about to leave."

"Sure," I say, leaning one hand against a window, "why not."

Not even fifteen minutes later, Alt has a glass in his hand and is sitting in the chair beside me as we both look out the window.

"You always have the best liquor. Hannah always insists on the organic, non-GMO bullshit that tastes like ass"—he takes a long sip, savoring the taste—"and not in a good way."

I laugh and shake my head. Hannah, his wife, is a decade younger than us and she is always on him about his health, but it's for the sake of their two children and the fact, in her words, *she doesn't want him dying early.*

"You're an old man now. She's gotta make sure you're around long enough since she's going to outlive you anyway."

"She is an amazing woman." He sighs, kicking his feet out in front of him. "She keeps me young, keeps me on my toes. God knows I don't deserve her; I don't know how I got so lucky."

"How are the kids?"

"Good. Josh just started middle school last month. The boy is whip-smart, loves science. And Elle is already running her fourth-grade class the second she walked in there. Just like her mother." He laughs, shaking his head. "She's going to give me a run for my money; I can already feel it, and everyone else does too. She'll be running my firm someday."

"Sounds like life is good then." I can't hide the pathetic jealousy in my voice. I sound like the depressed Debbie Downer friend over here.

"Okay, we covered me. So I'll ask again." He looks over at me. "Who is *she*?"

I swirl the whiskey around in my tumbler, bringing it to my lips and knocking back the final mouthful.

"She's my best friend's daughter. Jonas Ramsay." I stare straight ahead as I say it, not even wanting to hold back or hide it anymore.

He laughs, then looks at me, his smile falling as he realizes I'm not joking.

"Holy shit, you're serious?"

"Yup."

He whistles and shakes his head. "I did not see that coming. How? Does he know?"

"You think I'd be sitting here with you if he knew?" I look over at him. "It's a long story but he asked me to hire her and I did. She's so smart, extremely driven, just graduated from Northwestern actually with her master's in forensic accounting. She found the fraud with that Pierce deal."

"No shit? She looking to work for a law firm? I could use someone like that."

"Nah, she's too good for all this shit we do for a living. She's starting a nonprofit to help children. Wants to invest in startups and volunteer."

"So she's Mother Theresa, okay. Where's the flaw?"

"I just told you, her father." I laugh and stand up to walk over to the window. "I feel like—no, I am an asshole. I knew better for sure. No way in hell it was ever going to end but like it did."

"So it's over?"

I nod, finally able to admit it to myself.

"And Jonas still doesn't know?"

"No."

"Why did it end?"

"Because I'm a fucking moron." He laughs and it makes me laugh. "Jonas wasn't in her life for over a decade. They've both worked hard to repair that relationship and by the way she talked, it seemed like a big part of her attraction to me was that it was forbidden. Like the fact that she was doing something behind her dad's back turned her on and I can't deny that it wasn't part of the draw for me too, initially."

"Ah, but somehow feelings got involved?"

"Yup. Don't get me wrong, it was a huge ego boost for me to have a twenty-four-year-old woman look at me the way she did, but it was more than that. I'm about to be forty-seven. I get that it looks like some midlife crisis bullshit but—" I let out a huge puff of air, finally saying the words out loud that I've felt for some time. "I'm in love with her."

"Whoa, so serious feelings then." He stands up and walks up beside me. "I know you're not looking for advice, but if the only thing standing between you two and happiness is her father, why not at least talk to the man? We both know Jonas has a wife half his age so he can't pull that shit."

"He didn't go after his best friend's daughter; that's where the issue will lie, or at least the more minor issue at hand."

"What else aren't you telling me?"

"It's a dumpster fire."

"Hit me," he says, tossing back the rest of his drink.

"Venus Davenport," I say and he looks over at me, well aware of my past with her. "She's pregnant and she says it's mine."

"Well, smack my ass and call me Judy. I didn't think this situation could get more complicated, but goddamn, Beckham."

"I know." I hang my head. "The crazy part is, I'm not—how do I say this without sounding like a hopeful piece of shit... I'm not positive the baby is mine."

"You're doing a paternity test then right?"

I shrug. "Brontë said I should, but Venus took her birth control out when we were together the last few weeks and didn't tell me. I just think if I do it and it turns out she is my daughter, I'll constantly feel awful about denying my own child. Not to mention, I know Venus and she'll run to daddy the second that court-ordered paternity test hits her hands. The last thing I need or want is Miles Davenport screaming at me about how I knocked up his baby girl and now I'm trying to deny it. He's never been fond of me, and I know he'd go spread that rumor around town so even if the baby turns out to not be mine, the damage will be done."

I explain to him how the timeline worked and how I found out.

"It's not that I don't want kids at all anymore. For most of my life I didn't, but with Brontë, she makes me want all those things I never gave a second thought to. And now, it's all gone to shit, and I don't know what to do."

"So your plan is to just bend over and take it? Where the fuck has the Beckham Archer gone that I've known for the last twenty-five years? Because this sure as hell isn't him."

I crook an eyebrow over at my lawyer.

"This isn't the kind of thing you just say well, I guess I'll just let it happen to me and figure it out later. What the hell, man?"

I know he's right. I'm the last person on this planet who would ever let someone manipulate me or pull the wool over my eyes, but I just feel so defeated after losing Brontë.

"I guess it's a broken heart talking. She told me there's no chance of us making things work and it just sucked the wind out of my sails. I've never felt this way before, Alt." I turn to pour myself another glass of whiskey and he reaches out to stop me.

"I'm getting a court-ordered paternity test. I'll have the forms completed and submitted to court tomorrow. Once they're processed, I'll go with you if you want, to serve Venus at her doorstep. You're not going down without a fight, Beckham."

I feel a burst of fight inside me rear its head.

"And then, when it comes out that she's lying, you're going to march your ass over to Brontë's house and tell that woman how you feel and make things right because this"—he wags his hand up and down my disheveled appearance—"isn't a good look on you."

I can't fight the smile that pulls at my lips.

"I was just trying to get through my depressed phase since it all just went down over the last few days, but thanks for lighting a fire under my ass, Alt." I reach out and grab his shoulder. "Now get home to your family so I can go back to drinking and sulking in peace."

THREE DAYS LATER...

I stare down at the summons in my hand from the court, ordering both Venus and I to submit to a blood-drawn DNA test to establish paternity.

"Do you want me to go with you?"

"No. I don't want to embarrass her or make her feel ganged up on. I want to handle this as civil as possible in the hope that it stays between me and her."

"You don't want her to be embarrassed? Beckham, this woman is a conniving liar. She deserves to be and *should* be embarrassed by this."

"Alt, I know you've never cared for Venus, but she'll feel ambushed and that will start a war."

"Fine," he says, backing away with his hands raised. "I'll be here if you need backup."

"Thanks," I say, leaving his office and pulling out my phone to send a text to Venus.

Me: *Hey, are you around? Was hoping I could stop by and talk to you if possible? I'd like to see you.*

I hate that I know she'll drop anything if I tell her I want to see her, but I can't let her get suspicious that I'm about to serve her with papers or she'll call her lawyer or worse, her father.

I walk out to my car and before I can even unlock it, she responds.

Venus: *Hey, yeah, I just got home. Come on by. Can't wait to see you.*

She signs off with a kissing face emoji. I slide behind the wheel and head over to her house in the Gold Coast.

"Hey." Her voice is flirty and airy; clearly, she assumes I'm here to talk about *us.* "You look handsome." She bats her eyelashes at me and reaches out to run her hand down my arm.

"Venus," I say warmly but it feels forced because it is. "I won't take up much of your time," I say, stepping inside as she closes the door behind me.

"I was just over at this designer baby boutique, working with a stylist to design the baby's nursery and figure out the color scheme of the wardrobe once she's here."

"You hired a stylist for baby clothes?"

"Not just the clothes, the crib and the decor. I really want to go for a neutral palette, like nudes and whites."

What the fuck? For a baby?

I don't have time to get into how weird and frankly depressing that sounds to dress a baby in nudes so I just smile and then get on with it.

"Venus, this isn't a social call and you're not going to like what I'm about to say, but at this point in our relationship or whatever the hell this is, I don't really give a fuck." I pull the court order from inside my jacket and hold it out to her. "This is a summons for both of us to submit to a DNA test to determine paternity."

The fake smile on her face falls instantly. If she could show emotion through her Botox, I'm sure her eyebrows would be scowling at me right now.

"Are you serious?"

"Read it."

She flips it open, scanning the paper before hauling off and hitting me in the chest.

"You bastard!"

I catch her fists and hold her in place, walking her backward till we reach a chair in the elaborate entryway of her house.

"Sit down and calm down. This isn't good for the baby." She obeys, her bottom lip pooching out like she's about to start crying, but I'm not falling for her little dramatic displays anymore. For years she pulled that shit on me to get her way.

"This is how this is going to play out, Venus. You have two options here. You can fight this, get your father and lawyer involved, but that is a summons and you have exactly three days to respond to it and submit your DNA. Or you can tell me the truth because I find it strange that if you honestly believed that I'm the father of your child, you'd be angry at me for showing up with this suit. In fact, if it were me and someone wanted proof, I'd laugh when they showed up with a summons like this because I'd know that when those results came back, *they* would be the one looking like a fool and not me."

Her bottom lip quivers and tears start to fall down her cheeks.

"Why can't you just love me?" she cries, looking up at me.

"Because that's not how life works, Venus. You can't force someone into loving you. You can't trick and manipulate them into it because that's not fair and it's not real. Is that what you want? A love that you forced me into? A relationship with someone who's in love with someone else?"

She wipes away her tears with the back of her hand, gasping as she shakes her head no.

I crouch down in front of her. "I'm not trying to be mean. I don't understand why you did this, but we both know that the truth will come out eventually and paternity case results are public. Whatever situation you got yourself into, you're extremely wealthy and you come from one of the most powerful families in Chicago, why did you think this was your only way out?"

She sniffs, hiccuping, and I walk to her bar around the corner to grab a bottle of water for her. I open it and hand it to her. She drinks down about half of it, finally gaining her composure.

"I wanted it to be yours," she says softly, not looking at me. "I really did love you; I still do. I wanted a family with you and I think I made myself believe that if I got pregnant, you'd realize you wanted it too and we'd figure it out together."

"I understand, but that's not my daughter, is it?"

She fiddles with the bottle, biting her bottom lip. I can see it turning white around the edges of her teeth before she shakes her head no.

"No." It's barely a whisper but it's there.

Relief washes over me. I stand up and pace the floor, trying to make sense of this. I may not have ever loved Venus like she loved me and we may have had an at times toxic relationship but this—I never imagined she'd do something like this.

"Whose is it?" She just shakes her head and starts to cry again. "Venus," I say sternly, "I need you to tell me who the father is and why he doesn't know."

"It's Mitchell."

"Reardon? Mitchell Reardon?" She nods her head. "You gotta be fucking kidding me." I laugh because I don't know what else to do. "So my assumptions about you two were true when we were together?"

She nods her head again.

"So you and he had an affair when we were together. Why not just actually be with him? Why stay with me and cheat?"

"I didn't want to be with him, I just... He showed me attention when you were pulling away and it just happened. I don't know. It wasn't an affair; it was like two times and he wanted more, but I told him I was in love with you." She flops her arms dramatically, like she's a bratty teenager trying to get out of trouble.

"And why does he not know that he's going to be a father?"

"He does know. He doesn't want anything to do with me or the baby."

"He what?" That instantly gets my blood boiling. "He got you pregnant, knows it, and told you he doesn't want anything to do with you now after being a complete dipshit to me for years because he wanted you?"

"Yes."

"That arrogant, waste of—" I turn and start toward her front door.

"Wait, where are you going?"

"I'm going to find that piece of shit and make him take responsibility."

I slam her door behind me and climb behind the wheel, pulling out into traffic and heading straight for Davenport Enterprises.

I march through the lobby, straight to the elevator, punching the button for the executive floor. I don't stop for any pleasantries; I don't even acknowledge Mitchell's secretary who jumps out of her chair and chases after me down the hallway toward his office.

"Mr. Archer, he's in a meeting!" she says in a high-pitched voice.

I turn the handle on his door and fling it open. It hits the doorstop and bounces back.

"What the fu—"

I don't give him time to finish his statement before I'm grabbing him by the tie and dragging him around his desk and down the hall toward Miles Davenport's office.

"Get the fuck off me!" he shouts, attempting to get away, but I wrap the tie around my fist tighter as several people gather in the hallway to see what the commotion is.

"Oh dear!" Marsha, Miles Davenport's assistant, says as I walk right past her and straight into Miles' office.

He's on the phone, but he stops mid-sentence, his mouth hanging open as I deposit Mitchell on the floor of his office.

"What is the meaning of all this?" He stands up and looks at me, then Mitchell, his thin, sallow face growing redder by the second.

"This piece of shit is the father of your granddaughter that Venus is carrying." I point down at a sweating, red-faced Mitchell in a crumpled mess on the floor.

"Sir, no, I can explain," he says, scrambling to get up, but I step on the tip of his tie that's resting on the floor and it jerks him back down.

"Your daughter made me believe the baby was mine. She told me it was mine, but now I know the truth. It's Mitchell's and according to Venus, he wants nothing to do with her or the baby."

Miles' eyes go from wide and shocked to seething slits as he turns his venom toward Mitchell.

"Is this true?" he spits out.

I don't wait around for an answer from Mitchell. I leave him groveling on the floor and march my way back out of the office to my car where I finally breathe a sigh of relief that this is done. But the relief doesn't last for long because I know that there's one other thing I need to take care of and it might ruin everything but I have to take the risk.

I drive to my office, half the day already gone, but ready to get back to some sort of normalcy.

I hold my breath as the elevator doors open and I walk past Brontë's desk, but she isn't there. I check the time. I guess she could have taken an early lunch, but then I notice her plant is gone. Maybe she took it to the break room to water it, I think to myself as I walk into my office and sink down into my chair. That's when I see it. A typed-out resignation letter.

Mr. Archer,

Apologies for not doing this in person but considering the circumstances, I couldn't bring myself to face you. I also hope that due to the circumstances, you will forgive my lack of professionalism in not offering a two-week notice.

Please consider this my immediate resignation from Archer Financial. Thank you for your kindness, mentorship, and the opportunity you provided me to work here. I have greatly appreciated it and will continue to only wish you the best.

Sincerely,

Brontë

Chapter 21

Brontë

I took the coward's way out, I know that.

My stomach is in knots as I leave Archer Financial. I know I can't avoid seeing Beckham for the rest of my life, especially with his role in my father's life, but right now, it's still too raw, too fresh.

I do hope that someday we can be friends. I like having him in my life. I appreciate his honesty and guidance, his advice. I still want to volunteer at the Archer Foundation as well, but right now, I just need time to heal. Time to myself to focus on building my nonprofit and finding some small companies to invest in.

I spend the rest of the afternoon winding my way around the city. I end up at the lakefront, one of my favorite spots. I find myself walking toward the Ferris wheel at Navy Pier. I buy a ticket and get in a bucket by myself, looking out over the lake as it rises, the sun dancing like diamonds on the water.

I try not to, but I can't keep myself from remembering the brief moments Beckham and I spent up here. I wonder if by chance, I somehow ended up in the same bucket we were in that night. I remember the way he looked at me, like his eyes were trying to warn me when he told me not to pull at that thread regarding *us*.

I should have listened to him. I should have realized that I was far too young, far too naive to think I could keep my feelings and emotions out of it. I sit back, my chin beginning to quiver as the floodgates open and I release all the pent-up hurt that I've been keeping locked away.

I allow myself to cry it out, hoping it's the cathartic release I need to move on, but I have very little hope that's actually the case.

By the time I leave the pier, it's going on five p.m. I told my dad yesterday that I would come by for dinner tonight. The boys have been begging me to come over so they can show me how big Lemon and Lime, their kittens, are getting.

I see a text from Sylvia when I check the time.

Sylvia: *Hey, girl. Been thinking about you. Everything okay? We haven't heard from you in a while. Let us know if you're down for brunch or something this weekend. Love you!*

I feel guilty. I've completely neglected them lately. I've been so wrapped up in my own drama. But also, I've been afraid to be around them because they'll see through me pretending I'm okay in an instant. I'm just not ready to rehash everything by telling them all the details. I type out a simple response and make my way to my parents' house.

Me: *Ugh, I know I've been an awful friend. I'm so sorry! Been crazy busy, got a lot to fill you ladies in on. Definitely down for brunch this weekend. Mimosas on me! XO.*

———

"COME WITH ME!" JENSON GRABS MY HAND AND PULLS ME through the entryway toward the staircase. "Lemon, Lemon likes to play with this ball and when I frow it he says eeeeyyyyoooowwww!" He gives me his best cat impression and it makes me laugh.

"Jenson, sweetie, let her get settled for a moment." Chantelle gives me the mom look and he sticks out his lower lip.

"Ooookay."

"It's okay. We'll go up and see the kitties in just a second, okay?" He nods and Silas runs over to give me a hug.

"Boys, you get fifteen minutes to play with the cats before we need to wash up for dinner."

"Moooom, that's like barely enough time," Silas groans.

"You can play after, you know that, but dinner first." She embraces me. "Hey, Brontë, you okay?" She looks at me suspiciously and I shrug.

"Been better."

She looks over her shoulder as my dad approaches. *We'll talk later,* she mouths to me as she steps aside, my dad's outstretched arms embracing me.

"Hey, kiddo, how are you doing?"

"Hey, Dad. I'm good."

"You sure?" He pulls back to look at me. "You're looking a little thin and tired."

"Jonas." Chantelle smacks his arm and rolls her eyes. "Man has such a way with women."

"She's my daughter, I'm worried," he says, chasing her down and pinching her butt, making her squeal. He catches her, spinning her around and dipping her before planting a big kiss on her lips.

"Grosss!" Jenson yells and Silas shrieks and covers his eyes.

It makes me smile, knowing my dad is happy and that the boys are getting a good example of love and what marriage and a home should be like.

"Okay, boys, let's go see some citrus," I say, taking a hand from each of them.

"What's citrus?" Jenson asks.

"That's what lemons and limes are, Jenson; they're citrus fruits."

"No, they're not, they're kitties!" He laughs as we climb the stairs to go play with the kittens for a few moments before dinner.

After dinner my dad and I head to his study to share a glass of whiskey, or rather, he drinks his whiskey and after a single sip, I simply swirl mine around in the tumbler till he drinks it as well.

"So, I have made a decision." I feel my shoulders tensing. I know my dad said I can be more open with him but I'm still nervous. "I quit working for Be—Mr. Archer."

"Oh? Did something happen?" He sits up, immediately into dad mode.

"No." I wave my hands. "I just know that it's not what I'm meant to do. After we had our talk the other day and you mentioned regrets, I just realized I was wasting valuable time. I've started developing my business plan for my nonprofit and I've found two really sound startups I want to invest in. I'd love your input on them, if you have time?"

"You are just like your mother." He smiles and it warms my heart. "She was a go-getter. That woman decided something and"—he claps his hands—"bam, she was doing it. I'm proud of you, sweetheart. And I'm not just saying that because of our talk about it. I mean it."

"Thanks, Dad. Seriously, that means a lot."

"I'm happy to introduce you to my finance guy; he'll be a real asset as you start planning things out, budgeting, and he'll help you with your own investments." He opens a drawer and pulls out a stack of business cards, shuffling through them till he finds the one he's looking for. "Here, this is him," he says, reaching to hand it to me.

"You're so old-school." I smile, sliding the business card into my pocket. "You know you can share his contact information to me via text."

"Bah, you millennials." He winks at me and takes a sip of his whiskey.

"Can I show you the startups I'm looking at?"

"Absolutely." He stands and drags his chair closer to me as I pull them up on my phone and tell him about them.

"You've got an eye, you know. A real aptitude for this stuff."

I shrug. "You think so?"

"I know so. That's why I say you're like your mother. She might not have loved the finance or business world either, but when she saw a potential, she was always right. You're wise beyond your years, B.

217

Don't doubt your gut or your decision-making. Listen to that intuition, it's God-given." He points to his head.

"Yeah, I think I'm still trying to find that confidence in myself," I say as I look down at my tumbler, still feeling like I didn't do the right thing by walking away from Beckham before we even got the chance.

"Are you sure you're okay, sweetie?" My dad looks over at me with concern.

"Yeah, I will be." I raise my glass and clink it to his, taking a small sip of the whiskey, instantly taking me back to when I shared a glass with Beckham.

"Knock, knock," Chantelle says as she opens the study door. "Do you mind if I steal Brontë for an ice cream outing? The boys are begging for me to take them over to Gerald's for a lemon custard."

"Not at all." My dad smiles as he looks down at his phone. "Perfect timing actually. Beckham just hit me up to join him for a drink. You ladies enjoy custard with the boys, and I promise, I won't be out too late." He winks at Chantelle, kissing her softly before giving me a hug and a kiss on the forehead.

"Come on," Chantelle says, looping her arm through my elbow as we walk out of his office.

We walk the block over to Gerald's and the boys get their custard. They're busy eating, Silas explaining to Jenson that *technically* custard is different than ice cream. Jenson seems completely confused and shrugs, shoveling a big bite of the creamy treat into his mouth and doing a little happy dance.

"You don't seem like yourself, are you okay?" Chantelle rubs my back as we sit on a bench a few feet away from the boys.

"I ended things with him," I say, my head hanging down as I kick at some loose gravel. "And I quit working for him."

"When?" She half gasps. "Did you—did he not feel the same?"

I shrug. "I didn't ask him. I put my resignation letter on his desk this morning. I'm not giving two weeks." I feel tears start to well up. "I can't do it. I can't see him every day and put on a fake smile like I'm happy."

"Oh, sweetie, why didn't you tell him?"

I don't know how to answer that. I don't want to tell her about Venus and the baby. It doesn't feel like it's my business to tell.

"I guess I just realized it wasn't worth it. After our conversation I just decided it was easier for me to walk away than bring all this chaos into everyone's lives."

"Are you sure? Maybe you just need time away from each other to realize what you want."

"Maybe, who knows." I feel like a shell of myself. My emotions stunted. "I think I realized that I do want the things that he can't offer me. I want what you have, a family and a husband but"—my lip trembles and a few tears begin to fall—"the shit thing is, I want it with him."

I hang my head in my hands, pressing the heels of my palms into my eyes to try and stop the tears. I really don't want Jenson and Silas to see me like this. Thankfully, they're still too preoccupied with their custard to notice.

"You deserve happiness, Brontë. I hope you know that. Maybe he wants those things with you too?" I look over at her and see real concern in her eyes.

"I don't think so."

"Did he fight for you? Ask you to stay?"

"Kind of, yes. He begged me not to go the night things kind of went to shit, then asked me later if we could ever work it out, get back together." She looks at me questioningly. "I said no. I did tell him when we last spoke that I loved him, but I left it at that. He didn't say he felt the same way so I walked away. I know that if I had stayed, I would have talked myself into settling for what we had been doing. I can't be another woman who stays too long, trying to convince myself that he'll change his mind for me."

"I understand." She wraps her arms around me and I lean my head against her shoulder. "Oh, Brontë, my heart hurts for you. I feel silly that I told you to tell him, to put your heart on the line. I truly believed—" Her words trail off and we sit in silence for several minutes.

"I think I'm going to head home. I'm exhausted. Tell my dad I said good night when he gets back?"

"Of course. Boys," she says, turning to her sons, "your sister is heading home so come tell her good night."

The boys run over, wrapping their stick arms around me. I squat down and hug them both so tight, holding on a little longer than normal.

"I love you boys so much," I say, planting a kiss on each of their cheeks before they run back over to finish their dessert.

Chantelle gives me a warm hug, then pulls back to look at me.

"Make sure you take care of yourself, B. I'm here if you need to talk or hang by the pool or cry into some wine." She smiles and I offer my attempt at one. "And if you two ever do decide to work things out, just know that I'll have your back. I'll stand with you when you go to speak to your father. Just talk to him. What can it hurt to ask?"

Her eyes search mine and I thank her, but I don't promise her that I'll ask him because I don't think it's something I can do. Maybe it's my ego, maybe it's my immaturity, but the thought of asking a man I love to love me back and have a life and family with me only to hear that no, he doesn't want those things with me or doesn't feel that way, sounds like absolute, soul-crushing pain.

When I leave, I take the long way home, winding my way down streets I never take. I don't want to go home. I'm scared to sit alone in my house for fear that I will call him and beg him for another chance.

I walk for an hour. My entire body aches from the tension, lack of sleep, and the amount of pavement I've walked today. I finally round the corner to my building. The sun has completely set and the street-lights have come on. I take the final steps to my building, my head down as I pull my phone from my pocket to check the time when I see seventeen missed calls from my father. I panic. I didn't realize my phone was on silent this entire time. I worry something happened to

Chantelle and the boys before they made it back home. I slide my phone open to see a text from my father.

Dad: *Call me now!*

My chest clenches as my thumb moves to the call button, but a voice startles me. I look up and sitting on the steps of my building is Beckham. Disheveled, hair a mess, suit coat in hand.

"I told him."

I blink several times, trying to make sense of everything that's happening right now. I shake my head as if that will help me understand, my phone screen lighting up again as my father calls for the eighteenth time.

"Told who?" I ask, not putting it together.

"Your father. I told him about us. I told him everything."

My mouth falls open, and a cold flush rushes over my body.

"What? Why? Is this—are you trying to get back at me for quitting?" I hate that that's where my mind goes, but I never thought for one second that he would tell him.

That's when I see it, the pain in his eyes. "You think I would do that to you?" He pushes up from the stairs as he steps toward me, his hands coming to cup my face as he looks down at me.

"Why?" I ask again, my voice shaking.

"Because I'm in love with you, Brontë, and I refuse to lose you."

Chapter 22

Beckham

"Say something, anything," I plead, my eyes searching her face for some sort of reaction. She stares at me, blinking, her face as pale as the moon in the shadow of the building.

Finally, she looks down at the phone in her hand that's still glowing, her father's name flashing on the screen.

"Are you going to answer it?"

She shakes her head and steps around me toward the stairs.

"No, I can't even think straight."

I follow behind her. "Can I come up?"

"Yes, you have a lot of explaining to do." She holds the door open as she walks inside.

The elevator ride is silent. She stares at the floor, clutching the railing so tight her knuckles are white.

"You don't look okay, Brontë." I reach out to tilt her chin upward to look at me, but she jerks her head away just as the doors open. She steps into the hallway and I follow behind her till she unlocks her door and we step inside.

"Hey." I grab her arm. "Look at me." She hesitates and I pull her toward me. "I said look at me, Brontë." My tone is harsh and commanding, but I don't care.

"You had no right," she says, glaring at me. "Things were going well with my father! I opened up to him about my life, my plans for the trust. I told him I quit your company and he was supportive!" Her tears are already flowing in rivulets down her cheeks, her face red with anger. "You had no right!" she screams again as she pounds against my chest.

I wrap my arms around her, holding her against me as sobs rack her body.

"I'm sorry you're hurting and scared but I'm not sorry I told him. You're mine."

She pushes away from me, wiping furiously at her eyes.

"I'm not yours. You don't want the same things as me. A life with you would mean what? That I'm just a hot fuck when you need a release?"

"Don't!" I shout, pointing my finger. "Don't you fucking dare reduce us to that. You know it's more than that; I saw it in your eyes that night we ma—" I swallow down my nerves. "That night we made love. I saw the way you looked at me. You saw *me* that night; you saw through all the bullshit and the fear."

"You have a baby on the way with someone else," she cries. "How am I supposed to sit by, wanting that with you, but you don't want it with me? You know how hard it is to watch that? To see the dream you had with someone play out, but it's not with you?"

"She's not mine," I say, stepping toward her, realizing I didn't tell her. How could I have let her continue thinking this? "She's not mine," I repeat.

"What?"

"I got a court order for a DNA test and when I went to her to serve her the summons, she fell apart and confessed everything."

"I don't understand."

"She lied; you were right. She cheated on me with a man that I knew about, that I'd confronted her about and she denied anything ever happened between them. When he found out she was pregnant, he bailed, wanted nothing to do with her."

"Oh my God." She sinks down on the ottoman behind her and I crouch down at her feet.

"I confronted him, took him to her father because he works at his company actually. It's done, Brontë." I reach out and clasp her hands in mine. "I want those things too, with you, only you." Her eyes rise to meet mine. "I never thought I'd meet someone who made me want marriage and children, but it's all I think about anymore. You as my wife. You carrying our child."

She stands up and begins to pace.

"Why couldn't you have told me this before?"

"I didn't think you wanted those things. I didn't think you wanted a relationship with me."

"So why now? Why go and blow up my life and tell my father after we've worked so hard to repair things between us?"

"Because you left me!" I shout. "You told me you loved me. I realized that I couldn't lose you; I had to fight for you. I fucked up, Brontë. Royally. I realize that but I'm not going to just walk out of your life because you're too scared to try and make this work. I'll fight for the both of us if I have to."

"What did he say when you told him?"

"He's angry. He shouted, threatened me."

"Shit," she mutters, beginning to pace again. "Is he coming over here?"

"I don't know."

She grabs her phone and taps around on it, then tosses it on a nearby chair. "My stepmom texted and said she's keeping him home. She knows, knew about us, before you told him."

"She knew? You told her?"

She shakes her head. "She picked up on it at my birthday party actually. She showed up at my house and told me it wasn't a good idea, but then after we talked, she said that if it was real, if there were feelings involved, we owed my father a conversation before we pursued something. Guess she was right."

I can't stand it any longer. I walk over to her and grab her, wrapping my hand around the back of her neck and bringing her mouth to mine. I kiss her deeply and I'm a little surprised at first when she reciprocates. Her tongue demands entrance to my mouth, but then she steps back.

"Do you still love me?" I ask, unsure what I'm going to hear, but she doesn't hesitate.

"Yes."

"But you're angry with me?"

She nods. "Yes."

"Then take it out on me." She looks confused. "One area we've had no problem communicating is with our bodies, so take it out on me. Fuck it out of me."

She opens her mouth to say something, then closes it again. I step closer to her, reaching out to make her look at me.

"When do you feel most secure with me? When do you let all your concerns and thoughts go?" I run my hand through her hair, settling it around her waist as I pull her back toward me to plant a kiss on the corner of her mouth. "When do you feel most alive? Completely lost in pleasure that all you can feel is what's happening to you?"

"I don't know how to start." She looks at me timidly and I know what she's asking; she wants me to take control.

"Take off your shirt," I command as I reach for the buttons on my own and start to undo them. She watches my fingers and I tip her chin upward. "Don't make me tell you again, Brontë."

She reaches down to the hem of her shirt and pulls it over her head, her tits bouncing with the movement. I stare at them as I pull my own shirt down my arms and toss it on the chair next to me. I reach for her arm, pulling her toward me forcefully and reaching around her to remove her bra.

"Don't be timid on me now, sweetheart. Be that naughty little tease I've witnessed before. Remember the other day when you came into my office, begging for my cock?"

"Stop being so bossy all the time." Her eyes narrow and she reaches down to slide her jeans and panties down her thighs.

I laugh. "You like it when I'm bossy. You like it when I tell you to get on your knees and be a good little slut for me." My belt is undone, my zipper down when she reaches her hands out and shoves me backward, hard. I stumble, falling back onto the couch as she follows me, climbing onto my lap.

"I'm in charge tonight." She grabs a handful of my hair and yanks on it as I feel her warm, wet pussy start to grind against my crotch. She slams her mouth against mine, her hand reaching down inside my pants to grip my cock and free it.

I moan into her mouth as she slides her hand up and down my length, her thumb brushing against the underside of my tip. She raises up on her knees, positioning me at her entrance before inching herself down the tiniest amount.

"Are you sure you're ready?" I grip her hips as she squeezes her eyes shut and slides down an inch more. "Baby, let me get you ready." I still her movements but she pulls on my hair harder.

"Just shut up and fuck me."

"Look at me." Her eyes dart to mine as I grip her hips. "This is going to hurt but you asked for it." I push her down my length, a strangled scream coming from her throat as I pick her up and repeat the process. It's tight at first, her body resisting me, but after a few times, I feel her wetness build as the movements grow easier.

"Is that what you wanted? You wanted me to force my way inside your tight little cunt, stretching you with my big cock?"

"Yes," she moans, her head falling back as she drags her nails down my chest. She rides me, sliding herself up and down as my hands grip her waist. Her tits bounce with the movement and I lean forward, going back and forth between each one, biting, sucking, licking her nipples.

"Harder," she says as I bite down and I oblige. She hisses through the pain and I release it, repeating the process on the other one.

"You want it rough, sweetheart?" She nods, unable to form words as her heavy-lidded eyes roll back in her head.

"Do you trust me?"

"Yes."

I move my hand from her hip to her throat, gripping her tightly as I force her down onto my cock harder. My thumb swirls circles around her clit, her body tensing, her groans strangled as I tighten my grip and lift my hips up as I bring her down.

"I—I'm comi—" She falls apart, not able to finish the statement.

I stand up, working my pants down my thighs before turning around to put her on her knees on the couch.

"Grab the back," I say, straining to maintain composure as I sink deep into her pussy from behind. I put my knee on the cushion next to hers for leverage, grabbing her shoulder and forcing her back onto me as I thrust forward. The sounds of our skin slapping against each other fill the room as I struggle to hold back.

I feel like an animal, raw and visceral, marking her, devouring her. I'm so close. I pull back and slide into her one more time before flipping her back over so she's staring up at me.

"Open your mouth!" I demand as I stroke myself two more times before I'm spilling my cum down her throat. It overflows her lips, dripping down to her breasts.

I blink rapidly, the room spinning with my release. We both pant, staring at each other as we try to catch our breath.

"Are you okay?" I ask as she wipes her mouth, looking down at my release marking her skin. She looks up at me, a naughty little smile on her lips as she nods her head.

"Fuck me, you look good like that." I reach down and cup her breast. "I don't give a fuck what your daddy says; you're mine and I'm never giving you up."

I lean against Brontë's headboard, her body half on mine after a few hours of makeup sex. After the first round in the living room, I brought her back to the bedroom where I spent time kissing every inch of her before making passionate love to her a few times.

"Oh." She winces as she stretches against me.

"Are you sore?"

She nods. "In the most delicious way."

"I suppose we should talk about when we're going to go face your father?"

She sits up, pulling the sheet against her body as she leans against the headboard next to me.

"Tomorrow?"

"Better get it over with."

"What are we going to say?" She looks at me with concern on her face.

"I'm going to tell him the same thing I told him earlier tonight, which is that I love you and I want you to be my wife."

She sits up, her eyes big and round. "You told him you want to marry me?"

I tuck her hair behind her ear. "I did. Does that scare you?"

"No," she says calmly and confidently. "I want you to be my husband."

"I like the sound of that." I smile lazily at her. "I think we should celebrate this little revelation."

"Yeah? How so?"

"Well, I would love nothing more than to have you swing this delicious thigh over my body and straddle my face so I can bury my face in your pussy."

She blushes and giggles, biting her bottom lip as she gets a devious look on her face.

"I will, but under one condition, Mr. Archer." I crook an eyebrow at her. "Beg."

I laugh and pull her toward me, kissing her.

"Please, soon-to-be Mrs. Archer. Sit this sweet"—I kiss her neck, sliding my hand down her body to slip my finger inside her—"wet"—I kiss her breast—"mouthwatering"—I pump my finger so slowly in and out of her, her eyes growing heavy with need—"pussy on my lips."

Chapter 23

Brontë

One year later...

"The Nadine Spencer Foundation is dedicated to serving the needs of the community through offering classes on business and finance and continuing education courses to young entrepreneurs. We also provide a wide network of connections and investors as well as dozens of scholarships, grants, and resources to help individuals fulfill their dreams and goals of bringing their business to life and to the market." I look around at the large group that has gathered on the steps of my foundation, named after my amazing mother. "And to each of you who believed in this journey and donated, I can't thank you enough for your support and action."

"I want to thank my father, Jonas Ramsay." I smile over at him as I give the keynote speech at the opening of my nonprofit. His eyes are filled with tears as he smiles back at me. "For believing in me and my mother's vision to help our community and give back in any way that we can. You have been so supportive and offered me invaluable advice in this journey. Also, thank you to my stepmom Chantelle and my amazing little brothers Silas and Jenson for being patient with me and allowing me to steal so much of Jonas' time away from you."

Beg For It

The crowd laughs and I turn my gaze to Beckham who's staring back at me in awe.

"And lastly, thank you to my amazing husband, Beckham Archer. I couldn't have done this without you by my side every step of the way. You've been my rock, my compass, my everything since the moment I met you, and I can't thank you enough for your compassionate and giving soul. You have shown me what it means to be a successful entrepreneur yourself, being raised by a single mother, to then turn around and give back to those around you."

I take the giant scissors and cut the red ribbon as the crowd claps and cheers. Beckham steps up to my side, taking them from me and leaning in to kiss my cheek.

"You were amazing, baby," he whispers, letting his hand come to rest on my six-months pregnant belly.

Tonight is a black tie event for the opening of the foundation. We've been working tirelessly, nonstop for the last year, and it's been worth every single second.

"We are so proud of you." Sylvia fans her face as Taylor dabs at her eyes with a tissue. "Seriously, B, how are you Wonder Woman? Pregnant, kicking ass, volunteering all while establishing this?"

"Not to mention eloping," Taylor adds on, both of them still bitter that they weren't invited to the wedding and didn't even know it was happening until after the fact. In our defense, nobody did.

We ran off to Hawaii, getting married on a gorgeous cliff in Kauai surrounded only by nature. It was breathtaking and exactly what we wanted. No paparazzi, no stressful plans. We got to enjoy it for what it was, the beautiful union of our lives coming together.

"I know, I know, but you'll be there when this little one is born," I say, encircling my belly. "Oh, she kicked." I laugh and Beckham darts his hand down to feel it.

Since finding out we were pregnant, he has been beyond excited. He confessed to me the shame he felt when he went with Venus to the doctor and felt nothing. We both talked through his feelings, and

231

I managed to help him realize it's okay, because it wasn't his daughter and it wasn't the right person.

When we first found out I was pregnant, he initially panicked, worried he'd be the same way but the second he heard the heartbeat, he was a different man. Since then, his world is me and his unborn daughter.

"Sweetie, you were fantastic up there. I don't know what you were nervous about." My dad pulls me into his arms and hugs me tightly. "Your mother was smiling down on you; I could feel it, we all could."

"Thanks, Daddy."

"How's my little granddaughter doing? She was a star up there too."

"She's good, been moving around a lot today."

"Hey, Beckham, you see that bastard Mitchell Reardon is here?" My dad rolls his eyes, thumbing over his shoulder to where Mitchell is standing next to Miles Davenport. "Can you believe that piece of shit knocked up Venus?" He shakes his head.

"Better him than me." Beckham laughs, draping an arm around my dad's shoulders.

The day we went over and spoke to my father together, you could say all hell broke loose. There were threats, yelling, and at one point my dad threw a brandy snifter at Beckham's head. But after Chantelle took him to his study and chewed him a new asshole, he came out ready to be more civil.

To say things just fell into place would be a lie. It took weeks and even months before they could golf together again without my dad either walking off the course halfway through or Beckham coming home with bent and broken clubs. But we stayed at it, showing my dad that we were serious about each other. That our love wasn't going anywhere and after a while, it just wasn't an issue anymore.

My dad realized that we were happy and eventually apologized for some of his outbursts, telling me that the only thing he really cared about was that I was happy. Weirdly, through it all, somehow, Beckham and my dad became even closer and the second we told my family we were expecting, my dad became the doting, emotional grandpa who shows up with toys and clothes by the handfuls every weekend.

"You ready to go shake hands and kiss asses for a few hours?"

I laugh and take Beckham's hand as we step inside and do exactly that.

"My feet are killing me," I whisper in his ear as I pop off one heel behind a high-top table and rub my toes.

"Why don't we get out of here. You've put in the time; everyone can handle it without you, baby." Beckham stands behind me, his lips at my ear and his hands on my now fuller hips.

"I feel bad," I moan as I lean against him.

"I can make you feel so much better though." He presses himself against me.

"Don't tease me," I say as my nipples harden beneath my dress. Since about day three of my second trimester, I've been insatiable. I'm talking four times a night and still fantasizing about my husband every other second of the day.

"I'm not teasing you, sweetheart. The moment I get you home I'm going to worship your body. How does a nice warm foot soak and massage sound?"

"Before or after?"

He chuckles, that low throaty type that I can feel in his chest.

"Are you feeling achy?" He runs his nose up my neck, his fingertips gripping me a little tighter as we look out over the crowd. "Needy for something?"

"Mm-hmm, something long and hard." I press my ass against him, wriggling it a little.

"Behave yourself, Mrs. Archer."

"I thought you liked when I disobeyed?" I reach around to grip his firm cock and he whimpers.

"Don't think I won't punish you just because you're pregnant, sweetheart. I have no issue teaching you a lesson in obedience with that riding crop again."

I step forward to spin around, but he grabs me and holds me in place.

"Easy, unless you want the rest of this room to see what I'm carrying in my pants right now."

I smile and spin around, placing my hands against his firm chest.

"You know what that tells me; you can't chase me down if I do step aside right now." I step just out his grasp. He steps behind the table, adjusting the tablecloth.

"You fucking tease." He shakes his head at me as I raise my hand, waving sweetly before I walk across the room.

Five minutes later I'm stuck in conversation with Mitchell Reardon, karma I suppose for how I left Beckham hanging. He's going on and on about how expensive his new boat is and that the one he originally wanted was just too small so he just had to get the two-hundred-foot one. I don't have the heart to tell him Beckham's is four hundred feet.

"We're leaving now." Beckham's hand is on my arm and he's pulling me away from Mitchell, down the hallway and out the door to his waiting Rolls-Royce.

He helps me into the back seat, sliding in beside me and slamming the door.

"Apologies, Carson, need a moment with my wife," he says through gritted teeth as he hits the button and the partition slides into place.

"Everything okay?" I ask with a big smile.

His hand comes down to rest on my thigh. "Do you think that was a nice thing to do to your husband, Brontë?"

I shrug. "You were teasing me too."

"Yes, well, I was trying to get you to leave so I could tend to you, take care of your needs. You thought it was funny to disobey me in public after I told you to behave."

He looks over at me and it's that look that makes my stomach do that little quiver. The one that makes my thighs tremble and my panties wet. The one that tells me he's going to spend the rest of the night taking it out on me.

"Sorry," I apologize.

"You really love trying my patience, don't you?"

"Anything I can do to make it up to you?" I drag my hand up his inner thigh, but he reaches out and stops me.

"Oh, sweetheart, you're absolutely going to make it up to me." His fingers slide up my bare arm, leaving a trail of tingles as he reaches my chin. He tips it upward, a devilish grin on his face, his lips coming within a centimeter of mine.

"Beg for it."

Love a filthy talking billionaire? Want another sexy age-gap romance? Check out Savannah and Warren's romance in *Just This Once*.

Keep reading for a sample!

I swore to myself that I'd never cross that line with her.

But when Savannah Monroe, my chief operations officer, shows up on my doorstep with a proposition that starts with her in my lap and a promise of *just this once*...breaking the rules suddenly seems so enticing.

At fifteen years my junior and the smartest woman I've ever met, she's by far the greatest asset at Baxley Tech.
From the moment I hired her, we had a connection—as friends, as a mentor.
A lingering touch.
A stolen glance.
An unspoken attraction that simmers just beneath the surface, threatening to boil over.

So when she reveals a painful secret she's been hiding from me that involves my CFO, I don't hesitate...I take care of it immediately.
Or so I thought.

But the lies and corruption go much deeper than I ever realized and now we're in a tangled web of passion and secrecy.

After our one night together, everything changes.
The thought of her in the arms of another man turns me into someone I don't recognize—insatiable, hungry.
Indulging in every filthy thought I've had about her for three years is one thing, but losing my heart in the process wasn't part of the deal.

But here's the thing about forbidden fantasies...they usually come at a price.
And this one, just might be deadly.
When a blackmailer threatens to destroy her life and everything she's worked for, I take matters into my own hands.

Because when it comes to Savannah Monroe, there is no negotiation.
No backing down.
No Limits.
No Rules.
No losing her.

We promised each other it would only be *just this once*. But now that I've had a taste...I want my fill.

JUST
THIS
ONCE

ALEXIS WINTER

Prologue

Savannah-Three Years Earlier...

"I got an interview!" I thrust my hands in the air in celebration as I stand up, my desk chair shooting out behind me.

I glance around nervously, trying to judge if anyone heard me. Probably not the best idea to be shouting about a new interview at my current job.

I sit back down and read the email again for a third time.

"Oh my God, I got an interview," I repeat in disbelief.

When I applied for the open Chief Operations Officer position at Baxley Technologies, I truly didn't expect a call back. Not to say I'm not qualified for the job; I feel I am, but most companies want to see at least fifteen years on your resume before they even consider you for the COO role.

I close my office door and grab my cell to call my best friend Callie.

"Hey, this is a lov—"

"I got an interview," I blurt out, cutting her off.

"An interview for—oh, for Baxley?"

"Yes!" I'm attempting to whisper but with my excitement it's

240

coming out more in a whispered shout. "I'm in complete disbelief, like me? Seriously?"

"Of course you, why not *you*? First of all, you're very qualified. Your insane work experience in just six years speaks for itself, not to mention the MBA and undergrad from an Ivy League school, both of which you got into on merit and not because your family had money."

"I know. It's just that I don't want to get my hopes up if they're not serious about me."

"These are billionaires, sweetie. They wouldn't waste their precious time if they weren't serious about you. Now stop doubting yourself and get ready to go out and celebrate tonight. Think about where you wanna meet for drinks."

I smile into the receiver. If there's one person who will always have my back and gas me up, it's Callie. She's been my ride or die since the day we met freshman year at Northwestern. I didn't think she'd associate with me at all. She comes from a very wealthy family, old money, from the North Shore and I... well, I'm an only child, that I know of, raised by my grandma after my mom went to prison and my dad abandoned me.

I put my phone on my desk and turn back to my computer to finish up my workday. I feel too giddy to focus, but if this interview does actually turn into a new career opportunity, I don't want to leave this startup I've been at for the last three years high and dry. I need to finish up a few projects before I officially leave this place.

I knew from a young age I wanted a career, a big one. I busted my ass in high school, opting for any and every extracurricular and after-school program, even summer school. I graduated early with honors and was accepted into Northwestern University with a focus on business and finance.

Even through high school and college I worked any and every odd job I could find that would pay my bills and give me experience. I started in fast food, working my way up to a management position and then the corporate office that happened to be located in Chicago where I lived.

Even through getting my MBA, I continued to move up the ladder until I was brought on as a project manager and financial advisor here at this software startup. In only three years we've grown from nothing to a multimillion-dollar company that's in the final stages of IPO.

I was determined to break the cycle of failure in my family if it was the last thing I did. Sometimes I still struggle with imposter syndrome when I look in the mirror. Like who is this girl who came from nothing and why does she deserve this opportunity?

I shake the thoughts from my head and power through the rest of my day before sending a text to Callie.

Me: *Leaving here in the next twenty. Mitzy's for martinis?*

Thirty minutes later I take the first celebratory sip of my dirty martini.

"Will Todd be surprised when you put in your notice?"

"If I ge—"

"When," Callie says emphatically with an arched brow.

"When," I start over, "I get the job, I think Todd will be sad to see me go for sure, but I think he knew from the get-go that I didn't plan to stay long term. I think when you jump in at the ground floor of a startup, it's a much quicker burnout period than other jobs, you know?"

She nods and takes a sip of her French martini, her eyes rolling back in her head for a brief second. "Yeah, for sure. You have literally put blood, sweat, and tears into that place. I hope he knows what he has with you."

"He does. He's always been extremely generous with pay, but as we all know, there's zero work-life balance when it comes to a startup. I'm only twenty-seven and I already feel like between school and all my jobs over the years, I've never had a chance to just breathe, enjoy life, and take some downtime."

I do feel a little guilty wanting to move on from Code Red Software, but I'm beyond excited that I even get the chance to interview at a tech giant like Baxley Technologies.

I SWALLOW DOWN THE FEAR IN MY THROAT AS I STARE UP AT THE massive mirrored building on Franklin St.

I close my eyes for a brief second and take in a deep breath. "You've got this. You deserve this. You're going to nail it."

I square my shoulders back, lift my chin up, and march up to the massive revolving door emblazoned with the world-famous gold BT symbol.

"Please have a seat, Miss Monroe."

I take a seat in front of a large table where six other people are sitting across from me. "I'm Pierce Denton, Executive Vice President here at Baxley." The rest of the individuals follow suit with their name and title.

Round table style interviews are nothing new to me. I had to do them for my MBA program and when I came onboard with Code Red, but this one is intimidating. Not only is it filled with department heads, but the collective net worth in this room alone is more than I'll see in ten lifetimes.

"Mr. Baxley won't be here today for this interview. If we decide to move forward with second rounds, he'll be present for that one," Mr. Denton says.

I nod and try to consciously make eye contact with each person while not looking crazy at the same time.

"You have an impressive background, Miss Monroe. I'm sure it's not the first time someone has told you that."

I smile. "Thank you. Yes, I have heard that from previous employers."

We go through some general questions about my background, education, and then come the fun ones... the ones about how I'd be an asset to the company, why I should be considered, what value I'd bring to the company... a fight for my life or basically a modern-day version of a mock execution.

But this is where I come alive because I'm not just trying to blow smoke up these people's asses; I'm serious about my career and where I see myself, and I see myself at Baxley Tech.

I feel confident as I stand and shake each of their hands.

"Great job today, kid." Eric, the CFO who introduced himself earlier during the round table, gives me a wink and touches my elbow.

An instant *ick* feeling settles in my stomach but I don't let him see.

"Thank you. I feel very confident about the next steps." I maintain solid eye contact with him, refusing to let him make me feel out of place with his subtle comment about my age.

I'm more than aware that I'd be the youngest person in an executive position at this company, but that doesn't scare me one bit. It just stokes the fire of determination inside me.

"I have no doubt we'll be in touch shortly," Mr. Denton says after walking me to the elevator.

"Thank you and I look forward to it, sir." I step into the empty elevator and press the button for the ground floor. The moment the doors close, I toss my hands in the air again and do a happy dance.

———

IT'S BEEN FOUR AGONIZING DAYS SINCE MY INTERVIEW AND I AM a nervous wreck. Every time I turn around, I'm either knocking something over or tripping over my own feet. My nerves feel like they've been juiced up with adrenaline and caffeine and all my breath work is for nothing.

I glance at the clock; it's 4:48 p.m. on a Friday. For most people, the workday is done already but for me, I'll probably be here till at least seven p.m. or later. I'm used to it at this point—that's not why I'm looking at the clock. I refresh my email for the fiftieth time, but there's nothing from Baxley.

"Hey, Savannah, doing anything fun this weekend?" Lynn, my coworker, pokes her head in my office.

I shrug. "Nothing on the books. Probably be here pretty late tonight. What about you?"

"Pete's uncle is taking his boat out on the lake so we'll probably join him. It's not exactly my cup of tea, fishing and drinking beer, but it'll be nice to get out in the sun."

"That does sound fun. And hey, maybe you can convince him to take you to that cute French bistro you saw the other week that you mentioned."

Her eyes light up, "You are so smart. I completely forgot about that."

I'm about to respond when my phone buzzes and I look at the screen.

Incoming call from Pierce Denton.

"Oh, I have to," I say, pointing to the phone, and she nods and waves, shutting my door behind her.

"Hello?"

"Hello, Miss Monroe. Apologies for the late callback. I know how annoying that is, but business gets in the way sometimes." He chuckles and I hold my breath. "Anyway, we would love to have you back for another round of interviews next week. That work for you?"

"Yes!" I attempt to readjust my volume as my excitement gets the better of me, "Yes, sorry."

"Great. I'll have Dorene from HR set it up with you. She'll send over an email with some proposed times."

"Will Mr. Baxley be there?"

"Yes, he will be—should be. You'll be interviewing with him and Eric Oliver, the CFO you met at the last interview."

"Oh, okay. Yes, I remember him." I try to sound positive, but I don't love the idea of having to speak to that man for several hours as these interviews can run long. At least Mr. Baxley will be there to hopefully correct him if he calls me *kid* again.

Per usual, I stay late tonight but with a little extra pep in my step. I double down and make sure I finish up as much as I can, knowing that there's a good chance I'll be gone from here in a few short weeks.

Normally, my Friday nights are a stressful battle between me trying to work late to finish things up so I'm not so stressed the next week and trying to appease my boyfriend via text with promises to spend every minute with him this weekend.

However, after several painful and teary conversations into the wee hours of the morning, Nick and I recently decided that after four years together, neither of us could offer what the other needed.

It wasn't easy but it was right, and we both agreed. The breakup was mutual and amicable, and I'm sure we'll stay friendly over the years. I promise myself that this time, I'll give myself at least a year off from relationships.

I grab my purse and head down to my car, already yawning. I received an email about an hour ago from Dorene with three times next week for my interview. I confirmed one for Monday morning so now I can actually relax over the weekend... at least until Saturday afternoon when I start panicking all over again.

———

I HOLD MY PURSE, PLANT, BOX OF KNICKKNACKS FOR MY OFFICE, and a bagel all in my hands as I walk through the revolving door of Baxley Tech, my new job where I, Savanna Grace Monroe, am COO. It still feels unreal.

Unfortunately and strangely, I have yet to meet Warren Baxley himself. He was called away on business before our interview so he was only able to attend via audio, sitting quietly on the call. I wouldn't have even known he was there if Mr. Oliver hadn't told me.

I purposely made eye contact with Mr. Oliver the entire interview because less than thirty seconds into it, his eyes dropped down to my breasts when I dared to look away for even a brief second.

"Hold it, please!" I say as my heels furiously click across the marble floor of the lobby. I dart through the closing doors of the elevator just as someone rushes up behind me to do the same.

I stumble as I feel two warm hands grab at my waist. I try to turn and see who it is when I hear his voice. "Whoa, kid. I'm sorry. Almost took a tumble on your first day." Eric Oliver flashes me a smarmy smile, acting like he isn't the one who caused me to stumble in the first place when his chest ran into my back.

I give him a slight smile and try to push my way to the back of the elevator.

"You need me to show you around? I can—"

"No, thank you. I know where I'm going. Much appreciated though." I shut it down before he can offer anything else. "This is me," I say, exiting the elevator the second the doors open.

But it isn't me. I glance down to my right, then my left. I spot a bench and place my stuff down to pull up my email again to check the floor and suite number of my office.

"Shit, two floors up." I walk back over to the elevator and press the button. This time when the doors open, it's empty. I let out a sigh and step inside, but it stops after one floor and wouldn't you know it, he gets back on the elevator with me.

"You sure you don't need some help there, little lady?" He chuckles and pokes at my orchid that bobs over the top of my box.

"I'm sure."

"Well, listen, I mean it. If you ever want to get lunch and get a feel for the company or need a mentor, I'm here for you." It's like he has zero control of his eyes that once again look down at my breasts at least four times in that one sentence.

I spin around and exit on my correct floor this time, finally finding my office and placing my things down. I straighten out my button-down blouse and pencil skirt, second-guessing my very professional clothing choice... Maybe I should have opted for a damn potato sack.

I don't have many personal items to display in my office, not because I'm particularly private but because I have no family to have framed photos of or gifts or sentimental knickknacks. Besides my orchid, which I place on the corner of my desk, the only thing I have is a small five-inch-tall Eiffel Tower.

I click the button on the back of my iMac to turn it on, but nothing happens.

"The hell?" I mutter as I do it again and still nothing. I look under my desk and see that it's not plugged in. I reach under my desk and plug it in. I grab my chair to help pull myself back up, but it swivels, so I launch myself forward and land right on my belly on the floor.

"Glad to see you found your office. Everything okay?"

I hear a voice behind me as I right myself. I'm on my knees, readjusting my ponytail I just knocked askew. I am really not in the mood for this man's continued attempts at flirting or whatever the hell he's thinking. Time to let him know this won't fly with me.

"Sir, let me be very clear," I say with my back still toward the door. "I'm not your midlife crises, okay?" I stand up and brush down my skirt. "This is a professional setting."

"No, you're not, but I'm pretty sure I'm your new boss."

My spine stiffens and I feel my eyes bug out as I slowly turn around to face the man standing casually in my doorway.

Warren Freaking Baxley, in the flesh.

Shit.

Warren

Present Day...

"He broke up with me."

Savannah flings her arms in the air before flopping down in the chair across from my desk, her silky chocolate hair pooling around her shoulders as she slumps down.

"Are you more upset that *he* broke up with you or that the relationship is over?"

I don't look up from the document in my hand. This isn't the first time Savannah has vented to me about her relationship woes and I'm sure it won't be the last.

We're an... unlikely friendship. She's outgoing and friendly, young and not afraid to voice her opinion. Whereas I'm fifteen years her senior and do everything I can to avoid human interaction outside of my business.

Yes, I'm her boss, but I'd say we're also good friends. Completely professional, of course, which is why I leave all the filthy thoughts that wander into my head about her, in my head.

"What do you mean?" The V between her brow deepens.

I put the paper down and remove my glasses, folding them in my hands.

"I mean, is it an insult that he's the one who dumped *you* or did you really think he was the one?" She chews her bottom lip as she considers my question.

"I'm not upset that he was the one who ended things because I can't handle being dumped. I'm hurt. We've been together almost a year and a half and this just came out of nowhere. I thought he was asking me to move in with him or maybe proposing at the—"

"Proposing?" That gets my attention. Sure, they've been dating that long, but I've never heard her speak about him like she's ready to marry the guy. I swallow down the panic that forms in my throat.

"Yeah, or moving in together. It's just—frustrating. Another failed relationship at thirty."

"Savannah, you have plenty of time to find *the one*. Stop putting that pressure on yourself and live your life. I'm sure Nick will regret his decision soon enough." I offer her a tight-lipped smile, but she just glares at me.

"Nick? Nick was my ex from three years ago. His name is Easton and you've met him twice."

"I have?"

I shrug nonchalantly, knowing full well that I met the smug prick twice. The first time he tried to offer me advice on my company's latest software launch by telling me that someone *my* age should be taking tech advice from someone in their twenties. And the second time, he was sloppy drunk at our office Christmas party and knocked over an entire table of champagne flutes.

"Maybe I'm not the best person for these kinds of talks."

She lets out a dramatic sigh. "No, you're probably right. I'll save it for overpriced martinis with the girls." She stands up and stretches her arms overhead, the bottom of her blouse lifting just enough to expose a sliver of her flat stomach. She pulls her long hair into a high ponytail, wrapping the tie from her wrist around it a few times.

"You doing anything this weekend?" she asks, coming around my desk to look at the paper I've been studying.

"The usual—work, maybe a round of golf or tennis at the club, and more work."

She leans in closer. The familiar scent of her floral perfume still lingers at the end of a ten-hour day. Her long, delicate fingers rest on her hip as she eyes the paper.

"This the Code Red proposal?"

"It is."

She picks it up and hikes one hip up to rest it on my desk. My eyes fall to where her hips flare out from her waist. It's a spot that I often fixate on with her. She has that classic hourglass figure that leaves me constantly desiring to run my hand over that dip in her body.

Sometimes I wonder if there's overt flirty undertones with her body language and actions, but I always settle on no because she knows how important discretion is to me. But also because I don't think for one second she sees me as anything more than a boss or mentor—fuck, maybe even a father figure in her life. It hasn't gone totally unnoticed by some of my male colleagues that not only is Savannah young and beautiful, but that I'm also rather protective of her.

"Good thing I didn't sell my stocks after they went public and I left the company. If this acquisition goes through, I'm poised to become a very wealthy woman. Might even knock you off the richest man in Chicago pedestal."

She winks at me and tosses it back on my desk. I lean back in my chair, attempting to put some distance between us.

"What about your weekend plans?"

I'm trying my hardest not to look down at her smooth, tan legs left exposed by her skirt riding up a little. Sometimes—okay, often—I wonder what her reaction would be if I simply reached my hand out and ran my fingertips up her silky skin.

In my fantasy, she parts her legs a little further for me, allowing me a peek at what she's wearing beneath her proper pencil skirts. In this particular fantasy, her on my desk at the end of a long day, she'd simply slip her panties off and hike her skirt up, offering me her sweet, wet pussy to devour.

"Oh, general wallowing I suppose now that I'm a single woman." Her response snaps me back to reality and I realize I've let my gaze settle on her thighs, but she doesn't seem to notice.

"I'm sure I'll let it all out with Callie and then rapidly go through the phases of grief, convincing myself I'm better off while I get it all out over a grueling spin class."

"That sounds miserable but I'll wish you all the best."

"You're welcome to join us for martinis at Mitzy's if you're bored." She smiles and while I know she knows I'll never take her up on the offer, I do appreciate that every weekend she offers to let me tag along on whatever crazy adventure she's up to.

"I'm afraid I'd be a bore. You don't want an old man, let alone your boss, to tag along with your friends." I wink at her and I swear I see a slight pink hue spread across her cheeks. For as much as we have kept things professional between us, once in a while it feels like these little tender moments are laced with flirty innuendo.

"Maybe I'll become a sugar mama. Find some twenty-one-year-old smoke show that needs beer money." She scoots back a little further on my desk so that she's now fully sitting on it and reaches down to pull off her heels. "You ever done that?"

"Been a sugar mama? Can't say that I have."

She slaps my arm playfully. "No, have you ever entertained someone considerably younger than you that you knew wouldn't be anything serious, just a fling?"

I debate on saying something to the effect of *no, but I'd be happy to if you're offering.* Instead, I answer truthfully. "No. I'm not really the kind of man who wants to be used for my money, but there's no shame in those who desire that kind of arrangement. It's just not for me."

"And what kind of arrangement does work for you? What is Warren Baxley looking for?" She crosses one leg over the other, briefly drawing my attention to her exposed flesh. I look up at her and she's leaning on one arm, palm flat on my desk as she waits for my answer.

"Who says I'm looking for anything?" She rolls her eyes. "I don't think I'm looking for an arrangement of anything. Just open, I suppose."

It's a vague answer, but the truth is I'm not sure what I actually want. I'm not exactly wanting to die alone, but what I want feels wrong. It feels selfish to want Savannah. She's young, has her entire life ahead of her, and I'm already in the second phase of my life. Besides, I've convinced myself that the things I'd want to do to her would scare her away.

"Look at us, both single with an amazing career, but no prospects." Suddenly her face drops and she lets out a groan. "Dammit! I completely forgot that Easton and I have our annual benefit dinner next month for the Northwestern University Alumni Association."

"I'm sure he'll behave accordingly if that's what you're worried about."

She shakes her head. "That's not what I'm worried about. I just hate having to make a public appearance at a place where everyone knows he and I were previously dating. It's like a public statement letting everyone know we failed. Like back when your friend would change their Facebook relationship status to it's complicated."

"I think you're being a touch dramatic, Savannah. And if it's really that uncomfortable, just don't go. Make him be the one who has to tell everyone there that he made the biggest mistake of his life and dumped the smartest, most accomplished, and beautiful woman he'll ever meet. He'll look fucking stupid."

Her frown morphs into a huge, genuine smile that reaches her eyes.

"Look at you, Mr. Sentimental." She pokes me with her bare foot, and I bat it away, but she does it again, this time trying to poke me in the ribs, but I reach my hand out and catch her foot. The warmth of her skin tingles against my palm. The moment we make contact, it's like something shifts between us. The air grows thick with unsaid desires and tension.

Her smile fades and I swear I see a sharp intake of breath between her open lips. I don't let go of her foot right away. Instead, I do something so stupid—I run my thumb up her insole and her eyelids flutter. Something is definitely happening between us, and it feels magnetic, like I couldn't stop it if I wanted to. But then it's gone when a soft knock brings us both back to reality.

"Hey, boss, got a min—oh, sorry, didn't mean to interrupt." Eric shoves his hands in his pockets as he looks between us.

"Not interrupting. Come on in."

Savannah jumps down from my desk and scoops up her heels.

"I'm heading home," she says to me as she slips on her heels. "Have a good weekend, gentlemen."

"What was that about?" Eric asks the moment she's gone. He walks over to the bar cart in the corner of my office and pours himself a generous amount of my liquor.

I shake my head like I have no idea what he's talking about. "Nothing. We were just talking about our weekend plans and Code Red."

"Last time I checked, my secretary doesn't sit on my desk when she's making small talk with me."

That irks me. I narrow my gaze at him and sharpen my voice.

"She's not my secretary, Eric. Those digs won't fly with me so cut that shit out."

I've always known Eric was a little more than jealous when I brought Savannah on as COO. He thought as the current CFO, he was a shoo-in for the position. He could have managed it—I have no doubt—but he's better with finances. He's not as good with the big-picture decision-making that Savannah does.

He raises his hand in a silent apology. "Speaking of Code Red, are things still moving forward?"

"As expected, yes. We'll make the announcement sometime in

the next two weeks. How's Kane doing? Still no interest in coming aboard Baxley?"

I stand and walk over to the bar cart to pour myself a tumbler of whiskey. I'm not a big drinker, maybe a drink a week, typically on Friday night. It's a ritual; usually after everyone has left the building, I pour myself a glass and slowly sip it as I put on a record, kick back, and watch the city below.

"I'm working on it. Kid still thinks he wants to focus on building his own app. I told him I'm all for it, but it could really help him to get a few years under his belt working here. Really help him land some connections, and then he could develop the app with us or sell it to Baxley."

"Well, he's still young. I'm sure he'll come around eventually. It's good that he's so ambitious though. Just like you."

Eric and I have known each other for the better part of two decades. He was my mentor out of grad school at my first major job. He was a director, and I was just starting out. He saw something in me, took me under his wing, and helped me become the man I am today. So when I started Baxley Technologies fifteen years ago, he was the first employee I hired.

"More like you. I still remember you telling me six months after you started at DataTech, you said *Eric, I give myself five years before I start my own company and ten to make it a billion-dollar enterprise.* I thought you were crazy but here we are." He raises his glass to me and we both drink.

"Shit," he says, looking at his watch, "the Mrs. will be calling me any second if I don't get home. Maybe if I'm lucky I can sweet-talk her into giving me some of that action you and Savannah almost had." He winks at me and I just ignore the comment. "Have a good weekend, boss. See you Sunday at the club. Nine a.m. tee off; don't be late." He points to me as he walks out of my office.

Eric is on his fourth, possibly fifth marriage at this point. I can't keep track. His penchant for chasing after his next wife while still married to his current usually lands him in divorce court every few years.

His comment about Savannah and me lingers as I dim the lights and walk over to my records. I leaf through them briefly, finally deciding on "Something Else" by Cannonball Adderley. The smooth sound of jazz fills the office as I take a seat in my chair. I lean back and close my eyes, allowing the melody to carry me away.

Keep Reading _Just This Once_.

Read the rest of the Chicago Billionaires Series

Those Three Words
Just This Once
Dirty Little Secret

Also by Alexis Winter

Slade Brothers Series

Billionaire's Unexpected Bride

Off Limits Daddy

Baby Secret

Loves Me NOT

Best Friend's Sister

Slade Brothers Second Generation Series

That Feeling

That Look

Men of Rocky Mountain Series

Claiming Her Forever

A Second Chance at Forever

Always Be My Forever

Only for Forever

Waiting for Forever

Four Forces Security

The Protector

The Savior

Love You Forever Series

The Wrong Brother

Marrying My Best Friend's BFF

Rocking His Fake World

Breaking Up with My Boss

My Accidental Forever

The F It List

The Baby Fling

Grand Lake Colorado Series

A Complete Small-Town Contemporary Romance Collection

Castille Hotel Series

Hate That I Love You

Business & Pleasure

Baby Mistake

Fake It

South Side Boys Series

Bad Boy Protector-Book 1

Fake Boyfriend-Book 2

Brother-in-law's Baby-Book 3

Bad Boy's Baby-Book 4

Make Her Mine Series

My Best Friend's Brother

Billionaire With Benefits

My Boss's Sister

My Best Friend's Ex

Best Friend's Baby

Mountain Ridge Series

Just Friends: Mountain Ridge Book 1

Protect Me: Mountain Ridge Book 2

Baby Shock: Mountain Ridge Book 3

Castille Hotel Series

Hate That I Love You

Business & Pleasure

Baby Mistake

Fake It

ALL BOOKS CAN BE READ AS STAND-ALONE READS WITHIN THESE SERIES

About the Author

Alexis Winter is a contemporary romance author who loves to share her steamy stories with the world. She specializes in billionaires, alpha males and the women they love.

If you love to curl up with a good romance book you will certainly enjoy her work. Whether it's a story about an innocent young woman learning about the world or a sassy and fierce heroine who knows what she wants you're sure to enjoy the happily ever afters she provides.

When Alexis isn't writing away furiously, you can find her exploring the Rocky Mountains, traveling, enjoying a glass of wine or petting a cat.

You can find her books on Amazon or here: https://www. alexiswinterauthor.com/

Printed in Great Britain
by Amazon

40089854R00155